WITHOUT A LICENSE

Also by Keith R.A. DeCandido,
from eSpec Books

The Precinct Series
DRAGON PRECINCT
UNICORN PRECINCT
GOBLIN PRECINCT
TALES FROM DRAGON PRECINCT

Coming Soon
MERMAID PRECINCT

Forthcoming Titles
PHOENIX PRECINCT
MANTICORE PRECINCT
MORE TALES FROM DRAGON PRECINCT

Other Titles
WITHOUT A LICENSE

*To Stephanie —
It was great hanging out with you!*

WITHOUT A LICENSE

THE FANTASTIC WORLDS OF KEITH R.A. DECANDIDO

eBooks
Pennsville, NJ

PUBLISHED BY
eSpec Books LLC
Danielle McPhail, Publisher
PO Box 242,
Pennsville, New Jersey 08070
www.especbooks.com

Copyright 2015, 2018 Keith R.A. DeCandido

ISBN: 978-1-942990-62-8
ISBN (ebook): 978-1-942990-61-1

All rights reserved. No part of the contents of this book may be reproduced or transmitted in any form or by any means without the written permission of the publisher.

All persons, places, and events in this book are fictitious and any resemblance to actual persons, places, or events is purely coincidental.

"Editorial Interference," first published in *Fedoras Literary Review* Volume 1, #2, copyright © 1996 Keith R.A. DeCandido
"A Vampire and a Vampire Hunter Walk Into a Bar," first published in *Amazing Stories* #608, copyright © 2005 Keith R.A. DeCandido
"Sunday in the Park with Spot," first published in *Furry Fantastic*, copyright © 2006 Keith R.A. DeCandido
"Under the King's Bridge," first published in *Liar Liar*, copyright © 2011 Keith R.A. DeCandido
"-30-" first published as part of the *Viral* novella miniseries, copyright © 2012 Keith R.A. DeCandido, reprinted with permission from Steven Savile
"The Ballad of Big Charlie," first published in *V-Wars*, copyright © 2012 Keith R.A. DeCandido (characters of Luther Swann, Yuki Nitobe, and Jerry Schmidt copyright © 2012 Jonathan Maberry; character of Danika Dubov copyright © 2012 John Everson; character of William Blevins copyright © 2012 James A. Morrow), reprinted with permission from Jonathan Maberry and IDW Publishing
"The Stone of the First High Pontiff," first published in *Defending the Future: Best-Laid Plans*, copyright © 2012 Keith R.A. DeCandido
Introductions and all other stories copyright © 2015, 2018 Keith R.A. DeCandido

Interior Design: Danielle McPhail
Front Cover Art: Angela McKendrick
Back Cover Art: McP Digital Graphics

Dedicated
to the memory of

JAY LAKE

who originally bought "Behold a White Tricycle"
and who was present for the creation
of "Wild Bill Got Shot."

We miss you, buddy...

Acknowledgments

Primary thanks to Neal Levin and Jess Novesteras at Dark Quest Books for shepherding this collection into existence, and Danielle Ackley-McPhail and Mike McPhail at eSpec Books for doing likewise with the new edition.

Secondary thanks to Jeff Berkwitz (who bought "A Vampire and a Vampire Hunter Walk Into a Bar" for what turned out to be the final issue of *Amazing Stories* under Paizo's stewardship of the magazine), the late great Jay Lake (who bought "Behold a White Tricycle" for *44 Clowns: 11 Tales of the 4 Clowns of the Apocalypse*, though that anthology sadly never saw the light of day), Jonathan Maberry (who created *V-Wars* and bought "The Ballad of Big Charlie" for the first anthology in that series), Brit Marschalk (who reprinted "A Vampire and a Vampire Hunter Walk Into a Bar" for the first issue of *The Town Drunk*), the aforementioned Mike McPhail (who bought "The Stone of the First High Pontiff" for *Defending the Future: Best-Laid Plans*), Jean Rabe and the late Brian M. Thomsen (who bought "Sunday in the Park with Spot" for *Furry Fantastic*), Steven Savile (who created *Viral* and brought me in to write "-30-"), and the collectives of the Double-Breasted Fedoras (who first published "Editorial Interference" in the short-lived *The Fedoras Literary Review*), the Circles in the Hair workshop (who reprinted "Editorial Interference" in the group's eponymous anthology), and the Liars Club (who published "Under the King's Bridge" in the *Liar Liar* anthology). Thanks also to Elektra Hammond and Deborah Grabien, who didn't actually edit, respectively, the "Precinct" and Cassie Zukav stories in this collection, but they edited most of the other fiction in those two milieus, and they deserve props.

Significant thanks to Christopher L. Bennett, who first suggested this collection's title, and the aforementioned Elektra Hammond, who suggested the subtitle.

Additional thanks to the late Harlan Ellison, whose short story collections were a formative part of my earliest reading experiences, and to the various other genre writers whose short fiction has also been an inspiration, among them Adam-Troy Castro, Laura Anne Gilman, Ursula K. Le Guin, Alice Sheldon (a.k.a. James Tiptree Jr.), and Jack Vance.

Great thanks to Wrenn Simms and GraceAnne Andreassi DeCandido (a.k.a. The Mom), who edited both "Partners in Crime" and "Seven-Mile Race" within an inch of their lives before letting me put them in this collection.

And finally huge-ass thanks to the Forebearance, for all the years of encouragement, love, affection, and shoving books under my nose when I was too young to know better, and thanks to them that live with me (human and feline) who bring me joy on a daily (if not hourly) basis.

Contents

Introduction / 1

Partners in Crime / 7
a Dragon Precinct story

The Ballad of Big Charlie / 27
a V-Wars story

A Vampire and a Vampire Hunter Walk Into a Bar / 87

Under the King's Bridge / 93

The Stone of the First High Pontiff / 117

Seven-Mile Race / 137
a Cassie Zukav story

Editorial Interference / 157

Sunday in the Park with Spot / 175

Wild Bill Got Shot / 189

-30- / 197
a Viral story

Behold a White Tricycle / 243
a story of the Four Clowns of the Apocalypse

About the Author / 245

Introduction

When I first sent Neal Levin of Dark Quest Books the proposed table of contents for the original edition of *Without a License*, he was surprised to only see eleven stories. "I thought you had a ton more stories than that," he said.

And well, I do. In fact, as I was first putting this collection together, I had 68 pieces of short fiction published, and in the three years since the first edition's release in 2015, I've had twenty more purchased for publication. The problem from the perspective of putting a personal short-story collection together is that a whole lot of those eighty-plus stories are media tie-ins—stories written in the worlds of (going alphabetically) *Aliens, BattleTech, Doctor Who, Farscape, Magic: The Gathering,* Marvel Comics, *Night of the Living Dead, Star Trek, Stargate SG-1, The X-Files, Xena,* and *Zorro*. I don't control the rights to those stories, so I can't include them in this collection.

Which is really too bad, because some of the short fiction I'm proudest of writing is in those media milieus.

There's "The Ceremony of Innocence is Drowned," a *Star Trek* story for the *Tales of the Dominion War* anthology in 2004. It was established in dialogue on a *Deep Space Nine* episode that Betazed—the homeworld of *The Next Generation* regular Deanna Troi, as well as her mother Lwaxana Troi, a recurring character on both *TNG* and *DS9*—was conquered by the Dominion. I wrote the fall of Betazed from Lwaxana's perspective, a story that was significantly informed by my living in New York City in September 2001.

There's "Arms and the Man," in the *Untold Tales of Spider-Man* anthology in 1997, where I got to significantly dig into the character of Dr. Octopus via a writer trying to pen Ock's biography. Tom DeFalco actually used some of what I established in my story in a Doc Ock story he later wrote for the *Spider-Man Unlimited* comic book, which always thrilled me.

There's "God Sins," a *Magic: The Gathering* story for 1995's *Distant Planes* that took a look at the Planeswalkers, the demiurges of the *Magic* universe, the actual players of the game who control the lives of the people in the world. They're like unto gods—so what happens when one wants to retire, but his worshippers won't let him?

There's "Back in El Paso My Life Would Be Worthless," a story I wrote for *The X-Files: Trust No One* in 2015, in which our POV character is a normal FBI agent forced to work with Mulder and Scully, and we get to look at how he viewed working with the two weirdos in the basement.

And then there's "Letter from Guadalajara," one of the stories I'm absolutely proudest of. Appearing in *More Tales of Zorro* in 2011, it was a tale that, like "Arms and the Man," had me wanting to examine the hero's primary antagonist, in this case Captain Monastario. The story started forming in my head when I was on the bus with a single line of dialogue: "You see, Zorro, while your mask frees you, my rank shackles me." From there, the entire story just core-dumped into my head, and when I got home I sat at the computer and wrote the entire story in about three hours, a magnificent outpouring of fiction that's never been matched at any point in my two-decade-plus writing career.

But I can't reprint those, or "Letting Go" (my look at the families of the *Voyager* crew that they left behind in the Alpha Quadrant when they were lost in space in the 2005 anthology *Distant Shores*) or "Diary of a False Man" (the secret origin of the obscure X-Men character the Changeling in 2000's *X-Men Legends*) or "Recurring Character" (a look at a thug who is regularly beat up by Xena in *The Further Adventures of Xena Warrior Princess* in 2001) or "Life from Lifelessness" (the First and Fourth Doctor both encountering the Golem of Prague in the 2007 *Doctor Who* anthology *Short Trips: Destination Prague*), or any of the other tie-in tales, as they're not mine to reprint. More's the pity.

To add a little insult to the injury, of the remaining stories, a whole mess are either *Dragon Precinct* stories or Cassie Zukav stories, and I wasn't about to do more than one from each of those worlds in the collection. And, in fact, to add a little value to this volume, I decided to write a new "Precinct" story and a new Cassie story that appear for the first time here in *Without a License*.

That left me with seven stories to reprint, plus I had two other unpublished stories sitting on my hard drive alone and forlorn.

However, while the eleven stories herein only comprise a fraction of my short fiction output, rest assured that you're getting some of my finest work in a variety of genres. From the urban grittiness of "The Ballad of Big Charlie" to the space opera of "The Stone of the First High Pontiff." From the modern-day thriller of "-30-" to the lighthearted cats-and-dogs-and-squirrels romp of "Sunday in the Park with Spot." From a murder mystery in a high fantasy setting in "Partners in Crime" to a murder mystery in a modern publishing setting in "Editorial Interference." From a tale of New York City occupied by magical creatures in "Under the King's Bridge" to a story of Key West, Florida filled with Norse gods in "Seven-Mile Race." Plus we get a few very quick hits in the short-shorts "A Vampire and a Vampire Hunter Walk Into a Bar," "Wild Bill Got Shot," and "Behold a White Tricycle."

So come on in, pull up a chair, pour yourself a drink, and let's go on a few journeys...

—Keith R.A. DeCandido
somewhere in New York City

Introduction to "Partners in Crime"

The characters of Torin ban Wyvald and Danthres Tresyllione have been bopping around in my head since college. I started playing Dungeons & Dragons in high school, and both Torin and Danthres were characters I'd role-played either in D&D (Torin, a ranger) or the early version of what was eventually released as the Wildside Gaming System (Danthres, a fighter). For years, I struggled with ways to use the pair of them in a story, but everything failed—

—until 2003, when John Ordover at Pocket Books asked me to give him something for a line of original SF/fantasy he was running. I hit on the notion of mixing two of my favorite genres in high fantasy (something I'd loved since being exposed to *The Hobbit* at a tender age) and police procedure (my love for which was cemented at a slightly less tender age by exposure to the TV shows *Barney Miller* and *Hill Street Blues*).

That led to the 2004 novel *Dragon Precinct*, which re-cast Torin, my intellectual warrior from a city of philosophers, and Danthres, my embittered half-elf with a chip on her shoulder a mile wide, as detectives who solved crimes in the city-state of Cliff's End as part of the Castle Guard. The result was an acclaimed novel that was set in a traditional high fantasy world, but the plot of which was a murder mystery. The mystery generally has some kind of fantastical element to it, but the drudgery and politics of policework remains the same.

The line John was editing was then discontinued, leaving *Dragon Precinct* kind of flapping in the breeze, but the rise of the small press came to my rescue. Dark Quest Books picked up the series, publishing *Unicorn Precinct* in 2011, reprinting *Dragon*

Precinct that same year, and continuing the series with *Goblin Precinct* in 2012 and *Gryphon Precinct* in 2013. The series has since been picked up by eSpec (publishers of this volume), who have reprinted the extant books and will be publishing the next three novels, *Mermaid Precinct*, *Phoenix Precinct*, and *Manticore Precinct*.

In the interregnum between Pocket and Dark Quest, I kept the universe alive in short fiction, which appeared in a variety of anthologies both from major publishers (*Murder by Magic, Pandora's Closet*) and the small press (*Hear Them Roar, Bad-Ass Faeries, Dragon's Lure, Release the Virgins!*). In fact, the world is pretty well suited to short fiction, and a short-story collection came out in 2013 called *Tales from Dragon Precinct*, which had four new stories in addition to the ones I'd done. I've also gone the crowdfunding route, having done three "Precinct" stories via Kickstarter, and we're planning a second collection, *More Tales from Dragon Precinct*.

The story you're about to read is a bit different from the others, in that Torin ban Wyvald doesn't appear. In one of the new stories I wrote for *Tales*, I introduced an elven guard named Aleta lothLathna, who helped Iaian with a case in "Catch and Release." She was also mentioned in "Heroes Welcome," and she wound up playing a substantial role in *Gryphon Precinct*. The latter novel established a certain amount of tension between Aleta and Danthres, and I decided to construct a story around it.

"Partners in Crime" is a story I wrote especially for *Without a License*. It's also the first story to take place after the upheaval that happened in the Cliff's End Castle Guard in *Gryphon Precinct*. I hope you enjoy it, and if you do, please do feel free to check out the other "Precinct" books and short stories.

Partners in Crime

a Dragon Precinct story

Lieutenant Danthres Tresyllione reveled in the quiet in the squadroom.

Normally at this time of day the eastern wing of the castle was bustling with activity. Sergeant Jonas would be going over the day's reported crimes. Captain Dru would kibbitz from the doorway of his office. Danthres and the other lieutenants who served as detectives in the Cliff's End Castle Guard would make comments, and Danthres would find most of them inane, with the only occasional exception of those from her partner, Lieutenant Torin ban Wyvald.

But this morning the squadroom was blissfully quiet. Danthres wished it was for a better reason.

The captain walked in, then, along with Aleta lothLathna, Danthres's least favorite member of the Castle Guard. Aleta had recently been promoted to lieutenant for reasons having to do with politics. Danthres hated politics almost as much as she hated magick, and she *really* hated magick.

Aleta blinked in surprise. "What are you doing here, Lieutenant?"

"I work here," Danthres said tartly.

Shaking her head, Aleta said, "I'm sorry, I just—I thought you'd be sick—"

Captain Dru then let out a sneeze that echoed throughout the unusually empty squadroom.

With a smile, Aleta finished: "—like the captain."

Danthres rose to her feet. "You should be home, Dru."

"No thanks," Dru said as he applied a handkerchief to his stuffed-up nose. "The house is full'a sick kids." Dru's wife opened her house to children who needed care during the work day.

"I'm surprised there *are* any kids. Shouldn't they be home with their sick parents?"

Dru shrugged. "It's a smaller load'n usual, but a few came by anyhow. And both the elf kids she watches are there, too."

Aleta moved over to her desk and sat down. "You'd think the Brotherhood of Wizards would have found a cure for Chalmraik's Flu by now."

Letting out a watery snort, Dru said, "Yeah, right. We get two-three outbreaks of this a year when somebody blows into town either on a boat or on a caravan from the forest and infects half the city-state, the Brotherhood puts out another new healing potion that they *swear* will work this time, they sell it by the caseload, and it don't work any better'n any other healing potion."

"Sometimes," Danthres said, "I think the Brotherhood deliberately doesn't find a cure because they make so much coin on the 'new' potions."

"The good news," Dru said as he slowly walked toward his office, "is that there ain't much by way of crime, since most of the humans, dwarves, and halflings're sick. Whole city-state'd shut down if the gnomes and elves weren't immune."

Aleta was sorting through some scrolls on her desk. "And, apparently, halfbreeds as well."

"What was that?" Danthres asked tartly.

"I'm merely surprised that someone with as much human blood as you did not succumb to the flu, is all."

"Sorry to disappoint you, but I've enough elf blood to keep me well." Suddenly, Danthres got a whiff of an awful stench, like rotten eggs mixed with meat that had been left out in the sun.

"Excuse me?" came a voice from behind her.

Turning, Danthres saw a gnome wearing a filthy outfit standing in the doorway. After a moment, she recognized him as one of Orvag's assistants in the body shop, the cave in the Forest of Nimvale on the outskirts of Cliff's End where unclaimed bodies were disposed of by fire.

"Erm, Orvag sent me," the gnome said, "and he said to bring back a detective. Says there's something funny about a body."

Dru nodded. "Okay, fine, you two go."

Danthres shot her captain a look. "Us *two*?"

"I'm sure," Aleta added, "that one of us can handle this just fine."

"It's a body," Dru said firmly, "and policy's always been that two detectives investigate when it's a dead body."

Danthres rolled her eyes. "Policy is also for six detectives to be on duty."

"If something else comes up, I'll take one of you off the body and put you on that."

"Captain, I will not work with *her*." Danthres folded her arms defiantly.

"Yeah, you will, *Lieutenant*, 'cause I ordered you to." Dru's tone would have been more authoritative if it hadn't been spoken through a stuffed-up nose and followed by another echoing sneeze.

"You do know what she is, yes?" Danthres asked.

Now Aleta stood up. "Excuse me?"

Danthres ignored her, continuing to stare intently at Dru. "She's Shranlaseth. She used to travel the countryside looking for halfbreeds just like me and executing them in the name of the Elf Queen."

"No, she isn't," Dru said simply.

Now Danthres laughed derisively. "Excuse me? Have you seen the tattoo on her neck? It—"

"You asked me what she *is*. What you just said is what she *was*. What she *is* is a lieutenant in the Cliff's End Castle Guard, same's you. An' that means sometimes you gotta work together." He made a shooing motion with his hands. "So go work together. That's an order."

With that, Dru retreated into his office.

Danthres turned to look at Aleta, who didn't look all that thrilled to be going on this call, either.

With a sigh, she said, "All right, let's get this over with."

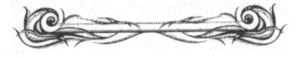

Aleta was nauseated by the smell as they approached the body shop. She had been hoping that exposure to the gnome would help prepare her for it, but it was as nothing compared to the overwhelming stench of decay as they came within sight of the cave.

Breathing through her mouth, Aleta followed both the gnome and Lieutenant Tresyllione into the cave. She let the halfbreed go first only because she would not, under any circumstances, turn her back on her.

A fat dwarf greeted them. Like his gnome assistant, he was wearing grime-covered overalls. The heat of the fire at the far end of the cave was enough to make it unbearably hot in her standard-issue leather armor, though at least the heat was a distraction from the horrid smell.

There were fifty pallets around the cave, all occupied by dead bodies.

Without preamble, the halfbreed said, "How is it you're not sick, Orvag?"

"Pfft." The dwarf waved the poker he was carrying around. "I've been exposed to every illness in Flingaria, never been sick a day in my life, eh?"

"Yes," Aleta said, "but this is a disease created by a wizard."

Again, Orvag said, "Pfft. Make me no matter. Anyhow, I have something for you, eh?"

Tresyllione said, "I haven't seen this many bodies piled in here since we had all those Bliss overdoses. What happened?"

Orvag shrugged. "Not everyone in Cliff's End has my constitution, eh? These people all died of the Chalmraik's Flu. All people from Goblin and Mermaid."

Aleta nodded in understanding. Goblin Precinct covered the slums of Cliff's End, and Mermaid Precinct covered the docks. It was where the poorest people lived, and they were the ones most likely to die of any illness.

Wandering over to one pallet, Orvag pointed at the body on it. "Except for this one, eh?"

Aleta followed Orvag to the pallet to discover that the body had the distinctive cheekbones and tapered ears of an elf.

"He can't have died of the flu," Aleta said.

This prompted a derisive snort from the halfbreed. "Brilliant deduction, *Detective*, it's no wonder they promoted you. Where was he found, Orvag?"

"On the River Walk. Got a wheelbarrow with a dozen people found on the River Walk dead. This one was mixed in with them, eh?"

Aleta stared down at the man's neck. Specifically, she noticed a bruising pattern on his left shoulder and on the left-hand side of the neck. Pulling off one glove, she reached down and felt the bones and muscles, then did the same for the left shoulder. The bumps and shards she felt under the skin confirmed what her eyes told her was likely to be the case.

Then she looked up. "Whoever this man is, I know who his murderer is. Or, rather, *what* his murderer is."

Tresyllione frowned. "What do you mean?"

"This man was killed by a technique that breaks the shoulder and the neck in a manner that is very painful for an instant before the person dies. The killer in this case was left-handed, since the attack is always from behind and was on the victim's left side." Aleta took a breath. "The technique is called *shan-shoora*."

The halfbreed nodded. "'The quick and painful death.' It's a Shranlaseth technique."

Orvag frowned. "What, the old elven special forces crazies? One of them's in Cliff's End?"

Tugging the collar of her armor to expose the tattoo on her neck, which contained the character in Ra-Telvish that signified the Shranlaseth, Aleta said, "Actually, there are three that I'm aware of. And perhaps now there's another."

Smiling sweetly, Tresyllione said, "Well, unless you killed this man."

Aleta didn't even dignify that with a reply.

The halfbreed then looked at Orvag. "Did you find anything on him that might give us a clue who he is?"

Orvag waddled over to a table and grabbed a very distinctive key, one Aleta recognized right away, and a bracelet, which she didn't. "Just these. Very nice key, eh? And I think the bracelet is gold."

"I know where the key is from," Aleta said. "There's a boarding house on the River Walk that caters to elves. I stayed there when I first came to Cliff's End. The locks are special ones they brought over from home."

"All right, we'll start there. Orvag, have the body sent to Boneen in the castle," Tresyllione said, referring to the mage on loan from the Brotherhood of Wizards who served as the Castle Guard's magickal examiner. He would keep the body from decaying with a Stasis Spell until the investigation was complete.

Danthres found the quiet as she and Aleta walked down Meerka Way toward the River Walk to be almost as pleasant as that of the empty squadroom. There were people on the thoroughfare, of course, but far fewer than usual, and most were elves and gnomes.

"I suppose," Danthres said as they crossed through Dragon Precinct, the middle-class district, "that it would be too much to ask that you all know each other."

"Most of us who were there at the end are at least acquainted, but I've no idea who else might have wound up here in Cliff's End beyond those two who are working as leatherworkers now. The closest comrades I had in the Shranlaseth are either out on Saptor Isle or—or dead."

"I'd ask if any of the ones you knew had murderous intent, but that would be all of you, wouldn't it?"

Aleta stopped walking. Danthres was tempted to just leave her behind, but she had obviously ceased her forward motion for a reason, so Danthres also stopped and turned around to see her fellow detective standing with her hands on her hips.

"You don't understand us at all, do you?"

"Don't I? You spent decades roaming the countryside carrying out the most vicious tasks the Elf Queen could provide—since, if they weren't vicious, they would hardly need you lot. You were trained to be ruthless and uncaring and loyal."

"Yes, but the Shranlaseth never committed murder."

Danthres couldn't believe what she was hearing. "Excuse me?"

"Every act we performed was at the behest of the Elf Queen, who was our rightful ruler. Murder is an illegal death. We were no more murderers than the hangman who carries out the magistrate's death sentences here in Cliff's End is a murderer."

For a moment, Danthres said nothing. Aleta's logic was infuriatingly impeccable.

Then, before she could pull a response together, Aleta went on: "Having said that, once the Elf Queen dissolved the Shranlaseth, we were left with very—specific skills." She shook her head. "Honestly, I wish more of us did come here. The Castle Guard is the perfect place for us, utilizing our skills in a way that still maintains order, not—"

"Not what?" Danthres prompted after Aleta cut herself off.

Aleta started walking. "Let's just say that our case may have nothing to do with the Shranlaseth directly. Some of my former colleagues have hired themselves out as assassins. They've mostly stayed back home, where there is still tremendous chaos, but..."

Her words trailed off, and she continued walking. Danthres caught up with her quickly. "So everything you did was simply because you were ordered to?"

"Of course. We were doing our duty."

"So why do you still treat *me* with contempt? The purity laws have been rescinded, the Shranlaseth are no more, and the Elf Queen is dead. You just said that you murdered—oh, sorry!" She held up her hands in mock apology. "That you *legally killed* all those infants and children who were of mixed blood solely due to the orders you received. But that means you shouldn't have an issue with me anymore, now should you?"

Aleta's mouth twisted. "I—"

"Don't contort yourself trying to explain your bigotry, Lieutenant. It's not becoming." With that, Danthres strode ahead of Aleta down Meerka Way.

The boarding house was a four-story structure on the western end of the River Walk, providing a view of the Garamin Sea as well as the docks. Danthres suspected that it was a lovely place to live, but she didn't care enough to ask Aleta about it.

The owners were an older elven couple, who greeted both detectives with a smile. Since Aleta actually knew them,

Danthres hung back and let the other detective take the lead.

"Aleta!" the woman said, her arms opening wide. She was wearing several necklaces and rings, so the action made the jewelry around her neck jangle. "So good to see you! And look at you, a lieutenant now!"

"Shiraia, Anthlam, it's good to see you both, but I'm afraid that Lieutenant Tresyllione and I are here on business."

Danthres couldn't help but smile at Aleta's transparency. Rather than lower herself to actually introduce Danthres to them, she just said each person's name out loud so they all knew who everyone else was.

"Oh dear," Anthlam said. "What is it?"

Aleta produced the key. "We found this on a dead body."

Shiraia put her hands to her mouth. "That's room 7."

Anthlam shook his head. "Feleth."

Danthres asked, "And who is Feleth?"

"It's Feleth lothHanthra. He's been living here for the better part of a year."

Even as Anthlam explained, Shiraia turned away. Danthres could hear her crying, though she tried to muffle it.

"We'll need to see the room," Danthres said.

"Of course," Anthlam said with a nod. "Anything you need."

Shiraia turned back around. "I want to see the body."

Anthlam winced. "There's no need for that."

Aleta nodded. "Anthlam is correct, it's not a very pretty sight."

"Actually," Danthres said, "there is a need. We only know that the dead body had Feleth's property. It would be good to have confirmation that it really is Feleth and not, say, someone who stole his key. We can take you to the castle after we look at the room—our magickal examiner should have the body soon."

At first, Aleta was glaring at Danthres, but her explanation seemed to calm the elven woman, as she voiced no objection.

Shiraia excused herself, obviously distraught. Anthlam took the lieutenants to the third floor. Each level had three boarding rooms, and the one marked with the numeral 7 in Ra-Telvish was the one Anthlam opened for them.

Danthres looked around and saw the usual toiletries and other items. The place was a bit disorganized, but no worse than that of any other person living alone who couldn't afford a house-cleaning service.

Anthlam said, "We hadn't seen Feleth in a few days, but that's not unusual in and of itself. He was an itinerant sailor. Never had a permanent job on any boat, but would do pickup work here and there."

Something niggled at Danthres, though, especially in light of what Anthlam just said. So she started going through his clothes. "When was the last time you saw him?" she asked as she picked up two pairs of boots. One set was well worn and pitted in spots, the other polished though equally worn on the soles.

"About a week ago." Anthlam snapped his fingers. "Oh, wait, I remember Shiraia saying she had bumped into him two days ago, right when the Chalmraik Flu hit. She said he was going to see if he could get some work given how many human and dwarven sailors were getting sick."

After dropping the boots to the floor, Danthres asked, "And he lived here alone the entire time?"

Anthlam nodded. "We charge more if a second person moves in."

"And he never had any relationships that you're aware of?"

"None. He would have told us, he was *very* honest."

Danthres nodded. "Thank you. Let's take you to the castle to identify the body." A picture was starting to form, and it wasn't what she'd been expecting.

Aleta found it to be almost physically painful to be in the magickal examiner's basement lair when Shiraia saw the body of Feleth and burst into tears. She'd always had an emotional attachment to her boarders, even the short-termers like Aleta herself. It must have broken her heart to see his body.

Through teary eyes, she said to Aleta, "He always wore a gold bracelet."

Nodding, Aleta said, "He was wearing it. We have it stored as evidence for the time being."

"I—" Shiraia glanced at Anthlam, and then started crying again.

Aleta was about to offer to escort them back to the River Walk, but the halfbreed spoke before she had the chance. "One of the guards can escort you back home."

"Thank you," Shiraia said.

After they left, having been handed off to a rookie guard named Tharanthi, Aleta looked at Tresyllione. "We're shorthanded as it is, and we have to go back to the docks anyhow to question the crews he worked with. Why aren't we escorting them back?"

The halfbreed shook her head. "We will do that, if we have to, but the first thing I need from you is a list of places a former Shranlaseth might hide. And I want to talk to the other two who are in town, those two leatherworkers."

Aleta shook her head. "What?"

"Feleth's body was found near the boarding house, so it's likely that the murder occurred either in the room or close by. And Feleth did *not* live alone."

"What makes you say *that*? Shiraia and Anthlam said—"

"Oh, I'm sure Feleth *told* them he was alone, because the rates would go up if he told them about his roommate. But there were two sets of clothes there, about half of which smelled of saltwater, and the other half didn't. Plus there were two sets of boots, and the set that wasn't pockmarked by salt were bigger than the pair that were. There were also two sets of toiletries."

"None of that proves anything. He could have another set of clothes that he wears on land, and one pair of boots could be the wrong size. Besides, is this phantom roommate going around bootless?"

"He could have a second pair," Tresyllione said. "Also, I'm fairly certain that Feleth and Shiraia were having an affair."

Aleta's eyes widened. "Based on what?"

"One of the necklaces Shiraia was wearing was an *erman* pledge necklace."

"I'm not familiar with those."

"They're common in the south."

Now Aleta made a face. "You mean in Sorlin?" Like most halfbreeds who survived to adulthood, Tresyllione had lived in that foul colony to the south, which had been a refuge for fugitives from the Elf Queen.

"Actually, I never saw one until I left Sorlin. A lot of the human lands to the south use them, particularly Treemark and Tomvale. And it's only the woman who wears a necklace. The man wears a plain gold bracelet."

That brought Aleta up short. "Like the one Feleth wore?"

Tresyllione nodded.

Then Aleta shook her head. "In that case—Anthlam may have been the one to hire a former Shranlaseth to kill Feleth in revenge for sleeping with his wife. He didn't seem as put out by Feleth's death as Shiraia was, even accounting for Shiraia's extreme reaction."

"That's possible."

Boneen came in a moment later. "What are you two doing here?" He followed that question with a sneeze. "Dammit, *that* spell didn't work, either."

The halfbreed smiled. "Boneen, I need you to go to the River Walk and cast a peel-back on room 7 of the boarding house on the western end of the road. We're fairly certain a murder happened there within the past two days."

"Oh, very well. Perhaps the sea air will do me some good." With that, he gestured and disappeared in a flash of light.

Aleta blinked spots out of her eyes.

Chuckling, Tresyllione said, "That's the fastest I've ever seen Boneen go to a crime scene. And he usually saves the Teleport Spell for the return trip. He must *really* be sick." She headed for the exit. "Come on, let's talk to those two leatherworkers."

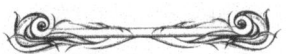

Danthres had expected the pair of leatherworkers to have an alibi, and they did. Whatever Danthres thought of them, they were well-regarded business people, and in any case, they were neither stupid enough nor financially desperate enough to take on an assassination contract.

However, they did mention that they'd heard a rumor that a former Shranlaseth had come into town a month ago aboard the *Sea Beast*, a cargo and transport vessel out of Saptor Isle.

Working their way down to the docks, Danthres was pleased to see that the *Sea Beast* was actually in dock, having arrived the previous day from its latest journey on the Garamin. The first mate informed them that Feleth had served as a bosun's mate on that vessel about a month or two ago, during which, among other things, they took some elven passengers from Saptor Isle to Cliff's End. The first mate couldn't say if any of them had neck tattoos, as he didn't interact much with the passengers.

Once they disembarked, Boneen met them on the River Walk. "The body I'm holding in—" He paused to sneeze. "—in the castle was in fact killed in that room by another elf." He handed Aleta a crystal. Upon touching it, she concentrated, and the image of an elf with the same neck tattoo as her own appeared over it.

"Recognize him?" Danthres asked.

Aleta nodded. "Only his face, though. We never went on any missions together. He was definitely Shranlaseth—and he was there when we were disbanded, I remember him being at the last gathering, and also at the port to sail into the Garamin a month later." Then her face lit up. "Wethran, that's his name." She turned to Danthres. "We should interview Anthlam. I still think he hired Wethran to kill Feleth."

Danthres rubbed her chin. "Either way, he may recognize Wethran's face."

Aleta nodded and put the crystal in the pouch at her belt. Instinctively, Danthres wanted to object to her holding onto it, but she swallowed it down when she realized that there was no reason for her to feel that way.

They proceeded down the River Walk while Boneen actually cast a second Teleport Spell. As they walked, Danthres said, "Hope we don't need Boneen for anything else. That's three spells in a row, he'll be napping for the next two days at least."

Anthlam was sweeping the walkway in front of the boarding house when the detectives arrived. "Lieutenants, what can I do for you?"

"We were wondering if you recognized this person." Danthres nodded to Aleta, who pulled out the crystal.

When the image of Wethran appeared, Anthlam stared at it. "He looks vaguely familiar—I think I saw him once or twice here at the boarding house. Why, is he involved with Fethel's murder?"

"You tell us," Aleta said. "When you saw him at the boarding house, what was your interaction?"

Now Anthlam stared at Aleta. "I'm sorry? Like I said, I only saw him once or twice."

"So you didn't interact with him at all?" Aleta asked.

"No. Look, what's this about?"

Danthres took over. "How are things here at the house? You have enough tenants?"

"Absolutely. It seems like every day there are more elves coming into town, and we provide a place that reminds them of home."

"And your marriage is strong?"

Anthlam hesitated. "I don't see how that's any of your business."

"It's a murder investigation," Danthres said, "that makes *everything* our business. And we're curious as to why your wife responded so strongly to Feleth's death."

"Shiraia is a very—very emotional woman. She cares for our clients a great deal."

Aleta said, "As I recall, she didn't react that strongly when old Theshnor died." At Danthres's quizzical look, she added, "Theshnor was living in the boarding house when I was here. He used to bring Shiraia tea every day. He was almost three hundred years old, so it wasn't a surprise when he died in his sleep. But Shiraia and he were very close, yet she didn't respond with half the energy she showed for Feleth."

Danthres wished that Aleta had mentioned this sooner, but said nothing in front of the suspect. "Yet there she was practically rending her garments over Feleth."

Anthlam held up a hand. "Enough. Look, Feleth and Shiraia were sleeping together. That's not a surprise."

That brought Danthres up short. "Excuse me?"

"Our marriage has been one of convenience for years. We stay together because we run the boarding house, but she has had many lovers over the years. Feleth is simply her latest. I myself have been sleeping with the couple in room 8 for the better part of two years."

Aleta felt deflated. She and Tresyllione went through the motions of questioning Anthlam, and then queried the couple in room 8 to verify that particular extramarital relationship.

As they left the room, Aleta noticed that the door to room 7 was unlocked. "Anthlam locked that door when we left earlier, didn't he?"

"He did."

The pair of them immediately went to the door, and stood on either side of it. Aleta put her hand to the hilt of her sword, but didn't draw it yet. Since she was on the same side as the handle, she counted down from three to one and then opened it.

Inside the apartment was the same face they saw over the crystal: Wethran.

"Don't move," Tresyllione said, but Wethran ignored the halfbreed's direction and ran toward the window.

Aleta went after him even as he jumped down the two stories to the ground. When Aleta reached the window she saw Wethran land, roll, and spring to his feet, just the way all Shranlaseth had been trained.

Taking a deep breath, Aleta unfastened her scabbard and tossed it out the window—the sword would get in the way—and did just as Wethran did, leaping out the window, landing while bending her knees with the impact and using her momentum to roll forward on her right shoulder and come up on her feet.

Room 7 looked out on the sea side of the house, so Wethran had run around the boarding house to the River Walk side. Aleta picked up her scabbard and followed him—

—only to find him standing at swordpoint, with Tresyllione's standard-issue longsword out and pointed right at his neck.

"Move one muscle," the halfbreed was saying, "and I slice that lovely tattoo of yours open."

Aleta was stunned. "How'd you get down here so fast?"

Tresyllione just smiled. "You two aren't the only ones with tricks. Wethran, you're under arrest for the murder of Feleth lothHanthra."

Wethran shook his head. "It was a mercy killing. He was a fornicator and an oath-breaker."

"Neither of those things," Tresyllione said slowly, "is against the law."

Laughing bitterly, Wethran asked, "What does the law matter? Laws change. A heroic act in war is a criminal act in peace. The only thing that *matters* is upholding what's right and punishing what's wrong."

Aleta shook her head. "So you were punishing Feleth?"

"Yes. And we're killers—it's what she made us—and so I punished him by killing him. That's what we do, after all. The immoral aren't people, they're things that must be destroyed—like *this* one." That last was said with a sneering look at the halfbreed.

Aleta started to speak, but Tresyllione put a hand on her shoulder and shook her head. After a moment, she nodded in return. It was better to let him ramble and incriminate himself.

"When I came to Cliff's End, Feleth gave me a place to stay. I thought he was a good man. I thought he was kind and generous. Instead, I found out that he was fornicating *with another man's wife*. Worse, the wife of the man who *housed* him! He lied and went back on his word. He no longer had the right to live."

"Everyone has the right to live," Aleta said, "until they're judged by the law."

"Oh, *please*," Wethran said. "The Elf Queen's law was that those who fornicated outside the marriage bed had broken the law."

"The Elf Queen doesn't rule here." Aleta actually smiled, then. "Laws change." The smile fell. "And at least with the Castle Guard, I know that there will be at least some measure of justice in the law."

Wethran gave another bitter laugh. "Justice. Spare me. There's no such thing."

Tresyllione grabbed Wethran and started pushing him forward down the River Walk toward Meerka Way. "Not yet. But we're working on it."

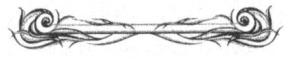

Danthres signed the scroll that contained the report on the Feleth murder. From across the squadroom, Aleta was just staring at the huge window on the north wall, which provided a view of the Forest of Nimvale, the setting sun painting the sky brilliant shades of orange and purple behind the trees.

On the one hand, Danthres had to admit that Aleta had performed well in this case. She had been promoted because she helped save the life of the king and queen, but based on what Danthres saw here, she had assets as a detective. It would probably be years before she was actually *good* at it, but Danthres was willing to admit that she had potential.

Admit it to herself anyhow. No way in hell she'd say it out loud.

The report complete, Danthres rose and summoned Ep, the imp who kept all the Castle Guard's files. The glass of the window twisted and turned and formed a giant face. "The Feleth case," she said.

"Which one's that again?" the face in the wall asked.

Snappishly, Danthres said, "The elf who died on the River Walk and was brought to the body shop."

"I don't have a case report for that yet."

"Because I'm handing it to you now."

"Oh."

Not for the first time, Danthres had to force herself not to put a gloved fist through the window. It wouldn't actually do Ep any harm, as he was magickally protected, and Captain Dru would probably take the cost of repairing the window out of her pay.

From behind her, Aleta said, "Some days, I really want to punch that imp right in the face."

Unable to help herself, Danthres laughed. "So has everyone in this castle."

"Honestly, I'd settle for punching *anything* right now." Aleta got up and started pacing the squadroom. "I just don't *understand* him."

"I'm assuming you don't mean Ep," Danthres said dryly.

"I mean Wethran. He and I both went through the same training, yet he turned psychotic. And what he said made no sense! If laws are mutable, if morality is mutable, why did he kill Feleth over morality? The morality didn't even make sense, Shiraia wasn't lying to Anthlam or sneaking around behind his back! Wethran said he doesn't believe in justice, yet he went and administered what he thought was justice."

Danthres just watched as she paced and ranted and raved and waved her arms around.

Finally, she stopped and looked at Danthres. "He did something we did all the time in the Shranlaseth, and we were praised for it."

"Killed a lot of adulterers, did you?"

Aleta shook her head. "No, the penalty for adultery was work prison. I meant using the *shanshoora* on someone. We employed it when we wanted someone to die quickly, but painfully. Our form of justice, I suppose." She blew out a long breath. "None of it makes sense."

"Our job isn't to make sense of things. It's to find out who broke the law and make sure they're brought to the magistrate to answer for their crimes. This city-state is filled with victims, and we're here to speak for them, to bring them at least a measure of justice. Sometimes it works, and sometimes it doesn't. But you're never going to do the job properly if you try to figure out why someone decided to commit a crime. Why isn't the point. Occasionally, finding out a perpetrator's motivation can aid in finding that perpetrator, but that's as far as it actually matters. And if you do keep trying to figure out why, you'll wind up like your friend."

"He's no friend of mine," Aleta said quickly and with disgust.

"I don't know, you have a lot in common. You were both Shranlaseth. You both found your way to Cliff's End. And you both think I'm an abomination."

Aleta looked up at that last part before quickly looking away. "The Elf Queen thought you were an abomination. She told us just what Wethran said: the immoral aren't people, and a union between an elf and an outsider was an immoral act. I spent most of my adult life believing everything the Elf Queen told me, so I didn't view those that I killed as *people*. I suppose that made it easy for those of us who became assassins to take on those jobs, and for Wethran to kill his friend without regret." She looked back at Danthres, her blue eyes intent. "But then the Elf Queen told us—told *me*—that the Shranlaseth were no longer to be trusted and she disbanded us. And now she's dead, her reign long ended. She was wrong about our trustworthiness. If she hadn't disbanded the Shranlaseth, she might not have lost the war. And if she was wrong about that, it's possible that maybe she was wrong about other things, too."

Danthres chuckled. "Possible, yes. C'mon, our shift's over. Let's head to the Old Ball and Chain and drink to another closed case."

Aleta hesitated. "You'd drink with a baby killer?"

"If you'll drink with an abomination." Danthres then pointed a finger at her. "Don't get me wrong, Shranlaseth, I still don't like you. But Dru's right, we have to work together, and today proved that we can work together. And that means another victim's been spoken for by the Castle Guard, another criminal is in the hole awaiting the magistrate's word, and *that* is something worth celebrating. Even with you."

Chuckling, Aleta said, "I can't argue with any of that. Let's go."

Introduction to
"The Ballad of Big Charlie"

Jonathan Maberry and I have been friends for years. Both of us are part of a cabal of writers known as The Liars Club (more about them in the introduction to "Under the King's Bridge"), and we've endeavored to work together where at all possible, as we're both very fond of each others' work.

Jonathan was invited by IDW Publishing—a comic book company that also does a variety of prose projects—to pitch an anthology idea. Jonathan thought it would be fun to do a shared-world anthology, where all the writers would contribute to a larger storyline. Years ago, Jonathan wrote a guide to vampire myths, and using that research he hit on a vampire story that would do something new by doing something old.

The conceit of *V-Wars* is that a virus that was frozen in the Arctic has been unleashed by the ice caps melting, and it activates dormant DNA in people—inlcuding the genes for vampirism. Every culture has vampire legends, and in *V-Wars*, those legends are actually true. But vampires were eventually killed off—until this virus came back. Now people are turning into vampires, but they aren't the vampires of Bram Stoker or Universal Pictures or Anne Rice or Joss Whedon or Stephenie Meyer. No, these are the vampires of folklore that Stoker used as the basis for *Dracula*, and that other 19th-century writers mined for their Gothic tales. So Greeks turn into *vyrkolatios*, Russians turn into *eretica*, Haitians turn into *loup garou*, etc.

Jonathan was insistent that there be no supernatural elements to the stories. This is a result of science, not magic. And so Jonathan and me, along with John Everson, Gregory Frost, Nancy Holder, James A. Moore, Yvonne Navarro, and Scott

Nicholson all penned tales of how these people with I1V1 (the "V-virus") deal with this change to their humanity—and how humanity reacts to these modern-day monsters in their midst.

For my part, what I was curious about was how it might affect politics. What if somebody running for office announces that he or she has the virus? What effect would that have on the campaign? Plus, there's a huge difference between local politics and national politics. We often see people running for local office who wouldn't last five seconds on the national stage. (To give an example from my own hometown of New York, Rudolph Giuliani was as successful as it's possible to be within New York City, but when he tried to go national, he crashed and burned pretty spectacularly.)

And so we have "The Ballad of Big Charlie," as Hugues Charles, a man of Haitian descent, and who is running for a fourth term as Bronx District Attorney, announces to the world that he has I1V1.

I had tremendous fun with this story, as I've always been fascinated by politics, and I'm always happy to write stories that take place in my home town. (This is one of five stories in this collection that at least partly takes place in New York City.)

I'm pleased to say that *V-Wars* was sufficiently successful as to spawn many spinoffs. IDW commissioned three more anthologies, Jonathan wrote monthly *V-Wars* comic book series for IDW, and a TV series starring Ian Somerhalder will debut on Netflix some time in the next year or so. I've written another story in the world, "Streets of Fire" in the third anthology, subtitled *Night Terrors. Daily News* reporter Mia Fitzsimmons is the protagonist of that story, and we get to see the NYPD's Vampire Crimes Unit in action.

The Ballad of Big Charlie

a V-Wars story

1

Walking into Bronx District Attorney Hugues Charles's office, it was easy for New York *Daily News* reporter Mia Fitzsimmons to understand how he got the nickname "Big Charlie."

The office, located in the rectangular edifice of the Bronx County Courthouse on E. 161st Street, was surprisingly cramped for the biggest prosecutor in the borough—and "biggest" took on a whole new meaning as his six-foot-eight frame unfolded itself into an upright position. The window behind him had a view of Joyce Kilmer Park alongside the Grand Concourse. On this sunny spring day, people sat out in the park, and cars zoomed past giant apartment buildings on the Concourse.

Big Charlie's shoulders were wide enough to land a plane on, and he loomed over the five-foot-three Mia. She approached his metal desk, which was covered in papers, a small Droid tablet, an iPhone, and two computers—a laptop and a desktop. His head was long and widened as you went down, with no obvious neck—it was as if his cheeks went straight into those gigantic shoulders. He held out a huge hand to shake that Mia almost didn't return for fear that her own tiny hand would be lost.

No wonder he's such a good prosecutor. If I had to face that in the courtroom, I'd plea for fear of being eaten alive.

Then he smiled, showing wide teeth, and suddenly Mia felt at ease. He spoke with a light Haitian accent. "A pleasure to meet you, Ms. Fitzsimmons."

She put out her own hand. "Thank you, Mr. District Attorney." His hands were warm and all-encompassing, but the handshake was gentle.

His face turned quizzical. "Or have we met before?"

Mia nodded, impressed at his memory. "At the opening for the Homeless Voices exhibit at the Bronx Museum of the Arts." It was one of Mia's first pieces for the *News* years ago before she got moved to local politics.

"Of course, I should have recalled," he said, though there was no reason why he should have remembered her. Indicating the guest chair with one enormous hand, he said, "Please, take a seat."

She sat in the guest chair opposite him, and fished her digital recorder out of her purse. "May I record this?"

"By all means."

After hitting RECORD, Mia said, "Yesterday, you announced that you're running for a fourth term for Bronx DA. First off, why'd you do it on Mother's Day with your Mom by your side?"

That prompted another smile from Big Charlie. Mia had missed the press conference, as she was having dinner with her own mother in Woodlawn. She was hardly the only one to miss the Sunday holiday presser, but she did see the footage on both New York 1 and Channel 12.

"*Maman*, she was seven months pregnant with me when she came here from Haiti," he said. "My father, he was killed by Papa Doc's *Tontons Macoutes*, and that was when *maman* decided to depart. She wanted what was best for her unborn child, so she boarded a boat and travelled to New York. She worked very hard to make sure that I had nothing but the best education, nothing but the best opportunities. It is due to her that I am here, and it is due to her that I am running again."

Mia nodded. "Is she also why you announced so late?" The primary was in September, after all, and while there was technically a general election, all local elections in at least four of the five boroughs were decided on Primary Day. Aside from Staten Island, this was pretty much a Democrat town.

Big Charlie got up and walked to the window, looking down at the park and the double-parked cars on 161st. "I was a boy in 1977. I recall watching the Yankees in the World Series on the television. The South Bronx—the neighborhood outside this window—was on fire. Howard Cosell was the announcer, and he said, 'Ladies and gentlemen, the Bronx is burning.'"

Mia couldn't help but chuckle at hearing the late sports announcer's trademark staccato monotone with Big Charlie's Haitian accent.

He continued: "I thought then that it was wrong that the place where law was made should be on fire like that. I wanted to protect this neighborhood so the law would still be made." Turning around, he hit Mia with the smile again. "I was a child, thinking childish thoughts, but they remained with me all my days. But once I had completed three terms, I was not sure of my ability to continue to fulfill that promise. It was *maman* who took me aside and said, 'Hugues, you're just being a fool, and I did not travel 3000 miles to raise a fool.'"

Frowning, Mia said, "Uhm, Haiti's less than 2000 miles from New York."

Big Charlie's laugh was deep and hearty. "Yes, I know. *Maman*, she has always been poor at judging distances."

"So she got you here and made it clear you wouldn't be a fool?"

"Yes." Big Charlie squeezed himself back into the leather chair behind his desk, the view of Kilmer Park framing his long face. "I grew up in the public schools, but then I received academic scholarships to the Bronx High School of Science, to Columbia, and to Fordham's law school."

"You spent all of three years in corporate law before becoming a Brooklyn ADA. Why'd you make the switch?"

"I recall my first case when I began working for the District Attorney's office in Brooklyn. I inherited a case that was going to trial—a drug case. It had been almost two years since the arrest. All the police officers on my witness list had been promoted—and this arrest was not a significant contributor to those promotions, as it was a standard buy-and-bust. It is the sort of crime that often leads to a plea-bargain so that a greater crime can be prosecuted.

"But that did not happen here. Instead, this minor purchase of heroin was allowed to tie up the court system for two years. It was a colossal waste of resources, and one I swore would never happen were I to ascend to the position of District Attorney."

"Uhm, okay." Mia smiled wryly. "That doesn't actually answer my question."

He chuckled. "I suppose that I simply did not feel that my childhood dream of keeping the place of law safe could be accomplished behind a mahogany desk in an office with a view of downtown. I prefer the metal desk in front of me and the double-parked cars out my window. I feel more as if I am part of something rather than attempting to remain above it."

That came closer to answering the question, and Mia figured that was the best she was going to get. "We first met at an art exhibit opening, and that's hardly the only one you've been to. Every time there's an event at the Bronx Zoo or at a park or museum, there you are. That's a lot more dedication to the community than you see from your average DA."

"I did not wish my legacy to be that of someone who was 'tough on crime,' because crime-fighting is the job description. Being a District Attorney who is hard on crime is merely someone who has shown up for work each morning. I wish to be remembered as one who went above and beyond such."

"You've hired Barel Grindberg as your campaign manag—"

Mia was interrupted by Big Charlie's iPhone, which made a three-tone beep and lit up. He glanced down at the status, and then winced. "I am sorry, Ms. Fitzsimmons, but that is one of my ADAs and I'm afraid I must contact her immediately. Let me just say that Barel has managed all my campaigns to date, and she has done a superb job. I am quite fortunate to have her again."

With that, Mia hit STOP on the recorder, dropped it in her purse, once again lost her hand in Big Charlie's oversized paw, and beat a hasty retreat out of his office. She'd been hoping to ask more about Grindberg, who'd been a player in New York politics for years, but the quote would be enough for the op-ed piece she was doing. It wasn't as if she was going to be digging any kind of dirt in this interview. Maybe later, but for now, she was doing a puff piece that would make the candidate happy enough to give her more access.

Then, if dirt materialized, she'd be in a better position to find it. And if it didn't, then she would have the inside track of a beloved community figure's candidacy. She won either way.

2

NEWS ARTICLE IN THE BRONX SECTION OF THE NEW YORK DAILY NEWS.

Several residents of the Edenwald neighborhood have reported a large dog or wolf roaming Needham and De Reimer Avenues near Baychester Avenue and Boston Road. Many garbage cans were turned over with the bags ripped open, and one resident—who asked to remain anonymous—said that the wolf or dog injured her cat.

NYPD's Animal Control has been notified, and a source at the 47th Precinct has stated that uniformed officers are keeping an eye out. No animals have been reported missing from the Bronx Zoo.

3

"The field's completely clear at this point. Ayala was the only holdout, and he's on board now, especially if you give him that promotion you've been promising him for a year."

Barel Grindberg looked up from the notes on her legal pad to see that Big Charlie was staring at the display on his iPhone, which sat on the conference-room table. "Uhm, hello? Coulda sworn we were having a meeting here."

"Hm?" Big Charlie looked up. "My apologies, Barel, I am simply concerned about *maman*. I have not heard from her all day, and it is rather unlike her to be out of touch for this long a period. What were we discussing?"

"Bernie Ayala. He agreed to drop out and endorse you if you give him that promotion to homicide."

Shaking his head, Big Charlie blew out a breath. "I only have refrained from promoting him due to the budget. If he's willing to accept the job title without the salary bump—"

Barel grinned. "He'll pretend to be pissed, but he'll take it. He wants murders so he can run when you finally get around to retiring."

"That should be four years from now."

"Yeah, right. That's what you said four years ago."

"*Maman* changed my—"

Holding up a hand, Barel said, "Please. Save it for the reporters. By the way, I loved that op-ed piece Fitzsimmons did for the *News*."

That got the trademark Big Charlie smile. "As did *maman*. And she generally has very little use for reporters."

Barel filed that away. While she did tease her boss about it, Marie Charles's likes and dislikes often had a profound impact on her son's decisions. If Fitzsimmons was someone Marie liked, it meant that Big Charlie was likely to give her access. She jotted down a note to have her guys vet the reporter.

Running a hand through the mess of steel wool she laughingly referred to as her hair, Barel opened her mouth when she saw something out of the corner of her eye.

The conference room of their Boston Road campaign headquarters had windows on the east wall that looked out on the rest of the main campaign office. On the far end was the glass door to Boston Road, which flew open to reveal Judy Alejo, the DA's press secretary. A tiny Latina woman, Judy had a lovely round face that looked disarming and charming most of the time—all of the time if she was in public or anywhere near a journalist or camera.

The only way she betrayed her mood was if she was biting her lip. The right side meant she was nervous or concerned about something. Having the left side between her teeth meant she was pissed.

"This isn't good," Barel said as Judy made a beeline for the conference room. She was holding a round disc in her hand.

"You're not gonna believe this," the press secretary said without preamble as she threw the door open.

"What is it, Judy?" Big Charlie asked.

But Judy didn't say anything, instead walked over to the DVD player on the table against the north wall and pushed the open button. After dropping the disc in, she grabbed the remote and turned on the flatscreen that was mounted to the west wall.

It was a Channel 12 news report. Based on the stamp in the lower-left-hand corner of the screen, it was just aired a couple of hours earlier that day.

"If you thought the Bronx DA race was over when three-termer Hugues Charles announced that he'd be running again, you'll have to think twice. Big Charlie has a challenger, and it's long-time activist Mickey Solano. Nishan—"

"You have *got* to be fucking *kidding* me." Barel was livid.

Judy hit pause. "I thought you said you took care of him."

Trying not to grind her teeth, Barel said, "I thought I did, too."

In a much calmer tone than either of the two women in the room with him, Big Charlie said, "I do not believe that it is entirely bad. Play the rest of the story, please, Judy?"

Nodding, Judy hit play. For her part, Barel thought she was, if anything, underreacting, but said nothing, wanting to see the rest.

"—da Henry has the story."

The image cut from the anchor desk to Nishanda Henry, a tall, striking African-American woman. Barel had always thought she was wasting her talents on the local level, as she had good instincts and camera presence. But she actually said she liked staying in her own borough.

"Mickey Solano hasn't been a practicing trial lawyer in many years, although he is a full partner in a local law firm, but now he's running for Bronx District Attorney."

Barel rolled her eyes. "That *momzer* was never a trial lawyer. Only time he saw the inside of a courtroom was when he got called for jury duty."

Now the image was that of the square jaw, slicked hair, and wide eyes of Mickey Solano. "It's time for a change. Hugues Charles is a good man, and he's done fine things for this city, but most of them have very little to do with being the man who prosecutes crimes in this borough. Mr. Charles has done a great deal to streamline the process, to unclog the courts, as his press releases would have you believe, but it's come at the expense of truly punishing those who deserve to be punished."

Rising to her feet, Barel gestured at the television. "That fucking *pisher* better not be pulling the death penalty *mishegoss* out of his *tuchas*."

Judy stared at her a moment, then looked at Big Charlie. "Okay, that's four Yiddish words in a minute. *Now* will you agree that this is bad?"

"When did I use Yiddish?" Barel asked, confused.

Having paused the DVD again, Judy smiled. "*Pisher, mishegoss, tuchas,* and *momzer.* I don't even know what a *momzer* is. I mean, I can guess from the context, but—"

Waving her arms back and forth, Barel rolled up the sleeves of her cardigan and said, "Play the damn tape, would you please?" She hated when she started sounding like Uncle Eli.

Nishanda was back on: "Solano was an advocate of New York's death penalty statute that was passed in 1995, and w—"

"Did I call it?" Barel asked.

"—as a vocal opponent of the state supreme court ruling of that statute being unconstitutional in 2004. He has dedicated a large amount of time and money to advocating for the reactivation of the statute and allowing the death penalty in New York once again."

"*This* is what the *momz*—" She caught herself. "*This* is what the asshole's going with? Elect me DA so I can enact a death penalty that never got used during the ten years it was legal?"

Solano was talking again. "It's all well and good for Mr. Charles to point to the reduced crime rate, but that's simply him taking credit for a citywide and nationwide drop in crime since he took office. Advanced technology, better crime-fighting procedures, COMPSTAT—these are what reduced the crime rate, not a man who happened to be in the right place at the ri—"

Judy talked over Nishanda. "Can you believe that shit? He lobbied *against* COMPSTAT for three years, and now he's talking about how it did your job for you?"

Solano was talking again. "—ave nothing but respect for Big Charlie. I like him a lot. But this isn't personal. This is business, and I'm putting myself in the business of giving the Bronx a better District Attorney."

Barel turned to Big Charlie, who was staring at his iPhone. "So do you agree that it's bad? He's a legit threat to you. That was why I thought he was dealt with—the whole thing was that you'd run this year and he'd make a run in four years. So what the fuck changed?"

Big Charlie looked up, with a sad expression. "Nothing changed, Barel. He simply was upset when I announced, after the conversation we'd had in April."

Glowering at him, Barel simply said, "What conversation in April?"

"I told him that I was not going to be running. He was going to announce on Memorial Day."

"And you were going to share this with me, when, exactly?" Barel asked tightly.

"Or me?" Judy was chewing pretty hard on her left lower lip. "Jesus, Charlie, you can't just leave shit out. We need to *know* things like that. We can't afford to be blindsided."

"If it makes you feel any better, Mickey is not particularly pleased with me, either." He held up the iPhone, and Barel snatched it out of his hand.

Staring at the display, she saw an e-mail from Mickey Solano. "I guess you seen the news. I'm sorry, Hugues, but you TOLD me you wasn't running again. I ain't gonna air your dirty laundry in public, coz I don't play that, but damn, man, you said you wasn't running! You KNEW I had an exploratory committee, you KNEW I was scouting out campaign locations, so why do you wanna do me like that? Well, I'm sorry, but I been planning this for way too long to give up now. It's my TURN, and you ain't taking this away from me, no way, no how."

"Dirty laundry?" Barel handed the iPhone back to Charlie. "Is he kidding? Did you actually promise him anything?"

Big Charlie shrugged his immense shoulders. "I said only that I was not planning to seek re-election—which, at the time, I was not—and that the field was open to him if he wished."

Judy shook her head, and Barel feared she would draw blood from the left-hand side of her lip. "Why would you even do that? Especially to Mickey? He's a snake."

"He's not a snake." Barel was shaking her head. "He's the guy the snake sends to the bodega to buy his cigarettes. And now he's gonna be crawling up our tuch— our asses. Hope you're happy." She tossed her legal pad aside. "Well, that's useless now. It doesn't matter who dropped out, because it's a race again."

"It was always a race, Barel."

"No, it was a cakewalk. Your only opposition were the down-ballot nutjobs. We weren't even going to have to debate those—those guys." She managed to swallow another Yiddishism. "Now, though, we have to actually have a debate."

Big Charlie stood up, looming over both women. "Then we shall have a debate." And then he strode out of the conference room and headed to the front door.

"I guess he's going home. Great." Barel looked at Judy, who was now chewing on her right lip.

"I'll do up a press release, saying we welcome the competition, the airing of issues, and so on. Y'know, the usual bullshit."

"Yeah." Barel shook her head. "You know Mia Fitzsimmons at the *News*?"

Judy nodded. "Yeah, we went to the same high school."

"Friends?"

She grinned. "Not then. I was the cool Latina chick, she was the brainiac Irish girl."

"Well, she did a nice job on the announcement, and I think we should give her more access. If Mickey's throwing his fedora in, we're gonna need all the favorable press coverage we can get."

4

Mia Fitzsimmons stood on the steps of the Bronx County Courthouse, the midday June sun blasting down on her, and wondered what this press conference was about.

Big Charlie and Mickey Solano hadn't even had their first debate yet, though it was scheduled (finally) for two weeks' hence.

Jack Napolitano approached, his jaw arriving half a second before the rest of him. He went from being an anchor on Channel 12 to a political beat reporter for Channel 5, the local FOX affiliate, and with his chiseled good looks, he was bound for an anchor there, too, if not something national.

In case Mia ever forgot all that, Jack was likely to remind her of it.

"So I heard it through the grapevine that you got the other question."

Mia frowned. "Excuse me?"

"Judy told me only two people are asking questions after he makes whatever big statement he's making, and a little bird told me that you're number two."

In fact, the impression Mia had gotten from Judy's e-mail was that she was the only one asking questions, but thinking back over the text of it, realized that she'd never been that specific. It burned her britches a bit that she had to share with *this* jackass, but Channel 5 was the most-watched local news channel, so she could understand the logic.

"So you have any idea what this is about? I've been keeping my ear to the ground, but everyone's lips are sealed."

"No idea."

"He's gotta be dropping out." Jack shook his head, and Mia felt the need to duck, as his jaw had quite the turn radius. "Why else would mum be the word?"

Mia shook her head. "He's not dropping out."

"How're you so sure?" Jack asked, sounding offended that she would disagree with him.

Were she speaking to someone she liked—or respected—or didn't want to sock in his oversize, cliché-spouting jaw—Mia would have said something like, "His mother wants him to run, and he's the world's biggest *maman*'s boy," but instead she just shrugged. "Call it instinct."

"If you insist." He let out a sigh. "I hope this doesn't take long. I've got an interview with RSN. I think I'm a shoo-in for that one."

Mia suddenly experienced a massive coughing fit, which covered her look of disgust. Yuki Nitobe had broken the "vampire" story for the Regional Satellite Network, and that got her a promotion—once she was released from the hospital, anyhow. Mia herself had been dubious about the whole thing, but then Mick McCarthy told her, and the rest of the reporters in the city room, about what he saw at Bellevue that night. Just Mick's descriptions of it had given Mia nightmares. She couldn't imagine what it must have been like for Yuki.

But she'd broken the story and now was the go-to girl for I1V1, the virus that was turning people into vampires. "The V-Event," some marketing dork at RSN had called it. Her promotion meant a job opening, and Mia was completely not surprised that Jack had dusted off his resumé to take his shot at it.

"It's showtime."

At Jack's words, Mia looked up to see Judy Alejo approaching the podium that was set up on the courthouse steps. Big Charlie was just a few feet behind her, looking far more solemn than Mia could ever recall the jovial prosecutor appearing.

Once everyone quieted down, Judy spoke. "Thank you, ladies and gentlemen, for coming. Without further ado, here's Bronx District Attorney Hugues Charles."

Mia blinked with surprise at Judy's clipped tone and terse introduction. She usually provided a bit more buildup than that. It was odd on several levels, not the least being that she never had anything but a happy face on for the fourth estate. The last time Mia saw such a sour expression on Judy's face, it was in high school when she lost the election for Latin American Club president to Paolo Sandoval.

Something bad's going on here. She jotted some quick notes on a small paper notepad. Jack, who was cradling a tablet, made a *tch* noise. "Paper? That's *so* twentieth century."

"Thank you, Judy," Big Charlie said. "I have spent my entire career—indeed, my entire *life*—being truthful with the people of this community, and I do not wish to cease this tendency now."

The plot thickens. Mia noted that the reporters were unusually quiet. If not for the traffic noise of cars and buses on 161st and on the Concourse, it would've been eerily silent.

"Many of you are, I assume, aware of the I1V1 virus that has been spreading across the entire world. Several people standing in front of me right now reported on poor Michael Fayne, shot down while in custody at Bellevue Hospital only a few months ago. I1V1 has been especially strong here in our great city, and it would seem that I am among those who are affected by it."

That broke the quiet. Everyone around her started bellowing questions at once, voices overlapping each other into a wall of meaningless noise.

But Mia was just staring at Big Charlie as he said, "Please, calm down, my friends. I will take questions once I have completed my statement. Thank you."

A million questions went through Mia's mind, the most prominent of which was: *How did I miss this?* She'd been around Big Charlie for almost a month now, and hadn't seen a single sign of this.

That, however, was not the question she could ask him when the time came.

Once the noise died down again, Big Charlie went on. "It seems that I have *loup garou* in my ancestry. My mother told me stories of men who could turn themselves into wolves—I had no idea that I would become such a creature myself."

Mia noticed Jack frantically tapping on his tablet, cadging a wireless signal from the courthouse to look up *loup garou*. Mia would do likewise when she got back to the office, but she could afford patience. Jack was going to be on camera in a minute, where Mia had until late evening to file her story.

"Let me assure you of several things. First of all, I retain complete control over the transformation. It is not triggered by the full moon or by stress or by any outside factors that are out of my control."

One of the reporters standing behind Mia muttered, "So not Lon Chaney and not the incredible Hulk." Mia snorted a quick chuckle.

"I can become the wolf purely by force of will. Indeed, I could demonstrate for you now—but the transformation changes my shape in such a way that it would destroy this rather expensive suit I am wearing..."

That got some more chuckles. Mia could see the trademark Hugues Charles disarming technique at work. The soft voice, the smile, the yes-I'm-massive-but-I'm-a-big-teddy-bear-really mien. But this time, she wasn't buying it.

"Secondly, I have gone to see a physician, and while there is much about I1V1 that remains unknown, I have received a clean bill of health. The results of that examination will be made public, rest assured."

That got a derisive snort from Jack. Mia looked over and saw that the Channel 5 reporter was salivating. This story would make a nice addition to the reel he sent RSN.

"Finally, I have not changed. I'm still the same man that ever I was. I am still the District Attorney of Bronx County, a position

I intend to retain for at least another four years after this one. Now, then, I can take a couple of questions." Several reporters raised their hands, even though Mia and Jack were, as far as she knew, the only ones who would get called on. "Yes, Jack?"

At first, Mia was annoyed that he chose Jack first, but then she realized she had no idea what to ask. All the questions she had prepared in her head were based on what she thought this presser might be about. Big Charlie being the latest victim of I1V1 never made that particular list.

"So just to verify—you *are* continuing to seek re-election?"

A dumb but necessary question, to which Big Charlie replied, "Of course. Nothing of consequence has changed. One more question. Mia?"

And just like that, she knew what she had to ask. "If you have full control over the transformation as you say, Mr. District Attorney—then why reveal the condition at all?"

Jack stared down at her with a look approaching respect.

"Thank you for asking that, Mia," Big Charlie said, and he sounded sincere. Mia couldn't help but put on a self-satisfied smile. "I have been a part of this community for my entire life. Except for my brief sojourn in Brooklyn, I have always been a child of the Bronx. I have never lied to the people of this borough, Mia, and I see no reason to start now. Some might say I have everything to lose by sharing this information, but what, pray tell, is the alternative? Yes, I could hide it—and then what? What if Mr. Solano or an enterprising defense attorney learns the truth and reveals it? I would no longer be able to do my job— more to the point, I would no longer be *worthy* to do my job. The truth is, the only way I lose is if I do *not* disclose this condition."

Mia jotted down a few more notes. She was witnessing political history here.

"There are men and women all across the globe who are being persecuted for what is truly only a medical condition. I am continuing with my life to show others that they can continue with theirs. Thank you all, my friends."

More voices blurted out with questions, but Big Charlie had left the podium, and a slightly-less-sour-looking Judy had returned. "Thanks, everyone, I'm sorry, but no more questions. No more questions!"

"Oh, there'll be more questions, you can bet the house on *that*," Jack said.

5

Judy Alejo had deliberately timed the call to her older sister for five minutes before *Top of the News with Helen Lashmar* started so she would only have to talk to her for five minutes. It meant Perla had to concentrate her questions about when Judy would get a boyfriend, start going to church again, and stop doing that awful job and do something *useful.*

"Look, I have to go," Judy said in Spanish when the closing credits for the morning talk show that was just finishing on RSN rolled.

"You always have to go so fast," Perla replied in the same language.

"I'm the press secretary for a district attorney running for reelection. It's busy now. It'll get better after the primary."

Barel walked into the office just then. The older woman was wearing yet another cardigan, despite summer coming around. She seemed to have an endless supply of them.

"You always say that, Judy, but—"

"I really do have to go."

"But—"

Judy pulled the phone from her ear and hit end. She turned to Barel and said, "That woman will drive me up a—"

"How's that again?"

Shaking her head, Judy realized she was talking to Barel in Spanish. Switching to English, she said, "Nothing. Let's see how this goes."

She'd been dreading this broadcast. The first story Lashmar would be tackling was Big Charlie, and her producers had assembled an impressive cross-section of pundits to pick the whole thing apart.

"Some good news," Barel said. "Judy Gomez cancelled, so they got Mia Fitzsimmons on."

Judy's eyes widened. Mia had been a godsend, giving them excellent coverage. More to the point, hers was the only coverage that had been about Big Charlie as a *person* rather than a cause or a thing. Of course, she'd been the only one paying attention to him prior to that, as a local DA election wasn't any great shakes. Now, though, everyone was on the story and everyone had an opinion—but very little of it had to do with Hugues Charles himself.

The opening music finished, and the camera cut to Lashmar—an attractive brunette in her thirties who looked great on camera and had done a superb job of never once having any kind of opinion. That combined with her strong interviewing skills enabled her to get really good guests on her show.

"Good morning," she said in her pleasant alto. "We start with our roundtable segment, where a panel will tackle the news of the day. Joining me today are John Generico of the Generico Politico blog, Mia Fitzsimmons of the New York *Daily News*, former Manhattan District Attorney and current columnist for *Newsweek* Allen Reimold, and the Rev. Michael Sookdeo, chair of the Religious Studies Department at St. Paul's College."

Judy frowned. "Religious Studies? What the hell?"

Barel shrugged. "The religious types've been coming out of the damn woodwork. Vampires, crosses..."

"Our first story," Lashmar said, "is from New York City. Patient Zero of I1V1 came from New York, and now the first politician to publicly admit to suffering from the virus has come out of the city as well. Bronx District Attorney Hugues Charles, known locally as 'Big Charlie,' has admitted to being a werewolf. We'll start with John—what do you think this means for Big Charlie's reelection chances?"

Judy noticed that Mia looked relieved that she didn't get the first question.

Not that she herself was all that thrilled with Generico getting it. He was either a textbook example of the triumph of Internet journalism, or proof that the Internet had destroyed journalism, depending on who you asked. Judy generally fell into the former camp, but Generico's bloviating blog was the exception in her mind.

He also had the proverbial face made for radio, as his wide mouth, twitchy gestures, and beady eyes meant he was better suited to carrying on where you didn't have to look at him. That didn't stop every cable news station from having him on since his blog passed a billion hits a week.

In response to the question, Generico said, "In the toilet. Seriously, did he think this would have any result other than total disaster? These people are being hunted down and shot—the ones who aren't hunting themselves. Plus, how do we know he isn't going around mangling people on the night of the full moon?"

Judy shook her head. "Here we go." The past few weeks had forced her to take a crash course in separating the wheat from the chaff of werewolf legends, but most people didn't go to that much effort, and just fell back on the obvious pop-culture stereotypes just as Generico was doing.

Mia spoke up. "Well, for starters, he has control over the transformation, and—"

Generico interrupted her. "We only have his word for that."

"We only have his word that he *has* the virus! And he didn't have any reason to tell anyone."

Dismissing her with one of his twitchy gestures, Generico looked at Lashmar. "He wasn't even sure he was going to enter the race. Now he's got cold feet, so he's admitting to the problem that probably led to his delay in entering the race in the first place. He probably just figured he'd have no opposition, then when Solano decided to run, he needed a reason to back out."

Judy's first job was in the mayor's office, and she'd met Allen Reimold when he was the Manhattan DA. She'd always liked him—certainly more than the jackass who had the job these days—and so she was cheered to hear him run to Big Charlie's defense. "Except he isn't backing out. If he was, he would have by now. In fact, he's increased his public appearances in the three days since the announcement."

Generico shook his head. "I still think it's butt-covering. He's been pretty popular, so he doesn't want to let the community down."

"He's not just 'popular'," Reimold said, "he's *good*. He's streamlined the DA's office, reducing the average time between arrest and trial by months. Now part of it's the lower crime rate. I tried to do what he did when I was in the Manhattan office, but I couldn't get it done because there was just too much backlog. But he's taken advantage of that to really do some good."

Barel was nodding. "Nice." The campaign manager had been bitching for days about this show, that it was going to be a hatchet job, especially with Generico on there, and Judy hadn't been able able to assuage her concerns.

Mia then joined in. "I think it's also important to recognize that he's doing something politicians almost never do: he's telling the truth."

Generico made a noise. "You think maybe there's a reason why they never do that? When they do, they fail."

"Actually, John, no, it's when they lie and get caught that they fail. We live in an age of a twenty-four-hour news cycle. Politicians—even local DA's—have reporters who follow their every move. Hell, I've been covering Big Charlie since he announced. With that kind of coverage, it gets impossible to have a secret life. End result, the bad stuff comes out. That's what killed Eliot Spitzer's career, just to give a recent local example."

Judy winced. Her mentor in the business worked for Spitzer's gubernatorial campaign and had really believed in him. The day the New York governor's career was torpedoed by a sex scandal, Judy had had to listen to a two-hour harangue over the phone over how you think you know somebody...

"I don't know about that, Mia," Reimold said. "I mean, you're right about Spitzer, but history is filled with examples of politicians who kept important health secrets from the public."

Barel snorted. "Generico's gonna mention either Woodrow Wilson or FDR."

Judy nodded. Woodrow Wilson had a stroke while in office, and his First Lady wound up doing much of the governing during the latter days of his presidency. Franklin Delano Roosevelt hid the fact that he had polio and was wheelchair bound from the world as he led the country through the second World War.

Sure enough, Generico said, "Woodrow Wilson."

"See?" Barel said with a smile.

"I was gonna say Roosevelt, but—" Reimold started.

Then, for the first time, Reverend Sookdeo said something. "FDR could still do his job, however."

Mia said, "Yes, but neither of them had to deal with television or the Internet. Wilson didn't even have to deal with radio, really."

Looking to the ceiling with glee, Barel said, "Oh, I could kiss her."

"Isn't anyone worried about what he'll do if he loses?" That was Generico. Judy figured he was suffering withdrawal from not having spoken in thirty seconds. "I mean, what if he goes all werewolf in the courtroom?"

Reimold laughed. "You've obviously never been a DA in New York, John. You don't have time to prosecute cases anymore once you reach the top office."

With a chuckle, Lashmar said, "Of course, he also might 'go all werewolf,' as John said, on his opponent."

"If that is the case," Sookdeo said softly, "then this is a truly grave matter."

Lashmar's smile fell. "I was kidding, Reverend."

"I know that, Helen," he replied, though Judy didn't think he did, "however, your joke does raise a reasonable question, and it is one that John raised earlier. We do not know the true nature of Mr. Charles's metamorphosis. Mickey Solano is one of Mr. Charles's oldest friends. Were Mr. Charles to attack Mr. Solano while in his wolfen form—"

Mia put in, "We don't even know what his wolfen form is *like!*"

"Isn't that the point?" Generico asked snidely. "We don't know anything about what he's turned into, but if he's anything like the werewolves I grew up reading about—"

"You didn't grow up with them, John, you saw them in movies."

"Nice one, Mia," Barel said proudly.

"That's not the point," Generico muttered.

Before Mia could reply, the reverend said, "Actually, it very much is, Mr. Generico, because Mr. Charles has not been transformed into a werewolf. He is a *loup garou.*"

"Forgive me, Reverend," Reimold said, "but isn't that just French for *werewolf?*"

Judy ground her teeth. If she had a nickel for every time someone had thrown that in her face, she'd be able to retire to the Bahamas.

"Not exactly." Sookdeo folded his arms on the desk, and suddenly Judy understood why a religious studies professor was on the panel. "There are many legends of the *loup garou*, but in many, the transformation is voluntary, and does not always come with the violent associations that the movies of Universal Studios would have us believe."

"What about—"

Lashmar, bless her, interrupted Generico's stupid question. "John, I'm sorry, I have to cut you off, as it's time for a break, and we still have three more news stories to get to. When we come back, what the origins of I1V1 mean for those who are against climate change? We'll be right back."

The screen cut to a commercial. Judy looked at Barel. "Whaddaya think?"

"I think we should get Mia a fruit basket. If this is the tenor the debate will take, we may pull this off."

6

SERMON GIVEN BY REV. JOSIAH MANN, THE BLESSED CHURCH OF ENLIGHTENMENT, DES MOINES, IOWA, BROADCAST LIVE OVER THE GOOD NEWS NETWORK.

The Bible states, "Thou shalt not suffer a witch to live." Except it doesn't actually *say* that, now does it? Y'see, the original Hebrew of Exodus 22.18 uses the word *mekhashefah*, which simply means someone who practices magic against people. Y'see, the Lord wasn't concerned about women in big pointy hats with green skin ridin' brooms. No, y'see the Lord was concerned about people who practiced unnatural arts. The Lord was concerned about people goin' against His will by usin' forces that were not meant for the people He created in His own image.

The Lord was concerned about people *usin'* magic.

Now, we have people all over the world who are usin' magic. The same scientists who try to convince us that we're descended from apes, the same scientists who lie about "global warming," as if God's Earth could possibly change because of man, are now tryin' to tell us that this is a virus. They give it a fancy name, I1V1, and they try to convince us that it's the flu. Just a little bed-rest and a couple aspirin, and you'll stop turnin' into a fanged killin' machine!

But y'see, this is *not* an illness! This is *not* a condition that people will get better from if they take antibiotics or if they pray or if they go to a hospital! This is people who are livin' in defiance of God!

And we have to be vigilant! Y'see, we have people—we have sorcerers, magic-users, and yes, *witches*—who are feedin' off of God's own creations. They're maimin' us, they're feedin' off us, they're *killin'* us!

And we cannot suffer them to live.

I am telling you now, ladies and gentlemen, that these are monsters. Y'see, they pretend to be the sick and the lame. They claim they have a virus, and they hope that they'll be healed the way that Jesus healed the sick people of Gennesaret. But these are *not* the ten lepers! These are *not* Lazarus needin' to be raised from the dead! These are mekhashefah, and they cannot be allowed to continue to contaminate God's Earth.

Now y'see, some may say, "Reverend Mann, I don't understand. I've read the 22nd book of Exodus, and it talks about fathers givin' away their daughters in marriage, and it talks about makin' sacrifices to other gods, and it talks about a whole lotta other things that don't matter in the world today." And ladies and gentlemen, people who say that are absolutely right. The Bible was written at a time when such things mattered. But y'see, Exodus 22 also speaks of not lyin' with animals, an act we *still* consider a sin. Exodus 22 also speaks of not stealin' your neighbors' belongin's, an act we not only consider a sin, but a crime. Exodus 22 speaks of startin' fires and of stealin' and of breakin' oaths—these are things that matter to us still.

Y'see, the 18th verse mattered to the people of the time as much as all that stuff about oxen and dowries and such. And for a time, people did not practice magic, at least not in the manner meant by the proscription in Exodus 22.18.

But y'see, ladies and gentlemen, times have changed. Foul magic is among us once again, and once again we must turn to the Bible, as the Israelites did so long ago, as we continue to do today to guide us in our daily lives, and we must follow the Lord's word.

Now y'see, there is a man who is currently in New York City. I know, I know—it is a den of iniquity in so many ways, but it is also considered by many to be the hub and heart of our great nation. It is where the Statue of Liberty resides, after all.

There is a man there who has been the District Attorney of the County of the Bronx, prosecuting the many criminals there, for the past twelve years.

Now y'see, I have no doubt that once Hugues Charles was a good man—*once*. But he has *admitted* to becoming one of these creatures. He has *admitted* to being able to unnaturally transform himself from a man made in God's image into something else—something wicked, something *horrible*. And he intends to keep his job. Y'see, even as I stand here talkin' to you all, Mr. Hugues Charles of New York City is runnin' for re-election. He intends to continue prosecutin' man's law even as his very existence remains an affront to God's law.

We cannot suffer this man to live.

7

"Have you seen this?"

Barel Grindberg blinked as she walked into Big Charlie's office in the courthouse and was hit with that question from its occupant. "Uh, well, if you're talking about the Reverend Mann thing, I e-mailed you about it half an hour ago. If you're not talking about the Reverend Mann thing, then I have no idea what you're talking about."

"I apologize, Barel, I have not as yet checked my e-mail. I have been too busy being livid about this. The man is calling for my death."

Unable to stop herself from grinning, she said, "I know, isn't it great?"

"I fail to see what there is to smile about, Barel."

"You kidding? This is *gold*. There's, like, a hundred different YouTube clips of it. They're all ripped from GNN. A bunch got taken down, but I think they finally gave up with the cease-and-desists after a day of fresh uploa—"

Barel cut herself at the expression on Big Charlie's face. She sighed. She supposed she shouldn't have been surprised that he didn't see the upside. "Barel—"

She held up a hand. "Look, I know it seems bad on the face of it."

Big Charlie was glowering now. "He is calling for my death."

"Well, technically, yeah, but it's not like he has an armed militia on his side. What he *does* have is a flock in the millions all throughout the midwest, which means that people all over the country are talking about you, and that means more press coverage that we don't have to pay for. Now the whole country's talking about our little DA race, and it's *you* they're talking about. If they even mention Solano, it'll be an afterthought."

"I suppose—"

She held up both hands. "Look, I get that you're concerned, but the people who hang on this asshole's every word are all out in the flyover states. None of them are registered Democrats in the Bronx, and those are your people, and they're the ones who're gonna get their backs up at some schmuck preacher calling for your head. The outrage votes alone'll knock us up five points."

Big Charlie stared at her for several seconds, and Barel honestly had no idea how he was going to respond to this.

Finally, he let out a long breath, and put a meaty hand to his forehead. "This is madness."

"Hey, you're the one who wanted to run with I1V1. We knew things might get crazy. May as well take advantage. I'm telling Judy to clear your schedule—I've already started getting calls asking for more appearances."

"And how am I to respond to people asking how I feel about this lunatic?"

"Well, for starters, don't call him a lunatic."

"Barel—"

"We take the high ground. Call Reverend Mann a decent, honorable man of God who was simply speaking his mind."

"Who wishes me dead."

"Trust me, I've dealt with the 'Blessed Church of Enlightenment' garbanzos before. They'll be spin-doctoring this puppy from here till doomsday. As soon as anyone actually *calls* them on their bullshit, they backpedal. We gain absolutely *nothing* by getting down in the dirt. Just stay above it all, and make use of all the new interview opportunities to point out how awesome you are."

That finally got Big Charlie to smile, his endless shoulders rumbling with a chuckle. "Very well." He tapped some keys on his computer. "Ah, I see your e-mail. Oh, and one from Mickey with the subject line of 'Rev. Mann.'"

That surprised, and concerned Barel. Solano at least claimed to be a devout Catholic, and she wasn't sure he'd come out against a man of God. Besides, Catholics were always going around forgiving people. "What'd he say?"

Big Charlie read off the screen. "'That's some serious bullshit right there. I won't be sayin nothin to support that asshole Reverend Mann nohow. Sorry you had to hear that shit.'"

Barel gave a quick fist-pump. "Perfect. Not only do we get free airtime, we get Mickey going around agreeing with you at a time when he needs to be ripping you to pieces. This is *great*."

"I hope you are correct, Barel." Big Charlie sounded as serious as he ever did. "The reverend's words did not come out of a vacuum, and I do not believe that he is the only one who has this particular opinion regarding those of us with I1V1."

"What did I always tell you?" Barel said with a glare. "In a campaign, there is no long term. Worry about that when it happens. For now, let's deal with the hand we've got, and Mann just gave us three aces."

8

Mia Fizsimmons sat in the press area for the debate between Mickey Solano and Hugues Charles. Normally, this sort of event would have a press section of about a dozen seats, and Mia would have had her choice of them, as maybe half would be filled.

But thanks to the Reverend Mann and his sermon—which Mia had now heard exactly two hundred times, she'd been counting for no good reason except perhaps so she could have a proper measurement for her suffering—the size of the press area was tripled and it was packed. She was squeezed between Josh, an overweight reporter from an Iowa paper ("Our readers want to know who the reverend was talking about—and hey, I'll take the free trip to the Big Apple"), and an overweight blogger whose name she never got who'd been writing about I1V1. She had no idea how he the latter managed to score press credentials.

And that was just journalists—camera operators were all over the place, with lights blinding anyone who looked anywhere near an aisle.

To her annoyance, Jack Napolitano—now working for RSN—had been chosen to moderate. To her surprise, they didn't provide an extra chair for his ego.

The debate had been going well, and the Iowa reporter was getting cranky at the lack of a mention of Reverend Mann.

"The next question," Jack read off an index card (this was still the Bronx, and a teleprompter wasn't in the budget), "is about the death penalty. Mr. Solano, you're in favor of reinstating it in New York State, and Mr. Charles, you've been very much set against it. Mr. Solano, can you explain your position?"

Solano smiled. He was dressed in a dark maroon suit. "Be happy to. When the Court of Appeals declared the death penalty law unconstitutional, they took a bullet out of every prosecutor's gun. The death penalty is absolutely a last resort, one that should be reserved for the most heinous of crimes—but it needs to be available for those. Now, Mr. Charles has never called for the death penalty, even though he had opportunities to do so while the law was still on the books. And you know what? *I agree with him.* There weren't any cases that came up in the Bronx during that time that called for the death penalty."

Points for Solano on that one. Mia jotted down a few notes.

"But I maintain," he continued, "that to rob prosecutors of that as a possible sentence robs them of the ability to do their job, and I have continued to lobby the Court of Appeals to reverse its decision. Having said that, if I am elected, I will, of course, abide by the law."

Mia snorted. *Stuck the landing, there, Mick...*

Jack looked over at Big Charlie, wearing a tailored charcoal pinstriped suit. "Mr. Charles?"

"There are no cases where the death penalty is called for."

And there's the sound bite. Mia jotted down the line in her notebook.

"Yes, you may provide historic examples like Adolf Hitler and Osama bin Laden, but these are not people who would ever be prosecuted at the Bronx County courthouse. But of all the arguments to be made against the death penalty, none are more compelling than the simple fact that innocent people have been found guilty of capital crimes. It is bad enough when the state condemns one of its citizens to death, but it is unconscionable that the state would do so to an innocent person. As for Mr. Solano's argument—prosecutors have dozens of options of punishments that fit the crime. The idea that the death penalty would cripple prosecutors in their jobs when Mr. Solano himself admits that it would not be used very often if at all, is ludicrous."

And there's the other sound bite. This time there were cheers. Jack whirled around to glare at the audience, as if their cheers were a personal affront. Then he read the next question off the index cards. "The Reverend Josiah Mann recently said during one of his sermons that Mr. Charles should not be permitted to live due to his suffering from I1V1. Mr. Charles, how do you respond to such a threat to your life?"

Next to Mia, Josh sat up in his chair, fingers hovering over his laptop.

"I do not believe any threat to my life was made. Reverend Mann is a devout, dedicated man of God, and I do not wish him any ill will. But he has said many things I disagreed with before last Sunday, and I daresay he will say more things I disagree with after this. He is welcome to his opinion, as are his followers. Since very few of them reside in the Bronx, I am confident that they will not be voting in September or in November, so my concern for his effect upon my chances are minimal."

"Oooooh," Josh muttered. "Burn."

"Well, he's right," Mia said.

"Oh, not complaining. Mann's poison, and I can't wait to tell my grandkids that I was there when he got put in his place by a werewolf."

"Mr. Solano?" Jack prompted.

"Mr. Charles is far more generous to Reverend Mann than I am. Yes, there are people out there suffering from I1V1 who are causing harm, and yes, those people are dangerous. But not everyone has decided to channel Count Dracula and suck people's blood. Some of them—most of them—are just people who are trying to go on with their lives. Mr. Charles is one of them, and he should be respected for that, not condemned. And anyone who does condemn him for that isn't a man of any God that I'm familiar with. Reverend Mann is a rabble-rouser and a scumbucket, and if he ever does come to the Bronx, he'll find out how we treat those kinds of people."

More cheers followed that, and Josh grinned. "My grandkids are gonna get a *great* story once they exist."

Again Jack impatiently waited for the cheers to die down. "The next question is for Mr. Solano. Are you concerned that your opponent has publicly stated that he is a werewolf, and is part of why you're running against him to prevent a self-described monster from running the prosecutions of this county?"

Solano actually rolled his eyes. "Let me ask you something—if Mr. Charles had had come out as a homosexual, would you even ask that question? I'm running for Bronx District Attorney because I think that it's time for new blood in that office after twelve years. I think that it's time for Mr. Charles to step down and give way to a different vision, one that can build on what he's accomplished. I think that the DA's office has become ossified and that I'm the man to apply the rust-off. That has nothing to do with whether or not my friend over there has a disease that allows him to change into a *loup garou*."

Mia shook her head. It almost didn't matter what Big Charlie said in response. Solano just had to support him before tearing him down. It made him seem noble, but she didn't think that was going to be enough.

The blogger to her right was just muttering, "Awesome, totally fucking awesome" to himself as he made notes on his tablet.

9

TRANSCRIPT OF "ON THE STREET" SEGMENT OF GOOD MORNING NYC

GOOD MORNING NYC: Today's "On the Street" asks the people of New York the question: Should Big Charlie be elected Bronx DA even though he's one of the many people suffering from I1V1?

PERSON #1: All's I know is, I can walk home at night without feelin' like I'm getting jumped by no crazy man, and it's been that way since he been DA. I don't care what he turns into, he's getting' *my* vote for *damn* sure.

PERSON #2: You kiddin' me? The guy's a freakin' *werewolf*. I ain't voted for him before, but I sure as hell'm votin' for him now! That's who I want a murderer lookin' at inna courtroom, know what I mean?

PERSON #3: God, no. Never. I mean, I don't vote or anything, but if I did, I would *never* vote for one of those people. Not *ever*.

PERSON #4: Not only am I not voting for him, I've given money to Solano—and I can't *stand* Solano. But seriously, the man is no longer even *human*. How can he enforce human laws when they no longer even *apply* to him? Christ knows I have *no* respect for that Mann guy, but he was right on the nose with that one. He ain't Big Charlie anymore, he's a monster, and he needs to be put down.

PERSON #5: You *know* he's the best BLEEPin' DA this town's seen, yo. He ain't even turned into no werewolf that nobody saw. So hell with that—I be votin' for him soon's I register, an' BLEEP.

PERSON #6: I admire him for coming out and telling the truth. God, I wish more politicians would do that. They spend so much time saying nothing that they don't say anything. This is a guy who came out and told everyone what happened to him. He didn't wait for a reporter or an Internet video or a police investigation to say, "Oh, yeah, didn't I mention that I snort coke off call girls?" or whatever. He probably could've gone the whole year without telling nobody, but he did the right thing. For that alone, I'd vote for the guy. But it's gotta wait until November, 'cause I'm an independent.

10

Oddly, Mia's second time on Helen Lashmar's show made her a lot more nervous than her first.

The first time was so last-minute, she didn't have the chance to get nervous. Now, though, she had the Bronx Zoo's entire butterfly conservatory in her stomach as she sat through makeup.

Next to her was Hannah LeBoeuf, a striking African-American woman who was one of the ACLU's lawyers. "You'll be fine," Hannah was saying. "You're good on camera."

Mia shrugged, which earned her a glare from the young man doing her makeup. "I appreciate that. I'm just worried about Mann's guy." Tim Markinson, the public information officer for the Blessed Church of Enlightenment, was on the panel as well. "They've just been..." She trailed off, unable to form words to do justice to her annoyance at the shitstorm Mann's sermon had caused for Big Charlie.

"I'll take care of Markinson. He's an empty suit that does whatever he has to to make sure the donations keep comin'."

"Thanks." The fourth panelist was Senator Alex Kapsis, whom Mia had met several times. *So that's two friendly faces, at least.*

Within a few minutes, they were seated around the table, cameras all around, lights shining brightly in her face. On the monitors in front of her, the closing credits from the previous show were running. The host had yet to arrive, but the other three panelists were present. Markinson wore a light blue suit that made him look like he was taking someone to the prom in 1952. Senator Kapsis looked like a college professor in his tweed jacket, and was on his cell phone.

"One minute to air!" somebody bellowed, and the butterflies started flapping their wings so hard in Mia's stomach she was sure they were changing history so the dinosaurs didn't die.

Last time, a PA had yelled at John Generico for talking on his cell phone in the studio, but he was an asshole and Kapsis was a U.S. senator, so the rules were probably different.

But when Helen Lashmar stormed in, staring intently at her smartphone as she walked, she said, "Okay, let's get this party started," which was apparently what she always said before the show began.

"In five—four—three—" The PA then held up two fingers, then one, then pointed to Helen. "Good morning. We start with our roundtable segment, where a panel will tackle the news of the day. Joining me today are Mia Fitzsimmons of the New York *Daily News*, Timothy Markinson, the public information officer for the Blessed Church of Enlightenment, ACLU lawyer Hannah LeBoeuf, and Senator Alex Kapsis of New York. I1V1 has been all over the news lately, with the Reverend Mann of the Blessed Church of Enlightenment calling for the death of Bronx District Attorney Hugues Charles, better known as 'Big Charlie,' and the discovery that murdered Chicago talk-show host Danika Dubov also suffered from I1V1." She shook her head and smiled. "A werewolf running for public office and a vampire hosting a morning talk show."

Helen was about to start a question when Markinson interrupted in a low, nasal tone. "I'd like to object to your characterization of the Reverend Mann's words, please, Helen."

"Of course, Tim, you—"

Markinson barreled forward as if Helen hadn't spoken. "The Reverend Mann did *not* call for the death of Mr. Charles. The Reverend Mann is a firm believer in the word of God, and the very words of God as handed down to Moses were that people should not commit murder. The words of Exodus 22 state that one should not suffer a creature of magic to live among us. A good analogy would be what King Saul did in the First Book of Samuel, driving all necromancers and magicians from the Kingdom of Israel."

It required all of Mia's self-control not to let out an interjection on the air that RSN's Broadcast Standards and Practices would not have been happy with. She had an entire bit on 1 Samuel ready to go, and this blue-suited Jesus freak just stole her thunder.

"When Saul contradicted his own order by consulting the Witch of Endor, he was condemned, and his army was soon defeated, leading to Saul's suicide."

Mia's words all but exploded from her mouth. "So what're you saying, Tim, that we should kick Big Charlie out of New York and send him, where, exactly?"

"He can no longer be in the community of God, and he must be removed from it as Saul did the magicians and necromancers."

The senator jumped in before Mia could respond. "Interesting, Mr. Markinson, so now you're saying that the Bronx is part of the community of God? Because I recall the reverend saying more than once—including after the September 11th attacks—that God had abandoned New York City. Given that, the Bronx would be the ideal place for someone you want to condemn to the same fate as the Witch of Endor."

Unable to help herself, Mia smiled.

Markinson looked nonplussed. "All of America is part of the community of God, Senator. What the Reverend Mann did in 2001 was express a *fear* that God had abandoned the city of New York."

Now Mia rolled her eyes. "So is this is what you do, Mr. Markinson? The reverend says something inflammatory and crazy, and you go on TV and tell people he didn't really *mean* that, what he *really* meant was *this*."

"That's not at all fair, Mia," Markinson said in his most condescending tone. *And you're "Tim" from now on, you self-righteous prick.* "The Reverend Mann's words are often taken out of context by a biased media and as public information officer, it's my job to clarify and explain when people misunderstand the reverend's words."

Hannah said, "I can't speak for Mia here, but I've read the reverend's words, Tim, every single one of them. Not once did he ever say 'cast out' or 'remove from God's community' or any of the other phrases that you've been using nonstop since the video of his sermon hit YouTube. He was calling for Big Charlie's death."

"Are you saying that the Reverend Mann doesn't have the right to speak his mind?" Markinson's condescension actually got worse, which Mia wouldn't have credited as possible a few seconds ago. "Because I would find that a *fascinating* position for a lawyer from the ACLU to take."

"Oh, I've got *no* problem with Mann speaking his mind, and I would defend his right to say it in court. But unless I *am* the one defending him, then I've got the right to say that he's full of it, and that he's calling for the death of a good man."

"Of course," Senator Kapsis said, "that raises the question of whether or not D.A. Charles still *is* that—a man, that is. Danika Dubov wasn't exactly what you'd call a paragon of journalism, but she wasn't a sadistic torturer, either—at least until this virus got her and turned her into some kind of vampire. The Chicago Police found dozens of people she'd been literally feeding off of for weeks. With all due respect to Mr. Markinson and the Reverend Mann, concerns about whether or not D.A. Charles is part of God's community is of less immediacy than his place in the human community."

Hannah shrugged. "Well, the human community in his home city seems fine with him. His poll numbers have gone up since he announced that he was a *loup garou*. And that's the point, this is a local election for a small part of one city. If that small group of people are okay with him, then I don't see the problem."

"Now hold on a minute, Hannah," Kapsis said, "we're not talking about a rural town with a few hundred people electing a sheriff. The Bronx has a population that is the same as that of the state of Alaska. And it's one-fifth of one of the most important cities in the entire world."

"With all due respect, Senator" Mia said, "I don't see what difference that makes. If it *was* a little town upstate, or if it is the Bronx—which, by the way, has *twice* the population of Alaska—the point is, it's up to those of us who live there to decide. It doesn't matter what we say or what some televangelist says. It's up to the people. And *that's* what matters."

"The Rev—" Markinson started, but Helen interrupted.

"I have to cut you off, Tim—"

Markinson interrupted right back. "The Reverend Mann is *not* a 'televangelist,' which is a term we find quite offensi—"

Sternly, Helen said, "Tim, *please*, we have to take a break. When we come back, a look at the president's new proposed budget."

Mia let out a long breath after the PA said, "And we're out."

"Nice job," Hannah said with a smile.

Looking over at Markinson, who looked like he'd eaten an entire lemon, Mia smiled and said, "Thanks."

II

Detective Hector Trujillo winced when he saw Mia Fitzsimmons from the *News* approach the crime scene.

At the moment she, like all the other reporters outside the Upper West Side apartment building where Senator Alex Kapsis had a co-op, was behind the yellow crime-scene tape. Two other *News* reporters were already there, reporting on the senator's murder, so Trujillo wasn't entirely sure what Fitzsimmons was doing there.

Fitzsimmons was talking animatedly to Officer Nugent at the tape. Nugent looked like he wanted to haul off and belt the reporter, and Fitzsimmons looked like she wanted to do likewise.

"S'okay, Nugent," Trujillo said. "Let her through."

Nugent gave the detective a dubious expression, but waved her through. She ducked under the yellow tape and approached Trujillo.

"Saw you on TV, Fitzsimmons," he said as she walked up to him. "Lookin' good."

"Thanks so much, Detective. God, it's been, what, two years?"

"Sounds about right," Trujillo said neutrally.

"When I gave you that witness that let you close the Rojas case?"

Again, Trujillo said, "Sounds about right." He didn't want to commit to anything until the reporter laid her cards on the table.

"Of course," she said with a smile, "I could've just sat on the witness and wrote the story, but no, I helped you out. You got promoted to second-grade after that, didn't you, Detective?"

So she was calling in the favor. "Can you stop fucking around and get to it, Fitzsimmons?"

"I thought you'd never ask." She took out her digital recorder.

Trujillo held up a hand. "Hold up—I ain't sayin' *nothin'* on the record…"

"Fine." She dropped the recorder back in her purse. "But can you tell me on the record that the senator was murdered?"

"The M.E. ain't made it official—but the bastard was ripped to pieces by teeth. Looked as bad as Bellevue."

Fitzsimmons nodded. Trujillo shuddered just from mentioning it. He'd gone to the Academy with Detective Jerry Schmidt, and had attended his funeral after he was ripped to pieces by Michael Fayne, the first vampire, at Bellevue Hospital.

The reports he'd read of what happened when Jerry was killed were frighteningly similar to what the senator's living room looked like right now.

But he wasn't about to share that with Fitzsimmons. He finally realized what she was doing here—she was on the Big Charlie beat, and when he last saw her on television, she was on with Senator Kapsis talking about the DA.

"Okay, look, we got a guy runnin' from the scene in custody now. The senator's nephew."

"Nate."

Trujillo nodded. It wasn't exactly a secret that Nathan Kapsis was a bad seed who had failed to appear for his day in court after he beat up his famous uncle. "He's FTA for the assault charge last year. Senator's wife said they ain't even heard from the fucker in a year."

"And he's got I1V1?"

"Looks like. Luther Swann said he's a—"

"*Vrykolatios?*"

"Gesundheit." Trujillo attempted a smile, but it didn't entirely work. "And yeah, I guess that's how you pronounce it. I got it in a text from Swann."

"It makes sense—cannibalistic, Greek."

Trujillo didn't care about any of that, he just wanted to close the case with a minimum of fuss. As far as he was concerned, this was a dunker—the nephew did it.

The only problem was the press angle, especially with the primary tomorrow. But at least now he had a way to repay Fitzsimmons.

A paddy wagon had pulled up, and two of the uniforms were leading a handcuffed Nate Kapsis to it. He was a skinny kid, with the muscle tone of a string bean.

Trujillo stared down at Fizsimmons. "We done here?"

"You said the senator was torn to pieces?" After Trujillo nodded, Fitzsimmons went on: "So how'd that little guy manage that?"

Shrugging, Trujillo said, "He's a vampire. Thought they was all super-strong and shit."

Fitzsimmons shook her head. "Not a *vyrkolatios*. They feast off family—"

"What, like that TV bitch in Chicago?"

"Yeah." Fitzsimmons let out a breath. "It's possible that Nate came on the senator and chowed down, but he doesn't have the strength to—"

Trujillo held up both hands. "I don't wanna hear it. I got me a dunker here, and you ain't fuckin' it up for me. The nephew did it—he's got the vamp disease, he's got a grudge against his uncle, and he's already a fugitive. It fits, and we ain't complicatin' this. Now we even for Rojas?"

"Sure." But Fitzsimmons barely seemed to pay attention to Trujillo. "It would need someone with a huge body mass to do something like that..." she muttered.

For his part, Trujillo didn't give a rat's ass. He had his killer in bracelets, he had a closed case to put under his name, and he no longer owed a reporter a favor. As far as he was concerned, it was a good night.

12

TRANSCRIPT OF "ON THE STREET" SEGMENT OF GOOD MORNING NYC

GOOD MORNING NYC: Today's "On the Street" comes from last night's Democratic primary for Bronx DA, as we asked people coming out of three different polling places in Riverdale, Morrisania, and Edenwald who they voted for, and why.

PERSON #1 (Riverdale): I'm sorry, but it's not any of your business that I voted for Big Charlie.

PERSON #2 (Morrisania): I ain't votin' for no werewolf, that's for damn sure. Solano all the way!

PERSON #3 (Edenwald): I grew up with Big Charlie. He's a good man—the best. I don't care if he turns into the Wicked Witch of the West, he's a good man. I vote for good men.

PERSON #4 (Riverdale): Oh, gosh, I just had to vote for Solano. I just don't trust Charles, y'know? The whole virus thing—it's just icky.

PERSON #5 (Morrisania): So he's a werewolf. So what? A woman turns into a monster from hell once a month, and I'd vote for a woman DA, so why not vote for Big Charlie, know what I'm sayin'?

PERSON #6 (Edenwald): You only be carin' 'cause he be a *loup garou*. He ain't no *loup garou*, nobody'd even be givin' no BLEEP if he was just bein' Big Charlie runnin' for office again. I voted for him three times, and didn't nobody come out to be askin' me who I voted for with no news cameras then, now, did they?

13

Mia Fitzsimmons was sitting in the Daily News city room writing up her story on Big Charlie's victory. It wasn't official yet, but the early exit polls made it look like Hugues Charles would win the primary in a walk over Mickey Solano.

Bart Mosby, her editor, walked up to her. "Looks like your guy's gonna do it."

"He's not 'my guy,' Bart."

"Bullshit. Just make sure the big guy remembers how far up his ass your face was during this campaign."

Mia made a face. "Bart, seriously."

"I am serious. The vampire shit meant he was good copy, and now the DA owes one of my reporters a favor. And with Kapsis's murder, it makes even better copy. People're eating this vampire shit up."

"Yeah." Mia was looking over the M.E.'s initial report on Kapsis's murder—it was fast-tracked, since he was a U.S. senator, and Mia had a friend in the medical examiner's office—and frowning. "It's funny, I thought it might hurt Big Charlie, but it didn't."

"What would?" Bart asked.

"Hm? Oh, the murder. I mean, it was obvious that someone with I1V1 killed him."

"Yeah, the nephew."

Mia shook her head. "I don't think so. He's a *vyrkolatios*. They just feed, they don't murder—certainly not like that. He doesn't have the strength to tear him apart like that, and the M.E.'s report says there were both teeth and what looks like claw marks."

"Who gives a fuck?" Bart asked. "He's a vampire. They can do that shit. Whatever, I'm gonna go get a cigarette. Worst day in the history'a the world was when they—"

The rest of Bart's harangue was lost to distance—though Mia had heard his railing against the laws that prevented indoor smoking since her first day in the city room—but she wasn't paying much attention.

Nate Kapsis didn't have claws. Something here didn't add up.

On the TV, Big Charlie was being questioned about the senator's murder outside his campaign headquarters. "Nathan Kapsis has always been a very troubled man. His violent tendencies go back many years."

"Yes," one reporter was saying off-camera, "but he's never killed. Do you believe that contracting I1V1 made him—"

"As I said," and now Big Charlie was sounding testy, "he was always a troubled young man. I1V1 did not change that. Recall, if you will, that he had failed to appear before the court in answer to an assault charge on the senator."

"But Senator Kapsis wasn't exactly your best friend," said the same reporter, and Mia was wondering who it was, now.

"The senator and I were friends for many years."

Mia winced. That sounded rehearsed.

"But he threw you under the bus on Helen Lashmar's show the other day. Do you think—"

Judy Alejo stepped in at that point and cut the questions off.

Kapsis certainly hadn't sounded much like a friend to Big Charlie on Lashmar. *Could that have been seen as a betrayal?*

She finished writing up her notes—both for the piece that would be in tomorrow's News and for the story about Big Charlie that she was finding herself composing in light of the senator's murder—as the night wore on.

Eventually, Bart wandered by and said the news story was in the queue. Curious, Mia called it up on her laptop.

Big Charlie won sixty-three percent of the vote, and the turnout was seventy percent of the registered Democrats in the Bronx. Mia wasn't sure, but she was fairly certain those were both records.

"Now it's just the election," she muttered.

Bart laughed. "Right. Are the Republicans even runnin' anybody?"

"No," Mia said, "but Escobar's gonna be on the ticket."

"Who's that?"

"The Right-to-Life candidate. Hell, Big Charlie's gonna be on the Conservative ticket, along with Liberal and Green."

"Right, so the election's gonna matter." Bart snorted and walked off.

It will matter if Big Charlie can't run due to being in jail for murder. It was a crazy thought—Mia had spent most of the last four months around Hugues Charles, and he didn't have a murderous bone in his body.

But neither had Nate Kapsis. Hell, neither had Danika Dubov or Michael Fayne.

Maybe there's no story here, but I have to play out the string in case there is one.

Luckily, Bart wouldn't have any problem with her sticking close to the DA's office moving forward.

14
OP-ED PIECE BY MIA FITZSIMMONS IN THE NEW YORK DAILY NEWS.

It started with Michael Fayne here in New York.

It's gotten far far worse.

In Los Angeles, a Laker Girl was attacked by an ape-like man who seemed to suck the very life out of her.

In Chicago, TV personality Danika Dubov kept victims in her home while Illinois State Representative William Blevins and his wife were horribly murdered.

In Paris, a massacre beneath the City of Light's very streets.

And here in New York, Anson Morris slaughtering his wife and best friend.

It's become impossible to turn on the news or read a paper like this one without there being some new vampire on the scene.

A year ago, Hugues Charles was sworn in to serve his fourth term as District Attorney of the Bronx. A year and a half ago, he won the Democratic Primary, as well as a virtually uncontested general election, despite having revealed himself to be a *loup garou*.

It would be hard to imagine Big Charlie succeeding in such an endeavor now. The lines are being drawn, human vs. vampire, and there's no real clear notion as to who will win.

Big Charlie knows which side he's on, though. In a press conference held on the first day of the Anson Morris trial, the Bronx DA, he said, "It does not matter that I'm a *loup garou* for the same reason that it doesn't matter that I have dark skin or that my mother was born in Port-au-Prince. What matters is that I was elected by the people of this county to prosecute criminals. Anson Morris is a criminal. It also does not matter that he has claws and fangs that he did not have two years ago. What matters is that he committed a heinous crime, and he will be punished for that."

The surety in Big Charlie's voice makes him a lone voice in the wilderness these days. Violence committed by people with I1V1 has skyrocketed, and it's been followed by increased violence committed against them, what one pundit referred to as "preventative self-defense."

So far, Big Charlie has stayed above the fray. The question is, how long can he remain there?

His response when I asked him that very thing, was typically candid. "There is no fray to remain above. I am here to do my job. It is the same job I have done for twelve years, and I intend to do for another four, at least."

That surprised me, as I recalled lots of talk about this being his final term.

"I do not wish to make predictions. Four years ago, I could not have imagined the circumstances that we face now. My presence as a prosecutor in a major city might well be important for people to see. Those of us who suffer from this virus—those people that have been dubbed 'vampires'—we are all simply people. So many barriers against prejudice have been broken in the last fifty years. Civil rights, gay marriage, an African-American president. But now we have found another group of people to oppress."

Of course the big question is what Big Charlie will do if the proposed "Vampire Registration Act" currently on the Senate floor passes. One of the bill's sponsors is Senator Emily Krascznicki, who was appointed to serve out Senator Alex Kapsis's term after his murder.

"My job as District Attorney is to prosecute to the full extent of the law. I swore an oath to uphold the laws of the county of the Bronx, the city of New York, the state of New York, and the republic of the United States of America. If someone in my county is in violation of any of the laws under which we live, then they shall be prosecuted by my office."

More thorny is the death penalty, which has been off the books in New York State since 2004. There's talk in Albany of bringing it back solely for I1V1 cases.

"Again, my job as District Attorney is to prosecute to the full extent of the law. I can say that, personally, I am not comfortable with any legal decision that discriminates against a particular group of people. Imagine if the governor proposed a law that stated that only black people could receive the death penalty, or only Jews could. It would never even be considered."

But Big Charlie won't let ideology stand in the way of doing his job. "If it is put into law, then—if it's appropriate—I will prosecute with the death penalty in mind. But that decision will have little to do with the virus and everything to do with whether or not that punishment fits that crime."

Let's hope that the state legislature's object will be similarly all sublime.

15

Barel Grindberg honestly did not expect to ever be walking into Hugues Charles's office in the Bronx County Courthouse again.

Big Charlie was on the phone, but he gestured for her to take a seat in the guest chair while he spoke. It was a lot of legalese flying back and forth that Barel didn't even pretend to understand.

Finally, he said, "Thank you, Amelia" and hung up. "My apologies, Barel."

"No problem," Barel said neutrally.

"How are you doing?"

Small talk first, then. "Keeping busy. I've been doing some consulting and some writing. Actually, a bunch of publishers have been approaching me about writing a book about getting you reelected. Just in general, that's enhanced my resumé."

"I am very glad to hear you say that, Barel, because I wish to hire you again."

Barel frowned. "The next DA race isn't for three years."

"Not for District Attorney. You are aware, of course, that Emily Krascznicki has declined to run for a full term, so Alex's seat is open. I would like to throw my hat into the ring, as it were, and I wish you to run my campaign."

Pulling her cardigan tightly around her chest, Barel took a deep breath in before replying. "Are you out of your *fucking mind?*"

Big Charlie recoiled as if he'd been slapped. "Not at all. I believe that, with my own profile increasing, this might be an ideal time to—"

"It is *not* an ideal time! It's the worst time in the history of the universe for you to be running for dog-catcher, much less U.S. senator! If you run, you will be absolutely destroyed. Remember what happened with Reverend Mann? Picture that *mishegoss* every single day. Public opinion on vamps is going down into the drain with every passing day, and if you try to run, you will be ruined. Hell, they'll probably force you to resign. People with I1V1 are getting *lynched* out there, Hugues!"

For several seconds, Big Charlie didn't say anything. His huge hands were folded together, elbows resting on his metal desk, staring at an indeterminate point to Barel's left.

"I appreciate your honesty, Barel. It is the quality of yours that I've always admired most."

"Thank you. So you won't do it?"

"I have not decided yet. In truth, I had not decided when I asked you. That you will not be willing to represent me—"

"I didn't say that." Barel spoke without thinking. She liked Big Charlie; she generally made it a rule not to like (or dislike) the people she worked for, but the prosecutor was such a teddy bear it was impossible to think ill of him. And she didn't want to disappoint him.

But after mulling it over for half a second, she realized she had to. "But I'm saying it now. It won't just be career suicide for you, it'll taint everyone who works for you. Don't do it."

There was some more small talk after that, and then Barel shook Big Charlie's enormous hand and left the office. She figured that would be the end of it. He had almost always taken her advice, and whenever he hadn't, he'd regretted it right afterward.

So she was stunned to hear the following as she watched *Good Morning NYC* over her morning tea: "Our top story on the hour: Big Charlie is running for Senate!"

"You have *got* to be fucking kidding me." Barel immediately opened up her laptop and started composing an e-mail to Big Charlie that boiled down to, "What the fuck is wrong with you, you *schmuck*?"

The man himself showed up on her screen as she frantically typed. "There has been an increasing call for more legislation against those of us who have contracted I1V1, and I believe that it is past time that those of us who have the virus had a say in how that legislation is crafted. Senator Kapsis lost his life to a family member who had the virus, and my announcement today is by way of reminding people that we are not monsters. We are people. Senator Kapsis's nephew was violent before he contracted the virus. And I was a District Attorney before I contracted the virus. I believe that I will be able to represent my home state in Washington regardless of whether or not I can alter my shape into a wolfen form."

"And faeries will come flying out of my ass," Barel muttered. Big Charlie's heart was in the right place, and nothing he said there was wrong. She made a mental note to send a well-done e-mail to Judy Alejo for that statement, as it was well put together.

But it wouldn't do a lick of good. Nobody was going to vote a vampire into office.

"State Comptroller Frank VanDerMeer has already announced that he will be running for the seat on the Republican side, but Big Charlie will have to survive a Democratic primary that already includes former New York City Mayor Aaron Barr, Manhattan Borough President Emma Jaffe, and State Senator Dianne Axisa. Oughtta be a fun race."

The one piece of good news was that no one on that list was going to scare anyone from running. Barr was far from the city's most popular mayor, a one-term wonder who created almost no impression, and Jaffe, Axisa, and VanDerMeer were bland career politicians who had almost no profile. Were it not for I1V1, Big Charlie could take the election in a walk.

As she was typing her poison pen letter to the DA, she got a notification of a new e-mail. It was from Mickey Solano.

Barel frowned and clicked on the icon to open that mail.

Then she decided she was going to need another cup of tea. Possibly with some whiskey in it.

16
TRANSCRIPT OF A COMMERCIAL PAID FOR BY "CITIZENS FOR HUMANITY."

By the people, for the people. This great country has always been about its people. But now it's in danger from creatures who may look like people, who may sometimes even appear to be people, but they aren't. Sadistic, brutal, vicious killers, with more of them every day.

And one of them is running for Senate. They call him "Big Charlie," but what they should be calling him is a monster. And he'll bring the monsters' agenda to Capitol Hill.

Don't let this happen. Let our country be for us, not the monsters who scare our children—who scare *us*. Make sure that when you vote for Senator, you *don't* vote for Hugues Charles.

Paid for by Citizens for Humanity.

17

Judy Alejo was on the phone with her sister when Helen Lashmar came on. So busy had she been with organizing interviews with Big Charlie that she hadn't even checked to see what she'd be doing, and she hadn't actually spoken to her sister in almost a month. Not that that was a bad thing from Judy's perspective, but now Perla was complaining to *mami* about it.

So Judy called her, and ignored the roundtable segment on Lashmar to listen to her carry on about how wonderful her two children were.

Just as she was about to bang her head into the desk, she caught Lashmar say, "—ther candidate threw his hat into the ring: Mickey Solano, who was Big Charlie's opponent in his latest reelection as Bronx DA. We've got—"

"Perla, I gotta go." Without waiting to hear her sister's objection, Judy hit end on her phone and dropped it on her couch while grabbing for the cable remote. Grateful for DVR technology, she rewound.

Lashmar was sitting at her desk with the I1V1 logo that RSN had been using for all their news stories on the "vamp sitch," as the vice president had insisted on calling it. "—ozens of Senate races starting to heat up, probably the one with the most heat is for junior senator of New York. The hottest of the hot-button issues is the vamp virus, I1V1, and the New York race has made it white-hot with the candidacy of Hugues Charles, an admitted vamp. Known as 'Big Charlie,' the current Bronx District Attorney has joined a wide field of Democratic candidates to replace Senator Emily Krascznicki. Today that race took a big turn when another candidate threw his hat into the ring: Mickey Solano, who was Big Charlie's opponent in his latest reelection as Bronx DA."

Cursing, Judy leapt from the couch to find her laptop.

The camera angle changed to one that had Solano's smug face on a screen while Lashmar turned to look at him. "We've got him here via satellite to talk with us this morning. Thanks for coming on, Mickey."

"It's my pleasure, Helen."

Yeah, I'll bet it is. She found her laptop on her dining room table and opened it.

"This is your second run at Big Charlie in two years. What makes you think that this time will be different?"

I'm an even bigger asshole? Judy thought uncharitably as she impatiently waited for the laptop to start back up.

"It's only been a year, but the world has changed a lot in that year, Helen. The vampires are a real problem, and we can't just nod our heads and say they're just victims. It's time to get tough. Honestly, Charlie's doing great in the Bronx, and that's where he belongs. Let him stay in the community he's been such a big part of, and leave the legislation to the rest of us."

I was right, he is *a bigger asshole. He didn't used to be this patronizing.* Her laptop finally came back online and found her apartment's wireless network. She started a new e-mail message to Big Charlie.

"Now you've hired Barel Grindberg as your campaign manager, and she ran Big Charlie's winning campaign against you."

"What!?" Judy rewound the DVR again to make sure she heard that right.

"—ired Barel Grindberg as your campaign manager, and she ran Big Cha—"

"That *bitch*." Judy had always liked Barel, and couldn't believe she'd stab them in the back like that.

"Hey, I was just happy that she was available."

Solano droned on, and Judy got more and more livid. She knew that Barel had specifically advised Big Charlie against running again, and now she wondered if that sage advice had come before or after she'd been hired by Solano.

She finished composing the e-mail and then realized she needed to talk directly to Big Charlie.

Solano was droning on as she grabbed her phone. "—can't help but be an advocate for the vampires, and that's not what we need. We need objectivity. Charlie's been on the front lines of it, both as a victim and as a prosecutor. Hell, a third of the criminal trials in the Bronx in the last nine months have been vampire-related, and a quarter of the civil ones."

Judy shouted at the screen, "The DA doesn't handle civil cases, you dumb fuck!"

Big Charlie's voicemail came on. With a sigh, Judy waited for the beep. "It's Judy—call me back the *minute* you get this!"

"—not part of the machine. I *am* part of the community. Mayor Barr, Emma and Dianne—they're part of the system, and that system ain't workin'."

Oh, sweet Jesus, he is not pulling that shit, is he? Judy went back to her laptop to finish the e-mail in case Big Charlie checked that before his voicemail.

Solano went on: "Humanity's at war with itself right now, and we need people who can step up. I've always stepped up when it matters, when the people of New York have needed me, both as a lawyer and an activist. And honestly, what I said about Charlie applies to the others, too, in that they're too close. They're part of the problem, so they don't see the solution. I can bring fresh eyes, eyes that have seen the reality of what the world is turning into."

Judy hit send on the e-mail she'd composed before trying to call, and then leaned back on her couch. In truth, she had also been against Big Charlie running for senator. Before I1V1, she had figured he'd be gunning for it when a seat came open, but now? It was madness.

But she also believed that he could do some good, so it was worth the shot.

She just hoped that she wasn't fooling herself. Or him.

18

Mia Fitzsimmons thought that Jack Napolitano was going to crawl out of his own skin.

"Can you believe that snake-in-the-grass is the one moderating?" He shook his perfectly coiffed head. "This was *my* racket."

Mia tried to ignore him, all the while cursing whoever sat the two of them next to each other in the press area. The debate among Democratic candidates for senator was being held at Fordham University, and campus security had insisted on assigned seats for the press—and indeed for everyone else, as Big Charlie's presence on the dais led to some serious security concerns.

Jack had said that between every question, and Mia swore that the next time, she was going to kick him. Either that or ask how she qualified as a snake in the grass when *he* was the one who took her job when she was promoted?

The moderator he was complaining about was Yuki Nitobe, who had been asked to moderate by several of the candidates—though notably *not* Big Charlie. Mia figured they were hoping that having the journalist who broke the I1V1 story do the moderating would have people talking about vampires even more, thus focusing more animus on Big Charlie.

The sad thing was, it would probably work.

"Mayor Barr," Nitobe said, "the next question is for you. Do you feel that the most important legislative agenda before Congress in the coming months will be legislation against the I1V1 virus?"

"Absolutely," Barr said without hesitation. "This virus is producing people who are running roughshod over, not just laws, but morality." Barr started doing the cup-your-thumb-in-your-index-finger method of pointing that politicians kept doing because somebody told them it made them look forceful. Mia was looking forward to the day when someone figured out that whoever told them that was wrong. "Plus they have abilities that were never accounted for in current jurisprudence," Barr added. "Now I'm not saying people should be rounded up or anything crazy like that. I'm talking solely about the vampires who have committed crimes—we need to come up with different punishments and different methods for arresting, incarcerating, and prosecuting that small percentage of those who do commit crimes."

As with every question, that resulted in applause. Jack started to make a comment, but Mia just glared at him, and he clammed up.

Nitobe waited for the applause to die down. "The next question is for President Jaffe. What would be your response to a vampire who—"

Big Charlie then cut in, which was a breach in protocol. All the journalists around Mia sat up. "Excuse me, but I am afraid I must interrupt. This is the fifth question in a row that has dealt with I1V1. One would think that a United States Senator had little else to deal with in his or her day-to-day life than legislating against those of us who suffer from the virus."

Nitobe looked positively nonplussed, but before she could say anything, Emma Jaffe, the sitting Manhattan borough president, said, "Oh come on, Charlie, do you really think it's not an important issue? Vampires have been running rampant with no control, and it's been worse in the big cities. The world takes the lead from New York, and we need to provide that leadership."

Mia snorted, since that was probably Jaffe's already-prepared answer to that question.

Dianne Axisa, a state senator, jumped in. "I think Charlie raises a good point. There's a budget crisis, we don't have enough jobs or true national health care, there are serious allocation and tax issues facing this country—and we've spent all our time in this debate talking about one issue. Yes, it's an important issue, but it's hardly the only one."

Wow, two voices of reason. Mia jotted down notes. *One more than I was expecting.*

Solano got that annoying smile of his. "I gotta say, Charlie, I think it's kinda disingenuous for you to complain, since the only reason you're running is *because* you can turn yourself into a werewolf."

"My reasons for running are many, Mickey. But the primary one is to make sure that those of us who suffer from this virus are given a voice in government." He pointed at the two female candidates. "It was less than a hundred years ago that Dianne and Emma could not even vote for a state representative in Washington, much less attempt to become one. It took almost a century and a half for women to achieve that right—I fear that achieving similar rights for my own kind may take as long, and that is simply *not* acceptable."

A gasp passed through the room. Solano put voice to what everyone was suddenly thinking. "That sounded like a threat, Charlie. And having I1V1 doesn't exactly take away your right to vote."

Big Charlie was sounding more—intense? angry?—than Mia had ever heard him. His voice was tighter and tenser than usual. "I have spoken with many who have faced problems, especially those who have had their appearance changed by the virus. They no longer match the visage that appears on their driver's license or passport and are denied simple rights—and not just to vote. We do require new legislation, it is true, but Aaron's solution focuses far too much on the negative and not enough on the positive. We need to take charge of our own destiny, and not let it be defined by others."

The applause that generated was much more subdued and guarded than that of the previous candidates'.

19

Emma Jaffe lay in her bed. The television was on, and her laptop was open, but she wasn't paying particularly close attention to either one.

It had been an exhausting day, the latest in a series. Her staff was handling most of the day-to-day of running the borough of Manhattan, which was good, because this campaign was taking up all of her spare time. Any other time, a senate race wouldn't be this brutal, but DA Charles made it a huge story. She was spending more time on camera than she ever imagined she would.

On the other hand, it was publicity you couldn't buy. People all over the country were talking about her. Even if she didn't win the race, she had recognition now, and could parlay that into something much bigger. If senator didn't work, there was always mayor next year.

She looked to the empty half of the bed. *You coulda been part of this, Steve.* But then, her career had taken off since the divorce, so maybe he couldn't have been. Maybe he really had been holding her back.

The TV went to commercial, and a deep voice said, "Michael Fayne. Anson Morris. Nathan Kapsis. What do they all have in common? They're all New Yorkers, they're all vampires—and they're all *killers*."

She grabbed for the remote and turned the volume up. She and her staff had gone 'round and 'round over this ad. Even once they finally agreed to film it, finding the right voice had been hard. Her initial thought had been for a gentle female voice, but her campaign manager had convinced her that the deep, scratchy male voice was the way to go.

"Nathan Kapsis murdered his uncle, Senator Alex Kapsis—and now another killer *just like him* wants to take his seat. You wouldn't let the fox into then henhouse. So why should we let a vampire into Congress? Whatever you do next Tuesday—*don't* vote for Hugues Charles for Senate. Vote life, not death."

Then her own voice: "I'm Emma Jaffe and I approve this message."

The key, of course, was that last line in the ad. "Vote life, not death" was the point she'd be hammering home on the rest of her interviews for the next week. Fear was her best weapon right now.

A crack startled her, echoing throughout her apartment. "Hello?"

Steve had taken the dog with him when he left her, so the apartment was empty. She threw the covers aside, pulled her bathrobe tighter around her waist, and cautiously walked toward the doorway. She left the bedroom door open, generally.

A familiar *clack-clack* echoed through the apartment: paws on hardwood. But she hadn't heard it since Steve took Muttley.

Then the clacking got faster, and Emma's heartbeat did likewise. "Who's there?"

A shape formed in the darkness of the hallway, coalescing into a giant, four-legged, hairy creature, breathing heavily and moving toward her.

Her heart pounded into her ribs. She realized that using fear against Big Charlie was a weapon that worked both ways.

A second later, the shape leapt toward her, and she screamed.

20
TRANSCRIPT OF "ON THE STREET" SEGMENT OF GOOD MORNING NYC

GOOD MORNING NYC: Today's "On the Street" is about the senate race currently playing out, as we went to Grand Central and asked commuters who they would be voting for.

PERSON #1: Yo, I'm actually *from* the Bronx, and I *voted* for Big Charlie every time he ran—but no way in *hell* I'm votin' for that motherBLEEPer now!

PERSON #2: Honestly, I've gone to every candidate's web site and read over their platforms. VanDerMeer's right out—the man's living in the fifties, honestly. Barr never impressed me when he was mayor, and his campaign feels like a desperate attempt to remind everyone he's alive, y'know? Solano's just a scuzzball lawyer. Jaffe and Axisa are okay, I guess, but they don't seem to have much substance. I'll probably vote for one of them, honestly. The only candidate I find myself liking and agreeing with is Big Charlie—but of course, I can't vote for *that*. That'd be crazy.

PERSON #3: I'd sooner vote for the love child of Manson and the Son of Sam than I would the werewolf guy from the Bronx, I'll tell you *that* for free.

PERSON #4: I'm kinda torn between VanDerMeer and Big Charlie. VanDerMeer because he actually knows how to get BLEEP done, Big Charlie because it would just be *awesome* to have a real-live werewolf in Congress!

PERSON #5: Well, you can probably guess from my white hair and claws that I've got I1V1. I'm actually a registered Republican, so I can't vote in the Democratic primary—which is too bad, because I think it's great that Big Charlie is trying to represent us in Congress. It's about damn time, if you ask me.

PERSON #6: Solano, mostly because I wish I'd voted for him for DA last year. Jesus, the way Big Charlie's been—it's like he's a totally different person! Did you hear him in the debate? I didn't see it, but I read what people were saying about it afterward, and it's like he wants to lead a revolution or something. Definitely Solano. Shoulda paid attention to him before.

21

Mia was surprised to see Detective Trujillo calling her. She never figured to hear from the detective again after he helped her out with the senator's murder.

"Hello, Detec—"

"Look, Fitzsimmons, we never had this conversation, okay?"

She frowned. "Uh, okay. What conver—"

"I caught the Jaffe murder, okay? And it's *seriously* fucked up. We're talkin' the exact same thing that happened to Kapsis."

Mia recalled that the borough president's apartment wasn't far from that of the senator—and both in the 24th Precinct. So it wasn't a surprise that the same detective caught both. "So what's the problem?"

"The *problem* is that this time we got footage. Jaffe had video surveillance on her place. Everywhere but the bathroom and bedroom's covered, and this was a fuckin' *wolf*."

Her heart leapt into her throat. "Big Charlie?"

"Nah, he's alibi'd. After that ad she ran? He was second on our list after her ex. But nah, he was in his office all night. Got footage'a *that* too. God bless security cameras, right?"

"So why're you—"

"'Cause somethin' ain't right. Look, Kapsis is closed, and it's stayin' closed. You don't reopen a senator's murder case if you wanna keep your job, so fuck that shit, but you? You ain't got nothin' to lose, and this ain't sittin' right with me. Come by the two-four when you get a chance—I got a DVD'a Jaffe's security footage for ya. Maybe you can use it."

Mia smiled. "I guess I owe you one now, huh, Detective?"

"Damn fuckin' right."

With that, he ended the call, and Mia's smile fell. If it was a wolf-like creature who killed both Senator Kapsis—who'd just criticized Big Charlie on the air—and President Jaffe—who'd just started a nasty ad campaign against Big Charlie—then things did not look particularly good for the Bronx DA.

The next morning, first thing, she took the bus to the 2 train, taking that to 96th Street in Manhattan, from which it was a short walk to the 24th Precinct. Sure enough, a padded envelope with a rewritable DVD was waiting for her at the sergeant's desk. Not wanting to wait, she went to a Dunkin Donuts on Broadway and opened up her laptop, putting the DVD in the tray.

Then she pulled out her phone and called her editor.

"Bart, I may have something. And I need to run it by you to make sure I'm not crazy."

"Okay," Bart said nonchalantly. He'd had reporters do this to him all the time.

"I got my hands on the security footage of Emma Jaffe's apartment."

"What?" Bart was less nonchalant now. "How'd you—"

"Never mind. The point is, I'm looking at what attacked her. It's a wolf."

"Shit."

"Yeah, and it gets better. Big Charlie isn't the only vampire out there who changes shape. You've got other *loup garou*, you've got *tlahuelpuchi, vârcolac, abchanchu*—"

"Get to the point," Bart said impatiently.

"Sorry." She'd been doing a lot of research lately, and she sometimes forgot that most people didn't care as much as she did. "Anyhow, the one thing that's constant with all the shapechangers is that they keep the same mass."

"Meaning?"

"Big Charlie is about 275 pounds. When he turns into a wolf, he's still 275 pounds. The wolf I'm looking at on this DVD is less than 200 pounds."

"You sure?" Before Mia could answer, Bart said, "Of course you're sure, you're quoting Eastern European vampire names at me off the top of your head."

"Actually, only the *vârcolac* is Eastern European. The others are—"

"I could give a shit. Look, Mia, where you goin' with this?"

She hesitated. "I don't know yet. But it isn't Big Charlie killing these people."

"What?" Bart's voice got distant.

"Bart?"

"Oh, fuck. All right, get Castro over there." His voice grew louder again. "Gotta go, Mia. And so do you—your guy's house just got torched."

22

PARTIAL TRANSCRIPT OF SPECIAL PRIMARY DAY COVERAGE ON CHANNEL 12.

CHANNEL 12: With ninety percent of the precincts now reporting in statewide, it appears that the race for senator is in a dead heat between Mickey Solano and the late Manhattan Borough President Emma Jaffe. The tremendous support for Jaffe coming after her brutal murder only a few nights ago is impressive. Even more impressive is that the less than one percent of the vote received so far by Bronx District Attorney Hugues Charles. Indeed, some reports are that Big Charlie—a self-confessed vampire—has received less than a hundred votes statewide, a historically low number. Quite a turnaround from his landslide victory in the Bronx DA race lasts year.

Speaking of Big Charlie, we have a breaking story in the Bronx. Nishanda Henry is on the scene. Nishanda?

NISHANDA HENRY: I'm at the home of Bronx District Attorney Hugues Charles—or, at least, what's left of it. The house, located on De Reimer Avenue in the Bronx, caught fire an hour ago. Firefighters have gotten the blaze under control. Although several members of the press and dozens of protestors have been present at Big Charlie's house fairly consistently since Manhattan Borough President Emma Jaffe's murder last week, no injuries have been reported yet.

I have to emphasize that "yet," because so far there are three people missing, and two of them are Big Charlie and his mother, Marie Charles. The third is Jack Kearns, a former NYPD detective who has been serving as the head of Big Charlie's security detail during the primary race. The lead firefighter on the scene, Lieutenant Eamon Mahony, had this to say.

LIEUTENANT EAMON MAHONY: We been through the entirety'a the wreckage'a the house, and we not only haven't found any bodies, we haven't found any evidence'a bodies. No blood, nothing. This was a slow burn, not the kinda thing that burns bodies so badly there's nothin' left. We responded in more'n sufficient time. It's a preliminary judgment, but I'd say that nobody was home when the fire was set.

HENRY: According to NYPD spokeswoman Jane Amundson, police have put out an all-points for all three missing occupants of the house, saying that they are wanted for questioning in the presumed arson. While NYPD has categorically stated that Big Charlie was not a suspect in the murder of Emma Jaffe, protestors have remained camped outside his house since that murder, with the threat of violence always there. It is unknown if one of them started the fire or not.

For Channel 12, I'm Nishanda Henry.

23

Judy Alejo sat in her office staring into space, biting the right side of her lip.

She had turned her phone off, and couldn't bear to look at her e-mail. Her laptop was open to news stories about the late Emma Jaffe's victory and the disappearance of Big Charlie following the firebombing of his house.

Someone knocked on her door. Probably her assistant. She ignored it.

"Judy, I'm sorry, but Mia Fitzsimmons is here to see you?"

She sighed. Had it been anyone other than her former high school classmate, she would have called security.

"Come on in," Judy said after a long sigh.

"You look like crap," Mia said without preamble.

That prompted a bark of laughter. "Yeah, well, the next time I walk out of this courthouse will prob'ly be the last. Ain't no way I'm keepin' my job. My boss has gone missing, and even if he didn't actually kill nobody, everyone *thinks* he did." She glanced over at her laptop. "Every op-ed in the city's about how innocent people don't run, and even if he didn't kill Jaffe and Kapsis, he prob'ly got one of his *loup garou* buddies to do it for him." She shook her head. "Christ, he didn't even *know* any other *loup garou!*"

"Well, he knew one." Mia sat down in Judy's guest chair.

Judy frowned. "Excuse me? I knew everyone he knew, and—"

"You knew her, too." Mia took a deep breath. "Okay, I don't have much by way of actual proof of this, but— Did you ever see Charlie transform?"

"Well—" Judy hesitated. It was funny, with everything they'd discussed, both among themselves and with the press and other politicians and lawyers, she hadn't even realized that she never saw the transformation. She'd been calling her boss a *loup garou* for over a year now without any empirical proof. "No, I didn't. But so what, he—"

"I don't think he actually *has* I1V1."

"That's crazy."

"Remember when he announced that he had it?" Mia was flipping through a note pad now. "He said he would provide records of his doctor visit."

"Yeah, so?"

"Judy, I never got those health records. Nobody did. We all kinda forgot about it in the mess of the race, and besides, it wasn't that big a deal. I mean, why would anyone lie about something like that, right?"

"He didn't lie!" Judy stood up, pacing her small office. "Jesus, Mia, do you really think he'd do something that crazy? Charlie's the sanest person I know, and he'd never do open himself up to all that bullshit—"

"Unless he wanted to protect someone he loved."

Judy whirled on the reporter. "Excuse me?"

"The cops are keeping it quiet, but the evidence points to the same killer for both Jaffe and Kapsis."

"I thought it was the nephew who got Kapsis."

Mia shook her head. "There's no way Nathan did it, he's a *vrykolatios*. He doesn't have the strength. I'll bet real money that his lawyer uses that when he finally goes to trial."

Shaking her head, Judy said, "I don't get it, Mia, what—"

"It's his mother. Marie Charles is the *loup garou.*"

For several seconds, Judy just stared at Mia.

Then she burst out laughing.

"Nice one, Mia. Marie's a *loup garou* and I'm the queen of fucking England. Now I remember why I didn't like you in high school. I'm calling security to haul your bony white ass outta here."

Mia stood up as Judy reached for her phone. "Please, Judy, hear me out. I don't like this either, but *it fits*. Marie doesn't actually have an alibi for either killing, and the wolf that killed Jaffe weighs about the same as she does."

Judy stared at her. "That's all you got?"

"I told you I didn't have anything solid. But I know him—and so do you. Look at what we do have, and think about how he feels about his *maman*. You really think he wouldn't do all this for her?"

Instinctively, Judy wanted to say no. But she couldn't. The woman sailed to New York from a violent country while eight months pregnant to save her son. And Big Charlie had always been one to repay his debts.

He'd try to avoid her being subject to the nightmare of press coverage of being the vampire mother of a politician. And he'd also try to fix it so that things were better for others of her kind.

"No wonder he wanted to run for senate so bad," Judy whispered. "Jesus, he kept insisting, no matter how many people told him it was stupid. And it never made sense. But now—" She looked at Mia. "How sure are you?"

Mia just stared back. "How sure are you?"

Neither woman said anything in response.

24

OP-ED PIECE BY MIA FITZSIMMONS IN THE NEW YORK DAILY NEWS.

"Ladies and gentlemen, the Bronx is burning."

That was the thought that went through my head as I stood in front of Hugues Charles' burning house two months ago. I had been on an errand in Manhattan when my editor told me that his house was on fire. I immediately hopped in a cab and high-tailed it to De Reimer Avenue only to watch Big Charlie's home go up in flames.

Back in 1977, Howard Cosell said those words when he saw the South Bronx on fire from Yankee Stadium. A young Hugues Charles heard them and swore he would protect the Bronx to keep it from burning.

On a Tuesday night in September, he officially failed. The Reverend Josiah Mann—a so-called religious leader who has never set foot in New York City as far as I know—called for his head, and TV commercials called him a monster and a menace. The day before her tragic murder, Emma Jaffe, one of his opponents, aired a commercial that called a vote for him to be a vote for death.

All of them missed the point. Big Charlie was just trying to protect the people of the city he called home from burning down.

It's been two months since that night that the Bronx burned, and while it was just one house on De Reimer Avenue, it was as devastating as those multiple fires were in October 1977. Big Charlie is still missing, with no sign of him or his *maman*. We can only assume that Marie Charles and her son are in hiding. We can only assume they're okay.

Today, Mickey Solano is the new junior senator for New York State. When he is sworn in early next year, he will be expected to vote on legislation against the very virus that gave him his job. After all, if not for I1V1, Alex Kapsis would have finished his term and likely been re-elected, opposed only by the same Frank VanDerMeer who only managed 30% of the vote against Solano. If not for I1V1, Big Charlie would probably have not been opposed by Solano in the Bronx DA race, which raised his profile.

Now the Bronx will have an inferior DA, New York has an inferior senator, and a good man whose only mistake was that he was powerless against a virus he couldn't help contracting, has disappeared, leaving only ashes in his place. Worse, those who have I1V1, who had put their hopes in at last having representation in Congress, have gone even further underground, villified even more by the Reverend Manns and Mickey Solanos of the world.

Ladies and gentlemen, the Bronx is *still* burning.

Introduction to "A Vampire and a Vampire Hunter Walk into a Bar…"

Having just done a modern take on vampires, we now turn to this little trifle, which is rooted more in pop-culture than folklore.

Hilariously, given its length, the tale you're about to read has been reprinted once (by *The Town Drunk*) and adapted into an audio drama by Gypsy Audio (which was nominated for an audio award, though it did not win). Not bad for an 1100-word story that's only dialogue between two characters. But then, I like writing all-dialogue stories (as we'll see again later in the book with "Wild Bill Got Shot," not to mention the *Dragon Precinct* story "Brotherly Love" that appears in *Tales from Dragon Precinct*).

Most of my short fiction has been for anthologies. This is one of the few that went to a magazine, and it helped kill it. "A Vampire and a Vampire Hunter Walk into a Bar…" was published in the final print issue of Paizo's run on *Amazing Stories* in February 2005.

A Vampire and a Vampire Hunter Walk into a Bar...

"About time you arrived. I already got your drink."
"Red wine again? Do you never tire of that joke?"
"Apparently I do not."
"Is it at least a Chianti? I'd hate to have to choke down one of those American atrocities."
"Of course. Do you take me for a philistine?"
"I take you for a Dutch lout with the taste of a pig."
"And you're an Eastern European dandy, but you don't hear me complaining."
"I've heard you do little else for the past several decades, my friend. And you have nobody to blame but yourself, you know."
"*My*self? If you'd been kind enough to stay dead just once, then maybe I wouldn't have sought out that Gypsy woman for that immortality spell."
"I could have warned you about the Romany, you know."
"As if I was going to consult *you* about finding a way to hunt you down more efficiently. And as if I would have listened to your advice in any case."
"It would have saved you considerable amounts of grief. And we would not be where we are today."
"No, I would be in the ground, and you would be out draining some young lass of her life's blood."
"It *is* what I do."
"I should have sued that woman."
"Sue the *Romany*? You are aware, are you not, that they are not overburdened with material assets?"
"Yes, but think how much fun it would be to subpoena them."
"I will take your word for it."

"*I'm* being sued, you know."

"You are joking."

"No. Some American woman I foolishly agreed to train. One of your kind killed her family."

"Not *another* revenge-obsessed last survivor?"

"Yes, another. Really, if you people insist on wiping out an entire family, the least you could do is be efficient about it and kill *all* of them. This business of leaving behind youngsters with visions of revenge dancing in their heads does get out of hand. All they do is cause trouble."

"This particular girl is taking legal action against you?"

"Yes. Apparently I violated the terms of our agreement, whatever *that* means. *She* came to *me* begging for help, and because I did not transform her into a reasonable facsimile of that blonde girl from television, she felt I did not perform my task adequately."

"The popular culture hasn't done either of us a favor, has it? It's been over seventy years, and I'm still living down that cape-wearing Hungarian drug addict."

"Well, you *did* wear a cape."

"Of course I wore a cape *then*! *Everyone* wore a cape *then*! I would hardly wear such an absurd anachronism now, yet everyone expresses shock because I'm not dressed in the same clothing I happened to be wearing in a previous century. I have always dressed at the height of *current* fashion."

"True. I understand suits of armor and bloody swords were all the rage in the fifteenth century."

"They were in the circles *I* ran in."

"Ran through, more like. Still, that Armani you've got on now looks good on you. I suppose it cost you someone else's arm and leg."

"At least I give some care to my appearance. Have you shaved at all since 1850?"

"What possible reason do I have to look good?"

"An excellent point. Why start now?"

"My line of work hardly requires it. Certainly not to the extent yours does. It's hard to convince beautiful young women to invite them into your boudoir if you look like—"

"An unshaven, slightly mad Dutchman with wild hair, battered clothing, and the lingering scent of week-old grime?"

"Touché."

"It should be pointed out, however, that I have not been able to enact such a scenario for some time. Gaining ingress to a lady's bedroom has gotten much more challenging with the advent of electronic security. It is difficult to mesmerize an alarm system."

"I hope you're not asking for sympathy."

"Quite the opposite—I view it as a challenge. I certainly get more joy out of that than the actual conquests. I find myself simply killing them more often than I do turning them. It hardly seems worth the time, given how tiresome they become."

"Oh?"

"We are creatures of the night. We are hunters, predators—killers. Yet vampires nowadays wish to loaf about and put their hands to their foreheads and bemoan how awful unlife is. It's revolting—they're so full of—full of—"

"Shit?"

"I was going to say 'angst,' but, yes, excrement fits the bill quite nicely. They have been given the gift of immortality, of power over others, and all they do is wonder about the meaning of existence and other such philosophical rot."

"Blame the literature. Or better yet, blame the Americans."

"Not that I disagree with the sentiment, but why them in particular?"

"Besides the fact that they produce the most egregious examples of the literature that propagates the very notions you're complaining about, the fact is that Americans think about things too much."

"I have been around since long before there *was* a United States, and I have never heard such a complaint."

"Of course not, because people don't pay attention. It's how your kind has survived so long, despite the efforts of men like me. But Americans, with their insistence on educating *all* their children rather than a chosen few, and their notions of universal literacy, have produced a race that does nothing *but* think. Most of them think only about the most foolish things, but they *do* think."

"That is a fascinating theory."

"Thank you."

"It is also utter rubbish. Nobody ever thinks. If they thought, they would go mad."

"Who says they have not?"

"An excellent point. Also my last. The sun will be up soon."

"So? This place is open twenty-four hours. It's not as if you're going to burst into flames."

"I still prefer to avoid the sun's gaze where possible. That, at least, is something for which I may thank the cinema. That German fool did our kind a great favor by perpetuating that burn-in-the-sun nonsense. Especially when dealing with *your* ilk. I do so love the looks on the would-be vampire hunters' faces when they expose us to the light and we *don't* catch fire. It's very amusing."

"You still needn't leave yet. You haven't even touched your wine."

"Nor will I. You have, as is your wont, put something in it that is inimical to my continued survival. As you always do."

"And you did not fall for it, as you never do."

"I do appreciate the irony, since I do not drink—wine."

"Indeed. Until tomorrow night?"

"Of course."

"Good-bye, my old enemy."

"Good-bye, my old friend."

Introduction to "Under the King's Bridge"

The Liars Club is a cabal of writers, most of whom live (or lived) in the Philadelphia area. Founded by Jonathan Maberry, the group's rolls have included the late L.A. Banks, Gregory Frost, Christopher Golden, Merry Jones, Solomon Jones, Don Lafferty, Marie Lamba, William Lashner, Jon McGoran, Edward Pettit, Kelly Simmons, Keith Strunk, Stephen Susco, Dennis Tafoya, Michael A. Ventrella, Chuck Wendig, and many others. The main focus of the Liars Club is outreach: supporting literacy and libraries and also assisting writers in any way that we can via workshops, panels, classes, etc. The Liars Club runs several Writers Coffeehouses in eastern Pennsylvania, Southern California, and New England areas, where scribes of any stripe can come by and gab at each other, discussing whatever issues might come up. The Coffeehouses (which you can keep up with at liarsclubphilly.com) are open to anyone, from aspiring writers still struggling with their first manuscript to multiple *Times* best-sellers and everyone in between.

I was invited to join the group in 2010, and in 2011 we put together a charity anthology, where each of us would provide a tale and proceeds from the sales of the book would go toward literacy-based charities. The members of the group write in a huge range of genres, from fantasy to mystery to thriller to YA to horror to literary and back again, so we decided to use our name as the theme. Regardless of genre, every single story would be about lying in some form or other.

In my case, I decided to take a character who'd been banging around in my head out for a spin. Bram Gold is a Courser, a person who hunts supernatural creatures, living in modern-day

New York. This story plays up on the history of the Marble Hill region of the Big Apple, as well as the appalling treatment of women throughout history, and the lies that it led to. The story worked well enough that it has led to more: WordFire Press will be publishing at least three Bram Gold novels, starting with *A Furnace Sealed*, coming very soon.

Under the King's Bridge

I gotta tell you, if I hadn't seen it with my own eyes, I wouldn't have believed it.

Usually, when commuters come out of the Marble Hill Metro North station in New York City during evening rush hour, they're rushing up the long, enclosed staircase to get where they're going like hamsters in those plastic tubes.

On this particular Friday afternoon, though, not so much. As I stood there next to the man who wanted to hire me, the mid-July sun bearing down on us, I watched a whole lot of them shamble up the stairs like the title characters in *Dawn of the Dead*.

Not all of them, mind you. Some were doing the usual mad dash, trying to get out of the airlessness of the covererd staircase as quick as possible. They scattered toward the gypsy cabs on 225th Street, or one of the bus stops on Broadway, or the shopping center across the street, or the 1 train on the corner. Like most New Yorkers, they moved quickly, not really giving a damn about much beyond landsharking their way to their (preferably air-conditioned) destination.

But all the ones who turned left toward the Marble Hill neighborhood that the station serviced were just—just *shuffling*. They barely picked their feet up. You expect that sort of thing to an extent when it's pushing ninety degrees, but not like this.

I turned to look at my companion, who regarded me with anxiety. "See what I mean, Mr. Gold? It's like you said—like they all started mainlining Prozac or something."

"Yeah." I nodded. "Last time I saw expressions that vacant, it was in a high school. All right, I guess I'll take the case."

I probably should back it up a bit. My new client had called me and made an appointment to see me in my office, identifying himself as Isaiah Daley. He was a tall African-American gentleman, arriving for the appointment wearing a New York Yankees T-shirt, khaki shorts, and moccasins. I let him in the front door, which had a nice black engraved nameplate that read: BRAM GOLD, COURSER.

First thing he asked when he walked in was: "So Mr. Gold, I have to ask: what *is* a Courser, exactly?"

I sighed. I always got this when people outside the game hired me. "It's a hunting term, actually. And hunting is pretty much what we do. Have a seat, and please, call me Bram."

Daley was fidgeting as he sat down in my guest chair. "Why not just call yourselves Hunters?"

I planted myself on the other side of the desk, the chair squeaking as my butt hit the cushion. "We *used* to be called that. Well, actually, we used to be called Slayers, but then *Buffy the Vampire Slayer* got popular in the Nineties, and everybody thought we were just role-playing or something. So we switched to Hunters, and then *Supernatural* got popular, and we finally just went with 'Coursers.' We figure no Hollywood writer's gonna know what *that* is."

"I'm sorry, Mr. Gold, but nobody else is gonna know, either."

I grinned. "Good point—and like I said, call me Bram. Anyhow, I'm assuming you didn't make the appointment with me to ask about my job title?"

"No, I—" He hesitated and fidgeted some more, then looked around at the blank gray walls and the big window that had a mostly uninteresting view of the Major Deegan Expressway. Part of why I chose the location on West 230th Street and Broadway in the northwest Bronx was that it was easy to get to: right off the Deegan, also the 1 train, about seven different city bus lines, and the aforementioned Marble Hill Metro North station. "This place is kinda dingy."

I winced. Besides the fact that he was stalling some more, he was also hitting a sore point. "I don't use this office all that much, truth be told. I mean, I got it as a maildrop, and a place to meet with clients, but all the mail I get is junk. And to be honest, Mr. Daley, you're the first person in six months who wanted to see me here. Most of my clients are either regular customers or they don't want to get together in public."

I didn't mention that I cleaned the place for the first time in six months for the two hours before he got here. Place didn't so much have dust bunnies as dust rhinos. And man was I glad that the air-conditioner in the window still worked...

"So, what did you—"

"Yeah, sorry, Mr. Gold, I just—" Another hesitation. "It's not 'Mr. Daley,' it's 'Reverend Daley.' I'm one of the pastors at St. Stephen's."

I nodded. St. Stephen's United Methodist Church was one of the oldest churches in the area, and one of the most popular. It had been at that location since the end of the 19th century.

"For the last week or so, Mr. Gold, lotsa folks've been acting—weird."

Deciding not to make a third offer to drop the formality, already, I folded my hands together and sat them on my desk. "Define 'weird,' please, Reverend Daley."

"Just kinda—lifeless. Like they're zombies, almost."

"Actual zombies or what everyone *thinks* zombies are like?"

Daley frowned. "I'm sorry?"

I kept forgetting that not everyone was in the game. "Actual zombies are corpses that are animated by a spell, and the person doing the animating has to maintain it, usually from pretty close proximity. They don't actually shamble across the terrain muttering, 'Brains...'"

"Well, uh, nobody's casting a spell on them, if that's what you mean. People can do that?"

"Way more than you'd believe."

"Okay." He seemed nonplussed, not surprisingly. Lots of religious types were in the game—my own knowledge of it came from my rabbi, who's also my aunt—but Methodists tended to be a bit too literal-minded to buy into it. "They're all kinda—listless, I guess. Just—like you said, shambling? They wander down to the Metro North station or the 1 train or whatever, then they go to work, then they wander home at the end of the day.

The worst thing, though, is that nobody's been showing up for services."

I scratched my chin. "Nobody?"

The reverend shook his head. "Been empty since Sunday."

I seriously doubted St. Stephen's ever had even a weekday service with no attendance in the century-plus since they opened. Hell, I doubt they ever got below a dozen. "I assume you went through the usual channels?"

"Oh yeah. Called the local precinct, they said people not goin' to church wasn't a crime, with which I respectfully disagreed. Called ConEd, in case it was, I dunno, a gas leak or something, but they didn't find anything, either."

Points for thoroughness. "So you called me?"

"One of the detectives at the 50th Precinct sent me to you."

I smiled. Detective Lyd Toscano wasn't in the game, but she knew about it, and she was more than happy to keep the rest of the NYPD as far away from it as possible. "All right. Before I take the case, I'd like to see what's going on for myself—see if it really is in my line. I don't want to take your money, and then discover that it's—I dunno, everyone doped up on bad anti-anxiety meds or something."

Daley seemed taken aback by that. "Really? Thanks. I mean, I brought a checkbook, I figured you'd—"

Waving him off, I said, "S'all right." Last thing I wanted to do was gouge a church. Tough enough to hire someone to fix something that you may not even really believe exists, but to take all their money before you even start? That's not how I like to do business.

"Why don't you meet me at the Marble Hill Metro North station when the 6:05 train comes in?" Daley asked.

Back at the Metro North station, the reverend asked me if he wanted to go back to my office.

"Twice in one year?" I laughed. "No, thanks." I quickly quoted him my rates, and he wrote me a check for the first day's work. Sweat dripped off his forehead onto lower-left-hand corner of the check, smudging the memo section. All he'd written there was P.I.

Strictly speaking, I wasn't actually a private investigator, but it wasn't worth trying to explain that. I was an expert in my field, and I *was* a licensed Courser, which was all that mattered in this instance. Besides, that was probably an easier sell to the church's bookkeeper.

"I take it this *is* something in your, uh—your line of work?"

"It's a supernatural creature, yeah." Sometimes it just didn't pay to beat around the bush. "If I'm right—and I'm pretty sure I am right—this is a lamprey."

Daley frowned. "Isn't that a kinda fish?"

I nodded. "Yeah, it's also a fish, but that's the name somebody gave to an animal that sucks energy out of people. In fact, you know that whole thing from Dracula about how vampires can't cross running water?"

"Uh, yeah."

"Total horseshit, but lampreys—who are kinda like energy vampires—are the ones who can't do that. Stoker mixed 'em all up."

Holding up both hands and shuddering a bit, Daley asked, "Hang on—vampires are real, too?"

"Yeah, but don't worry, they're total wusses."

Daley frowned. "What, Stoker's wrong, but Stephenie Meyer's right?"

"Not hardly." This time I shuddered. "No, I mean, they're long-lived and they heal most any wound, but they're also weak, sickly, pale people who don't like sunlight very much. Stoker got most of it wrong, and he took the avoids-running-water thing from lampreys, is all I'm saying."

"Damn." Daley let out a very long breath. "You're seriously messin' with what I know of God's world, Mr. Gold."

"You came to me, Reverend."

"That I did." He shook his head. "Just figure it out, please. I hate preaching to an empty room."

He headed in the general direction of St. Stephen's while I took out my smartphone.

Miriam Zerelli was the Wardein of the Bronx—she was in charge of all magickal activity on the peninsula. That meant she was one of those regular clients I mentioned, and also a handy resource.

Of course, I got her voicemail when I called. "Hey Mimi, could you do me a favor and see if there's any mention in the diaries of a lamprey in Marble Hill?"

I spent the next hour following around the various shamblers who came out of Metro North. The first clue that something was up was the simple fact that a tall, dark, and semi-handsome Jewish guy followed them home and they didn't notice.

Well, most of them didn't. This one lady who lived on the corner of Adrian and 225th was giving me a nasty look—and she was walking normally, too—and so was a little kid who was riding a tricycle over on Terrace View Avenue. Both of those were on the outskirts of Marble Hill.

The neighborhood was pretty tiny as it was. In fact, it was originally part of Manhattan. In the late nineteenth century, they cut through the land at the south end of Marble Hill so that the Harlem River would run straight across, thus making shipping a whole helluva lot easier. At first that made Marble Hill an island, but then around World War I they filled in the north side and it was physically connected to the Bronx. That also eliminated the object for which the Kingsbridge neighborhood was named, as you now went from there to Marble Hill by traversing a street rather than the King's Bridge over the river.

But because it used to be a peninsula—and then an island—it was pretty well enclosed, so it didn't take long to check the whole neighborhood. The southern and western edges—which included St. Stephen's—looked unaffected.

Next step was to figure out what the epicenter of the affected area was. Normally, I'd need a map, but Marble Hill was only about a thousand feet by eight hundred feet or so, and all of it wasn't hit with this potential lamprey.

Didn't take long to figure out that the middle was on 227th Street. What got my attention was the house that had a FOR SALE sign on the front door, along with a local phone number and a web site URL.

Nobody was home when I went up the stoop and rang the bell, but I saw plenty of furniture inside. I pulled my smartphone back out of my pocket and checked the web site. It belonged to Brauck Realty, a place that specialized in houses in Riverdale,

Kingsbridge, Marble Hill, and Inwood. I found the listing for this house, looked it over, then dialed their number.

"Brauck Realty, this is Tara," came a perky voice on the other end.

"Hi, my name's Abe Goldblume, and I wanted to inquire about the house on West 227th Street in Marble Hill? Any chance of a viewing this weekend?"

"Oh sure, we'd be happy to!" Tara sounded positively overjoyed. "We can't do it tomorrow afternoon, that's when the movers are coming, but any time in the evening or Sunday will work."

The movers coming meant the current owners might be present. Even if they weren't, I wanted to get a look at it *before* they took stuff away—or, failing that, during. "Actually, Saturday afternoon is the only time I *can* do it—I'm going out of town for a week tomorrow night. Too bad, the place was perfect for what I'm looking for. Oh, well."

"Well, wait, Mr. Goldblume." Tara sounded a bit panicky, fearing the potential sale slipping through her fingers. "Let's see what we can arrange. Tell you what, would you mind looking at the house while people are moving things?"

"Why should I mind?" I grinned. "Say noon?"

"Perfect."

We exchanged information, and then I disconnected.

Tara was now no doubt checking my credit history, which was why I had to use my real name. For Courser business, I call myself Bram Gold, because, let's face it: that's the name of a guy who can get stuff done. I mean, if you need someone to corral a werewolf or wrangle a unicorn or put down a nixie, you're not gonna hire some schmuck named Abe Goldblume, am I right?

I headed down Marble Hill Avenue to 228th, and then down 228th to Broadway, where I could catch the bus that would take me home.

Just as I got to the bus stop, Miriam called me back. I hit TALK on my phone and said, "Joe's Pizza, Joe's not here."

"You know, Bram, that joke wasn't funny the *first* thousand times."

"When has *that* ever stopped me?" I asked with a chuckle.

"I live in hope." Miriam let out a long-suffering sigh. We'd been friends since we were kids, when her Dad was the Wardein, and I was nephew of her Dad's best friend (my aforementioned aunt/rabbi). "I have good news and bad news. I've checked as far back as I can, and there haven't been any lampreys in Marble Hill—or anywhere else in the demesne—since 1914."

"That's a very specific date, Mimi."

"Noticed that, did you?"

"That's why they pay me the small bucks."

"Hey, c'mon, I pay you the same as any Courser. I don't even ask for a friend discount."

"You're all heart. Why the exact date?"

"Because prior to that, Marble Hill was an island that was still considered part of Manhattan."

I saw where this was going. Wardeins' demesnes were geographic, not political. Miriam's bailiwick covered not just the Bronx, but most of Westchester County to the north, and bits of western Connecticut.

Manhattan, though, had its own separate one.

"So," Miriam concluded, "if you want to know about anything prior to the first World War, you gotta talk to van Owen."

I let out a sigh that was even longer in its suffering than the one Miriam had hit me with. I hated dealing with Damien van Owen. He'd been the Wardein of Manhattan since roughly the Mezozoic. He also had had trouble with the digital revolution. Miriam was able to get back to me quickly because she had all the Bronx Wardeins' diaries digitzied and searchable. A few keystrokes, and she had the answer to my question.

But van Owen's records were still on paper. And sorted in his apartment on Central Park West in nothing like a meaningful fashion.

"I don't wanna talk to van Owen. He hates me."

"He hates me, too."

"That isn't especially comforting."

"Suck it up, *boychik*." I could hear her grin.

I winced. "Mimi, *bubbe*, please, don't bring the Yiddish."

"Then don't call me 'Mimi.'" And she hung up.

The bus arrived, and I hopped on, dropping my MetroCard into the slot. As the bus tootled down Broadway, I dialed van Owen's number.

He answered on the first ring, which made me at once happy and chagrined. The former because it'd move things along, the latter because I'd have to actually talk to the old bastard instead of just trading voicemails.

"What do you want, Gold?"

Charming as ever. "I need you to check back and see if there were any lampreys on Marble Hill back before World War I."

"Don't need to check—last lamprey sighting in my demesne was on Marble Hill in November 1913. Surprised you didn't remember, actually, given that one of yours was involved."

I frowned. "I'm sorry?"

"Elena Houk."

"Oy."

"'Oy' is one way of putting it, yes. Not exactly the finest hour in Courser history—but she had no business being granted a license in the first place."

The last thing in the universe I wanted to do was get into an argument with van Owen. "Fine, whatever. And 1913 makes sense, since it's in the window."

"Excuse me?"

I took some minor pleasure in the high-and-mighty Damien van Owen not undertsanding what I was talking about. "The sixteen-year window between 1898 and 1914 when Marble Hill was an island. Since the lampreys can't cross running water, best plan is to trap 'em on an—"

"Yes, yes," van Owen interrupted testily, "I'm familiar with the weaknesses of lampreys. If there isn't anything else, I have actual *work* to do."

"Knowing this stuff *is* your work."

"For *my* demesne, yes. Marble Hill regrettably now falls under the inferior supervision of your friend Miss Zerelli. So speak to her."

Before I could point out that I *did* speak to her and needed to speak to him to cover the pre-1914 stuff, he hung up on me.

That was when I *really* started giving it to him.

Okay, not really, but I thought about it. The only thing that stopped me was that I was on a bus full of people. Not that New York bus riders would think twice about a guy yelling obscenities into his smartphone...

I got off at my stop and walked home. Once I got inside, I called Miriam back.

This time, she answered on the first ring. "Don't tell me van Owen got back to you already."

"Yup." I filled her in on what her Manhattan counterpart told me.

"Crap. I should've remembered that. That woman..." She sighed. "There wasn't another female Courser for half a century because of her."

"I gotta tell you, I know she was the first female Courser—and the last one until the Sixties—but I don't know the specifics."

"It was a big scandal when she was chosen to be an apprentice. Her tutor was Secundo Tartarone, who was one of the best there ever was. Most of the other Coursers, and the local Wardeins, thought he was insane for taking her on—and then she got him killed. After that, her first job was to round up a lamprey, and after that, she retired, saying she couldn't handle it. Every single woman who tried to be a Courser for *years* was slapped down because Elena Houk was proof that women didn't have the fortitude."

"That's a load of crap."

"Hey, there's a reason why the first black baseball player was also great. If Jackie Robinson stunk up the place, it would've been decades before another black player cracked the major leagues. Why do you think it took two-and-a-half decades for another viable female candidate in a presidential election after Geraldine Ferraro? If you're gonna be a pioneer, you have to not suck at your job. And Elena Houk was a wretchedly awful Courser."

I let out a long breath. Miriam obviously felt pretty strongly about this. Not that I blamed her. She was the first of the Bronx Wardeins to be female since the first one was assigned back in the eighteenth century. Of course, that position was hereditary, so gender didn't really enter into how you got the position.

She told me she'd e-mail me the Bronx Wardein's diary entries that mentioned Houk, as well as the current password for the database, and by the time I fired my laptop up, it was waiting for me.

I spent the next half-hour reading over what the early-twentieth-century Bronx Wardein—a crotchety bastard named Gildo Zerelli, Miriam's great-grandfather—had to say about Houk, none of it good. She'd started her apprenticeship to Tartarone in June 1912, and a year later, she was licensed.

"Mr. Tartarone has explained that the woman he has been seen with is his apprentice, a Miss Elena Houk. He is not the first to accept an application from a woman, and I daresay that Miss Houk will fail as all the others did before her. The calling of Slayer is not one for the fairer sex." "Miss Houk's hysterical carelessness has resulted in the untimely demise of Mr. Tartarone during their pitched combat against a Water Elemental, though the Elemental was, at least, cast out." "Was called upon by Miss Houk with an offer of services as a Slayer. I provided her with tea as is civil, but politely refused, as her abilities are not adequate to the task." "Although Miss Houk displayed uncharacteristic cleverness in luring the lamprey to Marble Hill Island, thus effectively trapping it, before putting the creature to death, it was with a profound sense of relief that I learned of her retirement from the ranks of the Slayers."

Tartarone's death was in August 1913, not long after Houk was licensed. She trapped the lamprey on Marble Hill in November 1913, like van Owen said, and she retired right after that.

Meanwhile, I was wondering where this *new* lamprey came from. I switched over to the password-protected online database that Miriam maintained. The password was only given out at Miriam's discretion, and it changed every hour on the hour, and also changed when someone used it, so the same password never worked twice. Each password was a random collection of capital and lower-case letters, numbers, and symbols.

Sadly, there wasn't much on lampreys beyond what I already knew: they sucked energy, and they had about a billion teeth, so any time you tried to wrangle them, they'd bite the living hell out of you.

In particular, nobody had recorded anything about their life cycles, methods of reproduction, or anything else useful, beyond the fact that they usually lived for about a century, and their gray skin turned white when they were about to die. They weren't all that common around here, anyhow—they were mostly found in Europe. In fact, the one Houk dealt with was assumed to have come over as an egg on one of the many immigrant-bearing boats that hit New York Harbor on either side of 1900.

Weirdly, given their aversion to running water, they tended toward damp, dark places. They were sensitive to sunlight—something else they shared with the vamps—more so when hungry for life energy. They'd suck that out of people, sometimes to the point of death. But not always, interestingly enough.

I couldn't do much until the next day, so I checked Brauck Realty's web site again, finding a picture of Tara O'Neill. I knew to look for a blue-eyed blonde with long, curly hair tomorrow.

The next day, I put on a button-down shirt from Brooks Brothers and a nice pair of khakis—I wanted to look like I had money to spend, but I didn't want to die in the heat—and trundled back down to Marble Hill.

Since the appointment was for noon, I made sure to get there at eleven thirty. When I arrived, two harried-looking dark-haired people—one male, one female, very obviously related as they had the same eyes, nose, and cheekbones—were standing near the stoop. The woman was yelling at three burly Latino guys who were gingerly carrying a couch down the stoop while the man was futzing with a smartphone.

"Why you guys movin' so slow? Hello? Jesus Christ, you even *listenin'* t'me?"

Without even looking up from his phone, her brother said, "Nobody ever does, sis."

"'Scuse me?" I said tentatively. "My name's Abe Goldblume, I was supposed to look at the house?"

"Jesus Christ," the woman said, "that stupid *bitch*. We *told* her not to show nobody the house this afternoon!"

I smiled sheepishly. "Actually, that's my fault. I'm headed out of town tonight, and I honestly don't give a hoot if the movers are here, so I asked if I could come this afternoon. Just wanna see what the place looks like."

The woman put her hands on her hips. "It ain't convenient, all right?"

Finally looking up from his phone, the man said, "Ignore my sister—seriously, just totally ignore her, you'll live longer." He put the phone in the pocket of his jeans. He was wearing a tight T-shirt and tight jeans, showing off a too-sculpted physique that looked like it was the result of daily gym workouts. Offering his hand, he said, "I'm Val Dellucci, this is my sister Sam."

I accepted the handshake, shaking harder than he probably expected. I had a decent physique too, but I preferred to hide that particular light under a bushel, especially since I got it wrangling unicorns and getting beaten up by trolls.

"Whoa, that's quite a grip you got there, Mr. Goldblume."

"Thanks. So why you guys selling such a nice place?"

Sam answered before Val could speak. "It ain't ours. Belonged to our grandpa. Crazy old bastard. Never talked to nobody, wouldn't answer the phone, wouldn't do nothin'."

"He had Alzheimer's," Val added.

"No he didn't! Doctors checked him out, remember? Said he didn't have none of the signs, he was just—I dunno, listless or somethin'."

"The doctor was full'a shit—excuse my language," he added quickly. I waved it off, and he went on. "He was lyin'—if it was Alzheimer's, he couldn't run more expensive tests, the bastard."

I frowned, focusing on the use of the past tense. "So he died?"

Val nodded. "Yeah, last week. He was ninety-five."

A car pulled up 227th and double parked. Tara had cut her hair since she had her picture taken for the realtor's web site and straightened it into an above-the-neck bob that probably was more comfortable in the heat. She wore a white blouse and a black miniskirt that showed of a pair of legs that went all the way to the floor. If I had legs like that, and I was in the business of selling things, I'd wear miniskirts, too.

"Oh, Mr. Goldblume, you're early! Val, Sam, I'm so sorry, I was hoping to get here early to warn you—"

"It's fine," Val said.

"No it ain't!" Sam was livid. "Look, we don't want nobody seein' all of Grandpa's crap, all right?"

I waved my hand back and forth. "It's fine. You should see all the garbage my old man collected. When Mom and I sold their old place, it was a nightmare."

Actually Mom and Dad had almost nothing in the house, and after they were killed by a Golem—the event that led to my current calling—it took all of an hour for me to clean out the place.

Tara took me inside, walking past the death-glare of Sam and the eye-rolling of Val. It was a very nice Victorian, four bedrooms, a huge living room, a nice dining room—and, at the moment, a ton of boxes and smelly old furniture.

After looking around the downstairs and upstairs, and making all the right noises (including complaining about the kitchen, which looked like it hadn't been remodeled since Eisenhower was president), I asked, "Can I see the basement?"

"I don't think it's finished," Tara said weakly. "And there was a lot of stuff stored down there, so you really won't get much of a sense of it until the movers are—"

"It's fine. I wanna see it. I like basements, and I'll probably want to finish it and make it a workroom."

It took another thirty seconds of cajoling, but Tara finally remembered that the customer was always right, and she led me to the dark, creaky wooden staircase near the kitchen that led into the bowels of the house. Mildew and mustiness assaulted my nostrils as I went down the stairs, Tara's high heels clacking behind me.

The house was built into the hill, so the front of the basement was at street level. That end was mostly boxes, some in pretty wretched shape.

Two things caught my eye, only one of which I was in a position to do something about now. The first, which I left alone, was the trapdoor built into the floor. I did not want to open that while half a dozen civilians were wandering around.

The other, though, was a box that had a label that looked like it was typed with a manual typewriter. It was faded, but I could make out the words ELENA HOUK.

At this particular thickening of the plot, I turned to Tara. "Does that say 'Elena Houk'?"

She bent over and peered at it. "I think so. Why?"

"I need to talk to Val and Sam." I ran upstairs, a confused Tara following soon after.

Sam was bitching at the movers for moving so slowly, though I had a feeling that they weren't doing so on purpose, if what I thought was under that trapdoor was under it.

I looked at Val. "I'm sorry to bother you Mr. Dellucci, but—there's a box downstairs that has a name on it."

"Yeah, our great-grandma's shit—excuse my language. She was Elena Dellucci after she married our great-grandad, obviously, but Houk was her maiden name. Grandpa never let us touch her stuff, and it's all covered in mildew. Honestly, we're just gonna throw it out—it's useless trash."

"Do you mind if I take a look in the box? See, I'm kind of a genealogy buff, and there's this one relative we've never been able to find out anything about—her name's Elena Houk, and she lived somewhere in the Bronx after the first World War. But that's it. I'd love to see if it's her."

Val looked over at his sister, who was still haranguing the movers, now taking a coffee break. "If you want, yeah, go ahead, I guess. Just don't breathe through your nose."

I grinned, grateful for kids who don't care about the past. "Thanks."

Dashing back down the creaky stairs, I easily ripped open the decades-old paper tape that weakly held the box shut. Opening it, my nose was, as expected, assaulted by mold and mildew. Lots of yellowed paper, jewelry, mothballed clothes—and weapons! There was what was once a very nice crossbow, but with rusted metal and warped wood; a few daggers, also rusted; and a rapier that had rust and pits in the metal.

This was obviously where Elena Houk had packed away her life as what was then called a Slayer before marrying some guy named Dellucci and becoming a wife and mother like everyone told her she was supposed to.

But that still left the question of the lamprey.

I found a leather-bound book that had a rusted lock on it. Even if there had been a key in evidence, it probably wouldn't have worked.

Val came down the stairs. "Christ, what *is* all that?"

"Some rusted old stuff." I tried to sound dismissive. "Mind if I borrow this? I know someone who might be able to get this lock off." That someone was going to be one of the spellcasters I knew, but he didn't need to be told that part.

"Sure." Val shrugged. "Like I said, we were just gonna throw it out. Buncha old crap, y'know?"

"Thanks. I'll drop it off today, and it should be open by the time I get back from my trip."

I made a show of looking at some more of the house, then took my leave. Tara wished me a safe flight, as did Val. Sam made me very grateful for the lack of laser vision in the real world, since I'd have been zapped right there.

As soon as I was out of sight of the house, I whipped out my phone. I knew a mess of spellcasters who could do this, but the only ones who weren't pissed at me, on vacation, or already on a job they couldn't come away from were Teitelbaum—who wouldn't be working on a Saturday afternoon—and Velez.

I sighed. I hated having to call Velez.

By the time the bus brought me back up to my townhouse, I had spoken to Velez, and he said he was on his way. I also called Miriam and told her about my find.

When I got home, I changed into a T-shirt and denim shorts and sat down at the computer. I answered a few e-mails until the doorbell rang, and I buzzed Velez in.

I lived in the three-bedroom flat on the second floor of the three-apartment townhouse that I owned, with my cousin renting out the one-bedroom space on the first floor, and the top floor used for storage and a home office. José Velez slowly ambled up the stairs, huffing and puffing as he hauled his three hundred and fifty pounds against gravity.

When I showed him the locked diary and explained that I needed him to crack it open, he peered at me over his glasses like he was an angry teacher or something. "There's a locksmith that's, like two blocks from here, yo. The hell you haul my fat ass up here for?"

"This diary belonged to Elena Houk."

"Whozzat, your ex-girlfriend or somethin'?"

I sighed. "History's just a feature on your web browser, isn't it?"

"Kiss my entire ass, Gold."

"Houk was the first female Courser."

"Whoop-de-do. Can we do this? I got places to be."

I stared at him. "If you got places to be, why'd you take my call?"

Velez pointedly didn't answer, instead digging into his shoulder bag. He started setting out what he'd need: pestle, bottles of herbs, New York Yankees Zippo, a stick, and three different bottles of water. He put two of the latter back after staring at the labels.

"What, they're not all holy water?" I asked snidely.

He regarded me with his usual annoyance. "Very funny. Nah, for this I need the swampwater to soak the poplar root in."

I chuckled. Holy water didn't work the way most folks thought it did, something that really disappointed people who tried splashing it onto vampires. That only did damage if the vamp was wearing a silk shirt.

As for the poplar root, even I knew that that was a taproot, one that would go through concrete to find water. It was perfect for breaking through something

Velez dumped some herbs and the stick into the pestle, then poured in the swampwater, then lit the Zippo and ran the flame under the pestle.

I sniffed. "That mint?"

Nodding, Velez started murmuring something I couldn't make out.

Spells were out of my league. Or in a different league, really. I left that to the specialists like Velez.

After a few seconds, I heard a clicking sound, and the diary fell open.

"There you go."

"So, I gotta ask—what's the magickal power of mint?"

"Makes your iced tea taste better," Velez said with a grin. "I just add that up in there so it don't stink. Swampwater's *nasty*, yo."

I wrote Velez a check for his services, but he didn't leave. "You think I'm openin' this and ain't findin' out what's on the inside?"

I rolled my eyes. "Fine, whatever." I opened the diary up.

The first page I turned to had a detailed description of Houk taking down a werewolf. "Tartarone incapacitated from wine, as usual, and I was once again forced to hunt for him. Werewolf proved susceptible to steel bullets as much as silver ones, since Tartarone too taken with drink to provide location of latter."

That wasn't the part that blew me away, it was the date: "The fourteenth day of April, the Year of Our Lord, nineteen and ten." A good three years before her official apprenticeship started.

I flipped through more pages, which told of other exploits that most people probably thought were committed by Tartarone, but were in fact thanks to Elena Houk. "Tartarone, in one of his more lucid moments, has decided that I must be officially apprenticed. It is the only way to appease Zerelli, who grows suspicious of my presence. If I am to continue to act during Tartarone's ever-increasing bouts of intoxication, I must become a proper Slayer."

"Shit," Velez muttered as he read over my shoulder, "people really talked like that?"

Shrugging, I said, "Different time."

I kept flipping pages. Then I walked out the door while dialing Miriam.

Velez lumbered down the stairs behind me. "Where the hell you goin'?"

"You know any spells that can stop a lamprey?"

"Can imprison one for three days, but only if you got some more mint, 'cause that one stinks *bad*."

"We'll have to live with it. Where'd you park?"

"Excuse me?"

"You wanna follow along," I said as I went out onto the sidewalk, "you can drive me down to 227th between Van Corlear and Adrian."

"Shit." Velez led me to his bright red 3000 GT. I hopped in the passenger seat while he squeezed his massive frame into the tiny driver's seat. I never understood why a guy the size of Mount Rushmore owned an automobile that was only slightly bigger than a Matchbox car.

Miriam finally answered. "What is it, Bram?"

"You're not gonna believe this." I filled her in on what I'd read about Elena Houk while Velez blazed down Johnson

Avenue. "The thing is, she didn't get Tartarone killed, she'd been carrying his drunk ass for *years*. When he *did* get killed, it was because he was so toasted he was belligerent and forced her to take him with her when she went after the Water Elemental."

"That's not possible. Bram, Secundo Tartarone was one of the finest Coursers ever."

"No, Elena Houk was, and pretending it was Tartarone, while the finest Courser ever drank himself to an early grave. And that's not the kicker. Jesus, Velez, that's a *red* light!"

"You're in a car with *Velez*?" Miriam sounded understandably concerned.

"He got the locked diary open, and besides, I need to get back down to the house faster than the bus'll take me. See, the lamprey she claimed to put down? She didn't—it was an infant, and Elena couldn't bring herself to kill it."

"She left a lamprey alive?"

I nodded, even though she couldn't see it over the phone. "She couldn't kill a baby animal that was totally defenseless. It hadn't even developed any teeth yet. So she took it in. She hadn't been getting much work as a Courser anyhow, since everyone assumed she was the incompetent who got the great Secundo Tartarone killed."

"So—what, she kept the lamprey as a pet?"

"Sorta." Velez was driving down Kingsbridge Avenue to where the King's Bridge used to be—now it was just Marble Hill Avenue. "It lived in the basement under a trapdoor, and she and her family kept feeding it enough life energy to survive but not to hurt anyone. And that was all well and good, but her son just died last week at the ripe old age of 95, and the rest of the family'd moved out. Everyone thought the old man had Alzheimer's, but he didn't test for it."

"It was the lamprey."

"Uh huh. This place, with the for sale sign," I said to Velez as he drove down 227th. "Yeah, the lamprey just took from him until he started losing it. Now it's just sucking energy wherever it can now that its principal food source is dead. We're there, Mimi, I gotta go. I'll keep you posted."

"You'd better."

Velez parked right behind the moving truck. Sam Dellucci was now chatting amiably with her brother, and the movers were doing their work at a much brisker pace.

Sam's amiability dropped as soon as she saw me, of course. "The hell're you doing back here? I thought you were flying somewhere or something."

I ignored her and talked to Val. "I need to get back in the basement. *Now*."

"I don't—don't understand." Val looked back and forth to me and Velez. "Who's this guy?"

"Just call me the exterminator," Velez said with an unpleasant smile.

"Not helping," I muttered. "Look, there may be something bad down there. Trust me, you wanna sell this place? Let me see what's down there, and let my friend—my friend the exterminator take care of it."

Sam moved to stand in front of the stoop while Val dithered. "No way. I don't know who you think you are, but you already seen the place, and I ain't even sure you're a real buyer."

I started to tell my cover story—and then stopped. This whole thing started because Elena Houk couldn't tell the truth about her own abilities as a Courser or that her mentor was a drunk, and I'd been compounding it by lying to get into this house. Enough, already.

"There's a creature who's been feeding on people in this neighborhood for the past week. Your grandfather inherited it from your great-grandmother, who kept it as a pet down in the basement. Now, though, I'm worried about it."

"What is it?" Val asked.

"What the fuck're you *talking* about?" Sam interrupted.

Velez hauled out his shoulder bag. "*Hell* with this." He pulled out some ash and threw it in Sam's face.

She coughed, and then stopped moving completely.

Val panicked. "What'd you do to her?"

"She'll be fine in about an hour," Velez said. "C'mon, Gold, let's do this."

I stared at Sam's still form for a second before following Velez up the stairs. Val was still agog, and didn't acknowledge our entry into the house.

As I led the way down the creaky stairs, I asked, "Will she really be okay in an hour?"

Velez shrugged. "She'll have a bitch of a migraine, and ain't no detergent in the world gonna get that stuff out her clothes, but yeah, she'll be a'ight. 'Less she's allergic to shellfish. Then she'll prob'ly get a rash."

Before I could respond to that, the smell hit me. You know what a dead skunk smells like? This odor made me nostalgic for that.

I went straight for the trapdoor I'd seen before.

Opening it, the smell got much worse. Putting his hand over his nose and mouth, Velez said, "Shit, ain't enough mint in the world!"

Looking down into a good-sized crawlspace, I saw the long, snakelike form and giant teeth-filled mouth of a lamprey. It was surrounded by several well-worn cushions, a pipe that dripped water—lampreys took in moisture through the skin, so that was the equivalent of a water bowl for it—and a few other decorations that made it clear that this wasn't just a lair for the lamprey. This was the home of a beloved pet.

The lamprey was also white, not gray.

As soon as I opened the trapdoor, it raised its head toward me and bared its teeth.

I started to feel listless. It was sucking the energy right out of me. Fatigue started to smother me like a blanket, but I couldn't even work up the energy to care.

Then it looked at Velez, who was smiling. "Bring it on, bitch."

My own energy levels started to improve. The lamprey was obviously focused on Velez.

After a second, it let out a high-pitched wail, and then collapsed in the crawlspace, unmoving.

Peering into it, Velez nodded. "That is one dead motherfuckin' lamprey."

"What'd you do?" I asked.

"Nothin', just let it chow down. Thing was whiter'n you, so I knew it was too old to handle *my* mojo."

"Right." Spellcasters had considerably more life energy than the average person, and the lamprey probably gorged on Velez.

I should've been glad. I'd been hired to get rid of a lamprey, and now it was gone. Okay, I didn't actually *do* anything, Velez did, but still, mission accomplished. The lamprey wouldn't be sucking the energy out of people in Marble Hill. Between us, Velez and I would dispose of the corpse. Then I'd call Reverend Daley and tell him that he'd probably start getting folks back in St. Stephen's before too long.

But I still felt like crap. Elena Houk looked past what everyone was saying and saw a helpless creature. The same people who told her she had to kill it were the ones who told her she was the lousiest Courser around. So she showed it compassion instead, and it lived a long and happy life. But when her son died, nobody knew about it. Another lie, even though it was of omission.

"So, want me to incinerate this puppy?" Velez asked.

"No."

"Say *what?*"

"I said no," I snapped. "Let's give this guy a burial. Least he deserves. Least *Elena* deserves."

Velez shrugged. "Whatever, yo. Just so long's I get paid."

"Yeah." What he just did was above and beyond opening a lock, so he'd demand more money. Probably eat up most of my fee from Reverend Daley, but maybe I could justify hiring him as one of the expenses.

I gently pulled the corpse out of the crawlspace. The lamprey would get a proper burial.

And Elena Houk would get a proper legacy. Dammit.

Introduction to "The Stone of the First High Pontiff"

Like "Under the King's Bridge," "The Stone of the First High Pontiff" is a test-run for a setting/set of characters that I'd like to explore in more depth. In this case, though, I haven't had the time to sit down and write more of Jin the Human Finder.

A bunch of years ago, Mike McPhail, former Air Force and current co-publisher of eSpec Books, started up a military science fiction anthology series called *Defending the Future.* Mike invited me to contribute to the fifth anthology in the series, *Best-Laid Plans*, about stories where things don't go according to plan. (In the words of the great philosopher Jack O'Neill of the *Stargate* franchise, Plan A never works.) I figured that would be a decent opportunity to do a story with Jin and Timm and *Seeker* and a future in which Earth is a minor part of a larger interplanetary empire, having been conquered and subsumed by the Ashloj Collective. I always thought that would be more fun than an interplanetary nation in which Earth is the center. That's an understandable conceit, given that science fiction is written by humans and all, but it's fun to try it the other way, where we're the less technologically developed folks being conquered...

The Stone of the First High Pontiff

Jin yawned as she came onto the flight deck, and saw that the ship hadn't moved since she went to bed.

Timm didn't even turn to look at her, instead staring at the display on the nav. "No, they still haven't finished the maintenance on the Nimast Corridor. No, they haven't given us an estimate as to when it will be done. No, we can't just go on our own steam, as that'll take three decades."

Smiling as she took the copilot's seat on the cramped flight deck, Jin said, "Well, that answers two of my questions."

"Yeah, well, it wasn't until we entered hour number fourteen that I started plotting a direct course to Taksnaro, just for shits and giggles."

Jin shot him a mischievous look through hooded eyes. "And it'll take as long as three decades? You're losing your touch."

Timm shrugged and rubbed his smooth, dark scalp. "Well, that was at point-seven. Any higher, we start dealing with time-dilation, and *nobody* wants a piece'a that shit."

"On the other hand," Jin said with a sigh, "by the time thirty years go by, Brfnel might actually pay us."

"You are *such* an optimist."

"Are you sure we should be going to Taksnaro?"

Turning to Jin, Timm stared at her as if she'd gone Zlarix and grown a second head. "Excuse me? Did we not both agree, while sitting in these same chairs, right before we told Brfnel we'd find his daughter—again—that we'd go to Taksnaro for the opening-night performance of *Down Among the Stars*, assuming we found little Glarna before the twelfth? And is it not now the tenth, giving us two whole days to get to Taksnaro?"

Jin winced. "I know, but—" She sighed. "Well, Brfnel *hasn't* paid us. And this Corridor trip is going to take the last of our available cash."

Timm's nose twitched the way it always did when Jin started talking about the dire state of their finances. "You're telling me that new coil cost that much?"

With a snort, Jin said, "It wasn't a new coil, it was a used coil, and it cost a hundred. A new one would've meant going into the emergency fund—and before you ask," she added quickly as Timm opened his mouth, "we are *not* dipping into the emergency fund to pay to park this beast at Taksnaro."

"*Seeker* is *not* a beast, she's a good boat." Timm patted the console affectionately, which he always did whenever Jin told the truth about their tiny, cramped ship's rather dilapidated condition. He continued: "And we are too dipping into it if we have to, because you promised." He pointed an accusatory finger at Jin.

She sighed. "What if I promise to get you a HoloPlay of the performance when it comes out?"

"Three problems with that. One, HoloPlays are never as good as the live performance. Two, only place I can run the HoloPlay is the half-meter space over my console here, which ain't exactly the kind of immersive experience you get from live theatre. And three, you already promised we'd go to Taksnaro, so you promising to get me the HoloPlay in order to go back on your *other* promise is kind of unconvincing, y'know?" He got up from the pilot's chair. "Wake me if they actually put the damn Corridor back online."

Looking down at one of the displays, Jin saw that three messages had come in. "Did you check YourMail?"

"That is *all* I have done for the past fifteen hours. Not a single interesting thing there."

"We just got three—and one is from the Lighters."

Timm rolled his eyes. "Half the YourMail we got was from Lighters."

Jin grinned. "Which sect?"

"Both." He shuddered. "All the usual junk. Come to our side, we're more holy than the other side. Dunno why they blast it out to *everyone* like that. I mean, do they have *any* worshippers who aren't Vhaddish?"

"Probably easier to do that than just to target Vhaddish addresses." Jin shrugged. "Anyhow, this doesn't look like recruitment junk, since it's addressed to the 'human finder.'"

Timm grinned and Jin made a face. She hated being called that, but the appellation had stuck.

"It's from the High Pontiff himself," Jin said after tapping the YourMail logo to bring the message up to the screen. "He wants to hire us."

Timm put his head in his hands. "Oh hell, no, please, Jin, no, we do *not* want to deal with religious types. They're always asking for discounts, and—"

Jin cut him off. "They're willing to pay two thousand just to take a meeting, regardless of whether or not we take the job."

A several-second silence ensued after she said that. Finally, Timm spoke in a very quiet tone. "Say that again. Slowly."

Instead, Jin merely stared at him. She watched his face go through several emotions in succession, starting with annoyance at the need to miss the opening of *Down Among the Stars*, eventually modulating into a small smile at the thought of what he could spend his share of a thousand marks on.

Finally, Timm sat back down in the pilot seat. "Let me see it."

Before Jin could shoot the YourMail to his console, the Braslo InterShip beeped. Timm tapped it on; Jin noted that the call was from Nimast Corridor Control, and she hoped that it was good news.

A voice spoke in heavily accented Cwyar. *"This is Nimast Corridor Control. Maintenance is complete, and* Seeker *is in the queue for transit. Your registry indicates that this is a Revnen ship?"*

In the same language, Timm replied: "Yes, the co-owners of this vessel are Revnen, and we're both unbonded. If you want," he added impatiently, "I can provide proof of our—"

"That won't be necessary, Seeker, *you just need to be aware that there are four Sanashloj ships in the queue, and they're ahead of you."*

"That's fine, Corridor Control, we'll wait our turn. Out." Timm cut off the Braslo quickly, then looked at Jin. "Guess they have new folks in charge."

With a shudder, Jin nodded. Last time they'd come through Nimast, they'd had to provide proof that they were unbonded. Of course, that was right after all those Sanrevnen slaves on Fortinon had rioted and run away, and everyone was on edge.

Timm read over the mail from the Lighters. "Yeah, okay." He reopened the Braslo to Corridor Control.

"Nimast Corridor Control, go ahead Seeker.*"*

"Corridor Control, we need to alter our filed destination."

Jin had expected the receiving room for the High Pontiff of the Sacred Church of Enlightened Thought and Belief to be ostentatious, but her expectations were greatly exceeded. They had entered doors made of cast gravari, and inlaid with gold. The floor of the room was entirely made of fringelt—Jin felt guilty walking on it—and the ceiling likewise. The very long side walls were all decorated with hand-painted images of all of the previous High Pontiffs, going back to ten centuries before Jin and Timm's ancestral homeland of Earth was conquered by the Ashloj Collective. There were only about eighty of them—the Vhaddish were a long-lived people, although no one was appointed High Pontiff until they were already two hundred years old—but each was surrounded by acolytes.

The lengthy, open room was supported by pillars, which were also made of fingelt—however, one expected that, as every Vhaddish structure of any size used fingelt pillars—etched with scenes from the Lighters' holy texts.

Standing in front of each pillar was a Church Warrior—none of whom, she noted with amusement, were Vhaddish. It seemed they felt safer hiring non-believers to protect them for some reason. Each Warrior was armed with GranitoZap sidearms and covered head to toe in GranitoBlam armor. Jin had never been a big fan of firearms, but she knew from Timm carrying on like trash on the subject that Granito's goods were substandard—but also cheap, which probably was why the church went for it.

At the far end was the High Pontiff's throne, made of solid gold. Jin couldn't imagine it was in any way comfortable. However, it did make it clear that throwing two thousand marks around just to take a meeting wasn't even going to put a dent in their treasury.

Sitting in the throne was the round, tentacled body of the High Pontiff himself. His deep brown fur had been shaved into the pattern that indicated that he was the leader of the church.

Or, at least, the half or so Lighters who actually followed him.

Next to him was another Vhaddish whose white fur had been shaved into the pattern of a high acolyte of the church.

The white-furred one spoke in the Vhaddish language with his upper mouth as Jin and Timm approached. "Thank you for agreeing to the meeting, human finder."

"Please, you may refer to me as Jin," she said in the same language, hoping she was getting her pronunciation right—Vhaddish was created by a species with two mouths, each with a forked tongue, so it made for some entertaining sibilants—"and you paid us to have this meeting, so to this meeting we gladly attend. How may we refer to you?"

"I am the High Pontiff's Voice. And we shall refer to you as Jin. Our compliments on your facility with the holy language of the Vhaddish. It is rare to find an outworlder who speaks it so fluently."

"Thank you." Jin had indeed noticed that she was speaking the language more comfortably than she had in the past. It was yet another change that had come to her life since the circumstance that led to her becoming the so-called "human finder."

"I assume, Jin, that you are familiar with the schism that exists within the Sacred Church of Enlightened Thought and Belief, praise be to the church's wisdom?"

Jin nodded, then remembered that Vhaddish weren't very good at reading body language cues of non-Vhaddish. "I am aware of the schism's existence, and that each sect believes itself to be the correct one."

"So you are not aware of the cause of the schism."

"Forgive me, but I am not. I regret to say that I am not a student of your church's history."

Several of the Voice's tentacles vibrated at that. "Such is not part of our church's history, though it is, tragically, part of the history of the Vhaddish people. Long ago, in the earliest days of the Sacred Church of Enlightened Thought and Belief, praise be to the church's wisdom, there was a stone that had etched upon its surface the words of the First High Pontiff. The artifact was lost, but the words inscribed upon it were recorded in the holy texts. There are those heretics who believe that the texts are in error, and that the stone has words other than those recorded. That is the basis of the schism, and it has only grown worse over the decades."

Timm, who did not speak Vhaddish, was shifting uncomfortably from foot to foot. Jin cast him a quick apologetic glance, then said to the Voice, "Do you wish me to find this stone?"

The Voice's tentacles wiggled again, and three of his eyestalks turned toward the High Pontiff, who continued to sit upon the throne. If his lungflaps hadn't been vibrating, Jin would have thought the High Pontiff to be dead.

After a surprisingly long hesitation, the Voice said, "The High Pontiff, praise be to his great wisdom and knowledge, has learned of your exploits through the InformNet."

Jin somehow managed to avoid chuckling. That last word had been spoken in Yrak, the common tongue of the Ashloj, and the one used on the InformNet. Vhaddish had no word for that, so the Voice just appropriated the Yrak one. Jin had a hard time believing that the High Pontiff actually lowered himself to observe the InformNet.

"Based on all accounts, you have an enviable success rate. For that reason, the High Pontiff, praise be to his great wisdom and knowledge, wishes to engage your services to locate the Stone of the First High Pontiff."

Timm, who had been staring at the murals on the walls, looked over at those last words, which he apparently recognized.

The Voice went on: "The High Pontiff, praise be to his great wisdom and knowledge, wishes this schism to end, for all those who believe in the Sacred Church of Enlightened Thought and Belief, praise be to the church's wisdom, to once again be united under his guidance. The High Pontiff, praise be to his great wisdom and knowledge, believes that the retrieval of the Stone of the First High Pontiff, lost all these many centuries, may be what at last enables our deluded fellows to return to the fold, and make the Sacred Church of Enlightened Thought and Belief, praise be to the church's wisdom, stronger."

"If I am to accept this commission," Jin said slowly, "I will need to know everything about the Stone of the First High Pontiff. I will need to see not only the sacred texts, but also any heretical ones."

The High Pontiff's tentacles quivered at that, and the Voice quickly said, "That will not be—"

"Look, Voice—" She stopped, realizing she had gone back to Yrak. Taking a breath, she went back to Vhaddish. "In order to perform my task, I must have every piece of information about the Stone of the First High Pontiff, even information that is inaccurate. Even a lie may hold truths within it."

The High Pontiff's eyestalks all focused on Jin, and for the first time, he spoke. Unlike that of his Voice, the High Pontiff's words came out in a raspy whisper. "You speak the words of Samno. Good. Good."

Jin inclined her head in respect, though she hadn't the first clue who Samno was. The phrase was something one of her former owners used to say before she died.

Half the High Pontiff's eyestalks looked at the Voice, who then said, "We shall provide you with *all* the available data on the Stone of the First High Pontiff—even the data that is heretical and false."

"I apologize for forcing you to acknowledge heretical work," Jin said quickly, "but it is necessary to accomplish the task you have set out for me."

In Yrak, Timm muttered, "They tell us how much they're paying yet?"

Jin winced. She'd forgotten that part. She often did, which was why she preferred Timm to handle negotiations. After being a slave so long, the notion of being personally recompensed for work was still foreign to her. Her function as a slave had been to, among other things, handle her owners' finances, but that was for after jobs were done, not before.

"Assuming," she continued, "that we may properly negotiate payment."

The Voice's tentacles quivered. "Payment has already been made."

Jin frowned, remembering Timm's words about religious types trying to renege on paying their bills. "For this meeting, yes, payment has been made. We have fulfilled the terms of *that* agreement. If I am to find the Stone of the First High Pontiff, there must be recompense for *that* service."

More of the High Pontiff's eyestalks glanced at the Voice. Jin wished she knew more about Vhaddish body language.

The Voice then said, "We will only provide you with further currency if you complete the task. Therefore, another two thousand marks will be granted to you upon the return of the Stone of the First High Pontiff to the Sacred Church of Enlightened Thought and Belief, praise be to the church's wisdom."

Normally, this would be the part where someone haggled, but four thousand was more than she'd gotten for any *two* jobs. This would enable them to do *proper* repairs on *Seeker* and take a vacation besides.

Jin had never taken a vacation in her life. She rather liked the idea.

"Very well, I accept your terms," she said. "We will return when I have found the Stone of the High Pontiff."

"*If* you find it." For the first time, Jin detected an odd tone in the Voice. Was it humor? Skepticism? Jin wondered if the Voice didn't think much of the High Pontiff hiring some lowly Revnen from a conquered planet performing so important a task, and likely didn't think she was up to it.

Not that Jin cared what the Voice thought. Since she found the gem, she'd been able to find *anything*.

As they walked back toward the exit, under the many eyestalks of the previous High Pontiffs, Timm asked, "Please tell me you got us at least ten thousand for this."

Jin blinked. "What? No, I got another two thousand. That's four thousand, Timm, that's better—"

Whispering his shout so he didn't attract the attention of the High Pontiff or his Voice, Timm said, "You *what*? Look, I only know about ten phrases in Vhaddish, but one of them is 'the

Stone of the First High Pontiff,' and I heard you both using that one all over the damn place. That's what they want you to find, right?"

"Yes."

Timm shook his head. "You didn't do any transactions, so I'm guessing they'll pay the other two thousand when we come back with the stone?"

Jin nodded.

"Did you ask for expenses?"

This time, Jin shook her head. "Our expenses are never more than two thousand—in fact, they're never more than a few hundred, so—"

Waving her off, Timm said, "Doesn't matter. They can twiddle their tentacles all they want, we'll find it and sell it to the highest bidder. And I gotta tell you, the bidding will *start* at five thousand."

"No."

They got to the ornate fingelt door, which opened at their approach. Dozens of acolytes, as well as petitioners and other people waiting for a chance to see the High Pontiff sat with varying degrees of patience outside in the vestibule.

Neither Jin nor Timm spoke anymore of this until they reached the port where *Seeker* was docked.

Once they were safely on board with no prying ears around, Timm immediately went to the console and set the ScanBots to start a security sweep. Jin agreed with the sentiment. She wouldn't put it past the Lighters to plant a listening device on the ship to make sure they stuck to the plan.

Smiling, Timm pointed at the display, which showed that no fewer than three such devices had been placed on board. Jin was very grateful that they'd spent the money on the ScanBots—which she was planning to upgrade to the 6000 model once this job was done. After what happened on Siersee...

"All right, now that we can talk," Timm said, "let's talk. We can get so much more for—"

"No, Timm, I won't do that." Jin sat in the co-pilot's seat, relieved to be speaking in Yrak again. Her lips and tongue were exhausted from forming words in Vhaddish. "I will not become someone who reneges on a contract. It's been hard enough to find work. People don't believe that I'm as good as my reputation—"

Chuckling, Timm said, "If I didn't know your secret, *I* wouldn't believe you're as good as your reputation."

Jin nodded, conceding the point. "But I agreed to find the stone for the Lighters. And these are people who have a massive platform. Even non-believers can't get away from hearing from them all the time. If we go back on a contract with them, we'll never get another job."

"For that stone, we'll make enough that we won't *need* one." Timm sighed. "Yeah, yeah, okay, fine, we'll do it. But you should've talked him up another thousand at least."

Shaking her head, Jin stared at her console, which indicated new YourMail—one of which came from the same address as the Lighters' original message. Conjoined to that mail was a series of Inform files. "Okay, I'm gonna need to go through all this. Even with the gem, it should take me a few hours."

Timm nodded. "I'll take us out, then. Take a nice slow, leisurely journey to the Fearag Corridor."

Jin returned the nod and got up to head to her bunk. She was worried that Timm would just stay in the dock, but as she had pointed out many times, sitting in a dock cost money— flying in space was free.

At least, most of the time.

When she entered her cabin, she immediately stripped down to her underclothing—necessary in the heat. After upgrading the security system, her next priority after this job was done was to finally fix the thermostats in the bunks.

Discarding her coverall, she sat down on her bed and stared down at the gem embedded in her chest, right above her left breast, over her heart.

She still knew nothing about the blood-red gem, or what it was doing in that asteroid field, or why it embedded itself in her chest dangerously close to her heart, or why, since then, she'd literally been able to find *anything* she set her mind to find.

But shortly after she found the gem—or it found her?— her owners died, and she and Timm (who was free, but employed by Jin's owners) struck out on their own as "the human finder."

And she'd become more confident, more intelligent, more athletic. Her facility for Vhaddish had improved without any practice, and before the gem, if anyone had slapped her down the way Timm had, she'd have demurred and capitulated.

Something else she needed to do was find a good doctor. She'd allowed herself to be examined by medics she could afford, none of whom could figure out how the gem worked, how it was doing what it was doing, or much of anything else. One even offered to surgically remove it, which Jin quickly declined until she knew more.

But with the money they were getting for this, she could see a *talented* doctor.

Grabbing a tablet, she touched the implant on the back of her neck, and the Inform started to download right into her own mind.

Then, as always was necessary after that kind of download, she fell asleep.

As soon as she woke up, Jin knew everything there was to know about the Stone of the First High Pontiff, from the stories about how the First High Pontiff dug the stone out of a quarry with his bare hands, and why he chose the script he chose, and how his successors each placed the stone in a place of higher honor, how the stone was lost during the Pranik War when Vhad was destroyed, and the stories of how the stone was smuggled out by acolytes, and so much more.

She went back to the flight deck. Timm turned to give her an expectant look.

"Tell Fearag Corridor Control that we need to book passage to the Wosaphi Conclave."

The Voice of the High Pontiff sighed happily as he tossed the HebroGrubs—Hebro grew much more succulent grubs than the usual store-bought ones—into his lower mouth while dictating a memo in Yrak to the bishopric with his upper mouth. Computers couldn't really handle Vhaddish.

"Against my direct recommendation, the High Pontiff has continued to attempt to find the Stone of the First High Pontiff, despite the fact that the stone was obviously lost forever when

Vhad was destroyed by the heretics of Pranik. The legends that grew up around the stone were created to keep the devout from abandoning us following the destruction of our homeworld."

The Voice threw some more HebroGrubs into his mouth. They were particularly good today, and he made a mental note to compliment his slaves for getting a good bunch.

He continued to dictate his memo: "However, we can take some comfort in the fact that the High Pontiff has, of late, become quite fascinated with the so-called 'human finder.' He has become convinced that she will be the one to find the Stone of the First High Pontiff. To that end, I have liberated two thousand marks from the treasury to pay her off. She will search for it, never find it, and then the High Pontiff will finally let go of his obsession with using the stone to unite the factions. While the notion of bringing the heretics back into the fold in the abstract is a noble one, its practicality remains specious, especially since donations have increased a thousandfold since the schism. However, the High Pontiff continues to drone on about his legacy, that he wishes the Ninety-Ninth High Pontiff to be remembered as the one who healed the schism. With luck, the human finder's failure to locate the stone will end this foolishness."

As he popped the last of his HerboGrubs, he added, "And do not be concerned that the human finder will attempt to bring us a forgery. Providing a convincing forgery of the stone is far beyond her means. The materials alone for such a forgery would cost many thousands of marks."

With that, the Voice sent the memo off to the bishopric. He was looking forward to the imminent end of this obsession of the High Pontiff's.

The following morning, he awoke to a YourMail that the human finder had returned with the Stone of the First High Pontiff.

The Voice had to reread the message several times before he finally believed that it said what his eyestalks insisted it did.

"This isn't possible," he muttered as his servants tended to his fur before he met with the High Pontiff.

When he arrived for his audience in the High Pontiff's private chambers—to which only the Voice and selected sex slaves were allowed—the Voice was distressed at how joyful the High Pontiff seemed. His limbs were quivering, and his eyestalks practically bouncing.

"A great day for the Sacred Church of Enlightened Thought and Belief, is it not, my Voice?"

"So it would appear to be, Most Holy One. I am, however, surprised that the human finder was able to locate the Stone of the First High Pontiff so quickly."

"As am I, my Voice. It is proof that she is quite extraordinary. Come, let us not keep her waiting, for today is a great day in the history of the Sacred Church of Enlightened Thought and Belief."

The Voice followed several paces behind the High Pontiff as he entered the receiving room.

Once the High Pontiff was seated in his throne, the Voice instructed the computer to let the human finder in.

When she entered, the Voice had to once again be persuaded that his eyestalks were functioning properly. The human finder's face had several scars that were covered with DermalRep, her hair was considerably shorter than it had been when last she was here—and it looked as if it had been singed off—while her companion had a massive bandage on the crown of his smooth scalp.

The human finder was also holding a PlastiForm container.

"This is not possible," the Voice said without preamble, and before the human finder could say anything.

"On the contrary," the human finder said, "it is very possible. The Stone of the First High Pontiff was in a storage unit located under the ruins of Crivda."

Several of the Voice's tentacles quivered. "The Stone of the High Pontiff was in the territory of the Wosaphi Conclave?"

"Very deep within their territory," the human finder said, "but I was able to retrieve it, after a great deal of difficult searching." She exchanged a look with her taller companion.

Then she touched the side of the PlastiForm container, which slid open, and then she pulled out a round, engraved stone the size of her fist.

The Voice found himself unable to speak with either mouth at first. It looked very much like what the stone looked like in contemporary images. He'd imagined it to be larger, but—

But no, it had to be a forgery. Hadn't it?

His voice even raspier than usual, the High Pontiff reached out with several tentacles. "The stone," he said in Yrak, "it has been—found—at last—it has..."

Then the High Pontiff collapsed, rolling off the throne and onto the floor.

Stunned, the Voice stared for a second, then instructed the computer to summon medical help and activate the triage program.

The computer intoned a moment later: "All life functions in the Ninety-Ninth High Pontiff have ceased."

Quickly, the Voice stood up and spoke to the Church Warriors stationed at the room's pillars. "Remove these heretics! And have them take their forgery with them!"

"It's *not* a forgery!" The human finder was speaking in Yrak now as well. "I wouldn't have found it if it was a fake! That's not how it works!"

"It doesn't matter what you say," the Voice said in the same language, to make it clear that he would not be doing business with forgers. He had no idea how they'd managed to construct a fake, but it simply *could not* be the same one.

As the Warriors stood behind each of the humans, the woman said, "Our ScanBot verified that this was made of jeevon! There's only, what, half an acre's worth of jeevon left in the galaxy? Less? There's no way we could've gotten our hands on that. This is the real thing!"

"It doesn't matter," the Voice said again—and truly, it didn't. "The High Pontiff is dead, and his ridiculous quest to reunite the church has thankfully died with him. You are heretics and forgers, and you will remove yourself from this world as soon as possible."

"So, you do betray me," said a raspy voice, also speaking in Yrak.

All of the Voice's eyestalks turned in shock as the High Pontiff rose up.

"It—it—"

"Your treachery has been sent to the InformNet, so now the entire Collective is aware of your heresy."

With a start, the Voice realized that that was why the High Pontiff had been speaking in Yrak. Somewhere in the receiving room, he had sequestered CamDrones that were blasting to the InformNet.

"Remove the Voice and bind him by law," the High Pontiff said as he retook his throne.

The Warriors did as they were told. The Voice said nothing else, not wishing to make a further fool of himself to the entire InformNet. He would wait his time to speak his piece. Half the bishopric was on his side, and the High Pontiff would soon see his support erode.

At least, that was what he hoped. His own indiscretion would not sit well with his allies in the bishopric.

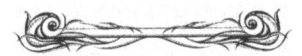

Jin had entered the receiving room thinking she was going to make two thousand marks—which was barely enough to cover what they went through to retrieve the damned stone. Then she thought she was going to be placed in a Vhaddish prison for the rest of her life. Then she thought they were going to get the money again.

So when the newly resurrected High Pontiff instructed the Warriors to escort them back to their ship, she was kind of surprised.

Speaking again in Vhaddish, Jin said, "Forgive me, please, High Pontiff, but we had an arrangement."

"You had an arrangement with my former Voice. That arrangement is no more. For all that I am aware, you were part of his plan to discredit me."

"His plan, High Pontiff, was for me never to find the Stone of the First High Pontiff. But I *have* found it."

"That is not possible." He switched to Yrak. "The stone was lost forever. I merely expressed interest in retrieving it to find out how deep my former Voice's treachery was. That stone must be a forgery—not yours, perhaps, but a forgery nonetheless."

"No, High Pontiff, *that* is what is not possible. My—my ability to find things can't be fooled by a forgery. *This* is what I found when I sought out the stone."

"Take them away!"

The guards each put their hands on Jin's and Timm's shoulders and started to guide them toward the exit. Jin supposed she should have been grateful that they hadn't unsheathed their GranitoZaps.

Deliberately speaking in Cwyar, Timm muttered, "*Now* can we auction this thing off to the highest bidder?"

Several months later, Jin lay on the sands of the Covert Beach, the twin suns of Covert gently baking her naked body. She had never taken a vacation before, and the last month on Covert had been magnificent. Never in her life had she been so relaxed.

Once the first of the suns went down, she decided to see what was happening in the Collective. Timm was due back the following day with the newly refitted *Seeker*, complete with the new ScanBot 6000, working thermostats, and shiny new coils—not to mention a general overhaul of parts.

Easy enough to do when you sell the Stone of the First High Pontiff to the "heretical" Relativist Sect for fifty thousand marks.

Touching her implant, she was able to get an AetherAir signal and do a quick InformNet download, bringing her up to date on assorted sports scores, news, and other stuff.

She noted an abstract of a piece on the resignation of the Ninety-Ninth High Pontiff, and activated that Inform.

"The surprise resignation of the Ninety-Ninth High Pontiff comes as record numbers of devout have left the Lighters, defecting to the Relativist Sect in light of that sect's revelation of the Stone of the First High Pontiff."

Jin couldn't help but laugh. It only would have cost the High Pontiff two thousand marks to keep the stone for himself. Instead, he let them leave with it, and it cost him his job.

"In the meantime, the Council of Elders of the Relativist Sect have announced that, with the great influx of new members to their church, they are considering electing a High Pontiff from among their number."

Jin went through the rest of the story only to find no mention of her whatsoever—indeed, that there was no mention that the Relativists *acquired* the stone, but that they simply had a "revelation" of it, whatever that meant. That was too bad—being the person who found the Stone of the First High Pontiff would be great for business—but she would have to settle for the large sums of money the Relativists paid her.

She also had a YourMail from the Ninety-Ninth High Pontiff. She wondered if he sent that before or after he resigned.

"To the human finder. It seems I owe you an apology. Or perhaps I owe you nothing, since you have received more money for the Stone of the First High Pontiff from those damned heretics. Either way, your skills are obviously greater than I gave you credit for, and in my eagerness to discredit my traitorous Voice I neglected the devout. I'll obviously never make that mistake again."

Jin smiled. Maybe public recognition didn't matter so much.

Introduction to "Seven-Mile Race"

I first created Cassie Zukav—a self-described "weirdness magnet"—for a short story I wrote for the *Urban Nightmares* anthology in 1997. In that story, Cassie—a grad student and scuba diving enthusiast in San Diego—encounters a strange sea creature, and seems to die at the end. However, I'd been wanting to revisit Cassie for a long time, and move her to Key West, Florida. The notion of Cassie stories in Key West bapped around my head for years. I had the whole setup ready to go. Cassie would live and work part-time at a bed-and-breakfast in the Old Town section of Key West, sharing her room with the ghost of a wrecker captain whom only she could see. She'd work part-time at a dive shop as a dive-master. And she'd spend her nights at one of the bars in Old Town, watching 1812, the house band, play, sometimes hanging out with an FBI agent she sorta-kinda might be interested in. Besides the ghost, other odd recurring characters include several Norse gods and an immortal barfly.

My original plan was for Cassie to just be a weirdness magnet, but when I submitted a proposal for Cassie graphic novels to BOOM! Studios, the editor, Matt Gagnon, told me that I needed something more definitive to explain Cassie's abilities. So I decided to make her a Norse fate goddess—one of the Dísir. As a Dís, she'd be able to see through artifice and notice things that others wouldn't.

I finally had a Cassie-in-Key-West story published when Deborah Grabien started up the *Tales from the House Band* anthology series, and I sent her "Ragnarok and Roll," which is the story in which Cassie finds out she's a Dís right before she has to help Odin stop Loki from bringing about Ragnarok. I did another Cassie story for the second *House Band* anthology, "I Believe I'm Sinkin' Down," a tale that involves the blues legend Robert Johnson, and another for *Bad-Ass Faeries: It's Elemental*, involving a water fae.

Deborah's publishing company, Plus One Press—who also published the *House Band* anthologies—then offered to publish a collection of Cassie stories. I already had three, plus the original from *Urban Nightmares*, and a I wrote a few more, including a big three-part epic about the ghosts of Key West being supercharged, plus one about Loki and Sigyn's turbulent relationship and one where Thor, the thunderer, shows up on the island.

After the collection, also entitled *Ragnarok and Roll*, came out in 2013, I have continued to spin Cassie yarns: from "Fish Out of Water" for the *Out of Tune* anthology, edited by Jonathan Maberry (him again!) and published by JournalStone, to "Down to the Waterline" for the online magazine *Buzzy Mag* to "William Did It" for StoryOfTheMonthClub.com (reprinted in the SMC compilation anthology *A Baker's Dozen of Magic*, edited by Jessica Branwer) to "Behind the Wheel" in the *TV Gods: Summer Programming* anthology edited by Jeff Young & Lee C. Hillman and published by Fortress Publishing.

For *Without a License*, I figured I'd do a new Cassie story (which takes place a couple of months after "Fish Out of Water"), one that's been percolating in my head since my fiancée, Wrenn Simms, suggested the dialogue exchange that you'll see between Cassie and the Ivaldi brothers on the subject of Thor's hammer. Past Cassie stories have featured several figures from Norse myth, including Odin, Loki, Sigyn (who's the drummer in 1812), Geirrod, and Thor, and this story adds Tyr, Eitri, and Brokkr to the list. It also features one of the great features of the Florida Keys, to wit, the Seven-Mile Bridge.

Seven-Mile Race

a Cassie Zukav story

I knew trouble was coming when I walked into Mayor Fred's Saloon on Saturday night and Thor was in the bar.

Having the thunder god back in Key West was just the perfect capper to this shitty week.

With the ramp-up to the Daytona 500, it was the beginning of spring tourist season on the island. This was great for the Bottroff House Bed & Breakfast on Eaton Street, where I lived and worked, and the Seaclipse Dive Shop over on Stock Island, where I just worked. It wasn't so hot in terms of keeping me from getting homicidal. From December to February, the tourists were mostly casual, just folks coming down to get away from the cold farther north. But Daytona signaled the beginning of the silly season that also included Bike Week in early March and the great horror that is spring break right after that. That was when *all* the crazies showed up.

And nobody was crazier than Thor, one of several Norse deities in my life. About six-foot-ten with shoulders the size of Ohio, Thor had a red crew cut and a thick red beard that made him look like half the bears on the island, except for the fact that he wasn't gay. I hadn't seen him since New Year's, and I really hoped he wasn't going to hit on me again. Or hit on anyone else. Or hit anything else.

Of course, he saw me as soon as I came in. The house band, 1812, was tuning up for their set, and Thor was sitting at the table by the big ficus tree that Mayor Fred's was built around.

My usual table.

To be fair, the Aesir had an affinity for the ficus. That was Key West's hanging tree in the nineteenth century, but the tourist web sites won't tell you that it's also a root of Yggdrasil, the world-tree that links the Nine Worlds together.

"Ah, fair and lovely Dís!" he bellowed. "It is good to see you again!"

I closed my eyes and sighed. I supposed it was too much to ask that he'd finally pay attention and start calling me "Cassie" like I'd asked him a billion times.

"Come join me, and we will toast to our lost comrades!"

There was no way to gracefully refuse, though I was tempted to gracelessly do so. Last April I discovered that a) the Norse gods were real, b) there weren't that many of them left, and c) I sorta-kinda was one: a fate goddess, one of the Dísir.

Since then, I'd saved the world from Ragnarok and seen two of those gods die. A toast to their memory probably wouldn't be too terribly bad.

As I sat in the chair next to him around the small round table, I shook my head. "I'm surprised to see you, Thor. As I recall, you swore after what happened at the Red Garter over New Year's that you'd never set foot on this island again."

Thor waved an arm. "'Twas but a trifle. The owner was a varlet and a knave—that lady was mine by right of conquest, and besides, I only broke one of those bouncer's arms."

Adina came by before I could comment. "Your usual, Cass?"

I nodded, and Thor downed the half-pint he'd had in front of him. "And another for me, sweet Adina."

She chuckled. "Youbetcha."

Thor watched her ass wiggle as she walked toward the bar. I just shook my head. Adina was a lesbian, which Thor already knew from the last four times he offered her the "gift" of his sexual favors. To be fair, he was incredibly drunk three of those times.

"So what brings you back?" I asked by way of taking his attention off of Adina's posterior.

"Tomorrow is the Daytona 500, and I wish to observe the festivities in a convivial atmosphere."

I nodded. Thor drove a muscle car, so of course he was into the race. Me, my car-nut days were behind me, and these days Daytona was just another event that brought the crazy to the island.

"Besides," Thor continued, "if my brother loses, I am in a fine place to celebrate. And should he win, this is the ideal locale to drown my sorrows."

I shot Thor a look. He'd told me once that Tyr was one of the gods who still lived, and he was also Thor's brother. "Tyr is in the race?"

"He uses the name 'Jamie McIntyre' for reasons known only to himself, but yes."

My eyes widened. "That pretentious asshole who always wears his driving gloves is really Tyr?"

"Indeed, that is he. Though he wears the gloves to cover the false hand that Eitri and Brokkr fashioned for him."

I recalled the story. After being told I was a Dís, I devoured everything I could on Norse myth, though the reality proved to only occasionally intersect with Snorri Sturluson. "That was after Fenris bit his hand off, right?"

Thor nodded as Adina brought our beers by. He raised his pint. "To Odin, the Allfather! To Loki Laufeyson, my devious cousin!"

I raised my pint as well. "Skaal!" I'd been there when both Odin and Loki had died, and it had been—well, very weird both times. I really hoped that was the last time I'd have to deal with that.

1812, as usual, played a spectacular set of rock-and-roll cover tunes. It being Saturday night, the bar was packed, and the band stuck with well-known classics, including plenty of audience requests. It being Daytona weekend, there were a lot of calls for Lynyrd Skynyrd, the Allman Brothers, Gov't Mule, ZZ Top, Molly Hatchet, and so on. Chet Smith, the bass player, had been bitching all week about how they were going to have to play all that "redneck shit."

After the second set ended, Thor turned to me. "Beautiful Dís, will you do me the honor of your company here on the morrow to watch my brother compete and—if the Norns are kind—lose horribly?"

I knew Ihor, the bartender, would be placing the big projector screen in front of the stage tomorrow and playing the race on it.

Normally I would have refused on principle, as I hadn't watched a race in years, and the last time I agreed to do something with Thor it ended spectacularly badly, but knowing that Tyr would be one of the competitors, I was curious. The owners of Seaclipse were race-car nerds; the Daytona was considered a holiday and the dive shop was always closed on that day, so I didn't have my usual Sunday afternoon dive.

"Sure, as long as you understand that we're staying right here in the bar. Under no circumstances am I accompanying you back to Summerland Key."

Thor sighed and shrugged. "'Tis your loss, superlative Dís."

"Do you keep a thesaurus around for new adjectives to use to describe me?"

He grinned. "Not at all. I simply find your beauty inspiring."

I had to admit, he displayed a certain charm. But I also had a first-hand report from one of his conquests that he wasn't exactly a master of the bedroom, no matter what he claimed.

I came to Mayor Fred's the next day, where Thor again waited at the table by the ficus. There was a big crowd of racing enthusiasts, plus a few tourists, and regulars like Larry, an immortal who'd been sitting at this particular bar since the day it opened.

To Thor's great disappointment, Jamie McIntyre won.

In his post-race interview, he spouted all the usual clichés, most of which I tuned out, but I did see the two members of his pit crew standing proudly behind him. They were both very short with huge noses.

"I also," he drawled with a southern accent that was way too exaggerated, "wanna thank my boys in the ol' pit crew, the Ivaldi brothers. I couldn't'a done none'a this without these two fellas."

Surprised, I turned to stare at Thor. "The Ivaldi brothers? His pit crew is Eitri and Brokkr, aren't they?"

"Of course," Thor said as if it were the most natural thing in the world.

Thor drank a great deal after the race, and tried to talk me into going home with him to his bungalow in Summerland Key, attempting to entice me by waggling his eyebrows and saying, again, that his hammer gets bigger if you rub it. I politely declined the first time and rudely declined the second time. I held a knee to the nuts in reserve for the third, but that sadly never came. I thought he'd found some other woman to set his sights on, right up until some tourist screamed that he found a body under the pool table.

That "body" turned out to be Thor, *very* passed out. We left him there until closing, and then Ihor, Chet, and I all half-rolled, half-carried his sorry ass out to the sidewalk.

Sure enough, his car was idling at the curb waiting for him. Thor had a 1964 Pontiac GTO, a make and model that was nicknamed a "Goat"—fitting for a guy who used to fly around in a chariot pulled by goats. Somehow, the car always knew when Thor was passed out drunk (which was fairly often), and just showed up for him and took him home. Once we poured him into the front seat, the car zoomed off down Greene.

The next few days were incredibly busy, as the island was flooded with tourists in the aftermath of the race. Seaclipse was booming, the bed-and-breakfast was full (I had to actually give up my room and sleep on the sofa in the lobby for two nights), and I didn't have the chance to get back to Mayor Fred's until Thursday afternoon. It was raining and windy, the water choppy enough that Seaclipse cancelled all dives.

This being Florida, by the time I drove back to Key West from Stock Island and walked to Mayor Fred's, the rain had let up to a drizzle, though it was still windy enough that the water was probably still a pain to dive in, especially for casual divers (who were the bulk of our clientele).

Two short men were holding court at the table by the ficus. They were surrounded by half a dozen people, mostly tourists I didn't recognize, but also Larry and one or two other regulars. Thor, I noticed, was nowhere to be seen.

I recognized the pair instantly as the pit crew who had been standing behind Tyr at Daytona. Both of them had shaggy brown hair and noses the size of cantaloupes. The only way to tell them apart was that one had a beard and one didn't. "Well, well, well," I said as I walked up to them, "if it isn't the sons of Ivaldi."

The two dwarves looked up and laughed heartily. The one with the beard said, "At last, it's Castor Zukav of the Dísir!"

Larry shot me a look even as I winced. "Castor? Is that *really* your—"

"*Yes*, that's my full first name. My parents named me and my twin brother Castor and Pollux because they're *insane*, and if *anyone* calls me 'Castor' again, I can promise that their fate will be drastically changed." I stared at the dwarves and pointed a finger at them. "That goes double for you two garbanzos."

Both of them held up their hands, and the clean-shaven one said, "We vow to forget we ever knew your full name, Cassie."

"That's better."

"Please," the bearded one said, "have a seat. You obviously know who we are."

"But not which is which."

The bearded one laughed while the clean-shaven one said, "I'm Eitri—the good-looking one."

"In your dreams, brother." Brokkr punched Eitri lightly on the arm to punctuate his point.

Larry took off his Rays ballcap and scratched his bald crown. "These two jokers have been telling tall tales."

Eitri raised a bushy eyebrow. "Is that meant to be a comment about our height?"

"Psh," I said as I folded my 5'11" frame into a chair and sat opposite the brothers. "You're all too short."

"If it is tales from tall people we will hear this night," Brokkr said, grabbing his pint of beer, "then it should be from the oversized Dís here. Part of why we came to this island was to hear firsthand of your adventures."

I used to be squirrelly about talking about my being a fate goddess in front of the general public, but after what happened over Christmas, pretty much everyone in the Keys knew exactly what I was. The ones who didn't buy it just chalked it up as another crazy Key West story like all the others they didn't believe.

So I told the story of how I stopped Loki from bringing about Ragnarok and how I helped Odin and Loki and Sigyn stop the spirit of the Calusa tribe from committing mass murder, at the cost of Odin's own life, and the story of how a mermaid got revenge on Loki for a long-ago crime by killing him, and a bunch more stories.

But I was curious about these two and the guy they worked for. "So you manage Tyr's cars?"

"Yes, we currently dabble in vehicular modification," Eitri said with a twinkle in his eye. "I assume you've seen Thor's GTO?"

I nodded. "And ridden in it."

"Our handiwork," Brokkr said proudly.

That explained why the car had a mind of its own, anyhow. "You made his hammer, too, right?"

"And Sigyn's snare drum. We understand that the troupe she performs with will be here this even, yes?"

"Yeah," I said. 1812's drummer went by Ginny Blake, but her real name was Sigyn, another of the Aesir (and also Loki's wife—though I guess "widow" was the better word now). She had a glorious brass snare drum that she guarded with her life. Now I knew why.

"Excellent," Brokkr said in reply to my positive reply. "We have heard her perform in the past, but not with these particular minstrels."

"Can we drag it back to Thor's hammer a minute? There's something about it that's always bugged me." Well, okay, there were a lot of things about Thor in general and the hammer in particular that bugged me, but I wasn't about to get into that. "You guys made weapons for a lot of the Aesir, right?"

"Of course," Brokkr said.

Eitri grinned. "All of the *good* ones, certainly."

"Nobody else that I know of among them used a hammer as a weapon. Neither did any of the Vikings. For everyone else, it's a tool. So why'd you make him a hammer?"

Brokkr rolled his eyes. "Because the big fool couldn't hang onto any of the others!"

"You see," Eitri said, leaning forward, "we kept making swords and axes and maces for Thor. And in less than a month, he would return to us with a tale of woe, that he'd lost it or broken it or misplaced it or gave it to some woman he was wooing."

"We take great pride in our craft," Brokkr added, "and take great care in the making, and we expect our clients to show similar care in their use. If they don't, then the care is, shall we say, reduced."

Eitri grinned. "Which is why we simply took one of our work hammers that was lying about the forge, made it indestructible, and put enchantments on it. He can't give it away nor can anyone else use it."

I nodded. "So he can't lose this one because it always flies back to his hand."

The dwarves exchanged glances. "Er, well," Brokkr said slowly, "if he gets his hand up fast enough, then yes."

For a couple of seconds I stared at them. Then I burst out laughing.

The Ivaldis joined in the laughter. "Either way," Eitri said between guffaws, "it was guaranteed to be the last weapon we'd ever have to make for him."

Ginny came in then, snare drum in hand—the rest of the drumkit was already set up—and broke into a huge grin at the sight of my table.

"Eitri! Brokkr! I despaired of seeing you after so many days had passed!"

"I'm afraid the post-race celebration was even heartier than usual," Eitri said with a rueful grin. "Indeed, Tyr is still recovering, though he claimed he would attempt to join us to see your minstrels perform this even."

Ginny chuckled. "We're actually referred to as a 'band,' and I'm much happier to see the two of you in any case."

"Likewise, my dear," Eitri said. "We were especially concerned after the trickster's demise. Are you well?"

"I wish people would stop asking me that," Ginny said a little too emphatically. "Loki was a terrible person, he hasn't even *been* a true husband to me in far too long, and this isn't even the first time he's died on me."

The rest of 1812 trickled in and they started setting up. Larry started telling some stories of his own from his decades of sitting in this bar and that went on until 1812's first set started.

They rocked the joint, as usual. Toward the end of the set, Bobbi Milewski, the lead guitarist, looked right at me and said, "This is for Cassie."

Then they dove into REM's "It's the End of the World as We Know It (And I Feel Fine)," which they'd been dedicating to me on and off for months now, ever since I stopped Ragnarok in this very bar. I just rolled my eyes, as the joke was starting to wear thin. On the other hand, it was a good set-ender.

Just as the band started to come down off the stage, a booming voice came from the entrance by the merch table, just as a different booming voice came from the other side of the bar near the pool table.

"Cassie!" one cried in a familiar bellow, while the other yelled, "Here I am, boys an' girls!" in the fakest southern accent I'd ever heard.

Turning, I saw Thor come in by the bar, while "Jamie McIntyre" walked in by the merch table. Tyr looked very out of place in his long-sleeved Daytona 500 shirt, khakis, and racing gloves. T-shirts and shorts were the usual dress on the island. It wasn't as if his fake hand would be a big deal—it wouldn't even be the only prosthetic in the bar, as the sound guy, Paolo, also lost his hand—but he insisted on standing out. Which, I suppose, fit his personality, both as a god and as an asshole race car driver.

Thor and Tyr noticed each other and their faces fell. They both came to the ficus and stared each other down

"Brother."

"Brother."

"I see you won. Again."

"'Course I did. What all didja expect?"

"Regardless of expectation, I was hoping for your ignominious defeat."

"Nah, I leave the ignominy to you."

"How dare you!"

As entertaining as this wasn't, I decided to interrupt. "If you two take down your pants to compare sizes, I'm having Ihor toss you both out right now."

Tyr turned away from Thor and looked at me with a spectacularly insincere grin. "Well, lookee here, if it ain't the Dís her own self? Pleased to meetcha, lovely lady."

"I prefer my actual name of Cassie, but whatever."

Ginny came over at that point looking nauseated. "I was wondering which of you two would arrive first. Leave it to you to turn up together."

"Ah, fair Sigyn," Thor said, "it is good to see you well after your loss."

"It wasn't that much of a loss," she said, sitting down next to Eitri. "I prefer not to speak of it."

"Yeah," Tyr said, pulling a chair from a nearby table, "show some respect to the lady, brother."

"If I do, brother, it will not be due to your desiring it!"

I rolled my eyes and excused myself to the bathroom. I didn't actually have to go, but there was a line, and I figured that standing on it would keep me away from the posturing for a bit.

By the time I got back to the table, 1812 was setting back up for the second set (it had been a really long line), but the two brothers were still standing nose to nose.

"Least I didn't go and get Hymir killed on a simple little old fishin' trip!"

"And I had the brains not to place my hand in a wolf's mouth!"

"'Bout the only time anyone'd say you had brains, truth to tell."

Thor opened his mouth to respond, but I cut him off. "Will you two shut the fuck up, already?" I looked at the dwarves. "They always like this?"

"No, usually they're contentious."

I snorted, then looked back at the two gods. "Now either sit down and shut up and enjoy the music, or you can both go elsewhere. Be assholes at Sloppy Joe's or Irish Kevin's." I deliberately suggested my two least favorite bars on Duval Street.

They both reluctantly sat down, arms folded.

Rolling my eyes, I sat as well, the five of us crammed around a tiny table.

1812 lead off the second set with Rockpile's "Play That Fast Thing (One More Time)," which opened with a big, complex drum bit. That, at least, got Thor and Tyr to stop being all pouty, and instead got them to stare at Ginny.

By the end of the song, they both had expressions on their faces that were making me nostalgic for pouty.

"She is a magnificent maiden, is she not?"

"Yeah, that's a mighty fine filly."

I'd rolled my eyes at these two enough times that I half-expected to see the back of my head. "For fuck's sake, she's isn't either of those things. She's a person."

"Who has suffered a great loss."

"Not that ol' Loki's all *that* much of a loss, really."

"She requires the gift of comfort and pleasure."

"Ayup. And I'm just the fella to give it to her."

"*You?* Do not make me laugh, Tyr, you could not bring pleasure to a concubine to whom you'd paid extra."

"Yeah, well, payin's the only way you're like to get any tail."

Eitri and Brokkr were just chortling to themselves. They were sure as shit enjoying this more than I was.

"Will you two shut *up*? All you do is bitch each other out. I mean, I get it, you're brothers, but I've got a twin brother, not to mention the brattiest little sister ever, and we're not *this* bad. I mean, hell, why don't you just have a race in those surrogate penises you call cars and have done with it?"

Both men turned with huge grins on their faces.

"Now that's a mighty fine notion there!"

"Agreed! A wager it shall be! And I shall trounce this lout with his puny vehicle."

Now Eitri spoke up. "Hey! We put together that puny vehicle, same's we did yours."

Thor put up a hand. "Of course, good dwarves, your work is doubtless superb. But a steed is only as good as his rider." That last was with a scowl at his brother.

I put my head in my hands. "Fuck me sideways, I've created a monster...."

"And the winner shall have the right to woo Sigyn!" Thor said while pounding his fist on the table, making everyone's drink shake and slosh onto the worn wood.

"Sounds pretty dang fine to me!"

"Uhm," I said slowly, "don't you think Ginny should have some say in this?"

"She shall have her say when the wooing commences," Thor said.

Eitri grinned. "So what track shall we use?"

Thor frowned. "No, no track. That is where this varlet plies his trade. It shall be on a proper road."

"Kinda obvious, ain't it?" Tyr said with a grin. "Gotta be the Seven-Mile Bridge."

"Indeed!" Thor's face broke into a grin of its own.

I put my head in my hands. The Seven-Mile Bridge was the part of the Overseas Highway that linked the Keys to each other, enabling you to drive from Miami all the way down to Key West. The bridge itself linked the seven-mile gap between Marathon Key and Little Duck Key. "You doofuses do realize that there'll be *other people* driving on it, right?"

Tyr chuckled. "Nah, little lady, I ain't talkin' the *current* bridge."

My eyes widened. "Are you kidding me?"

The Overseas Highway was originally the Overseas Railway. After a hurricane trashed it in the 1930s, the railroad sold the right-of-way to the state. Most of that old railway was now the highway, with one exception. They built a new Seven-Mile Bridge in the 1970s, but the old one was still there.

Mostly. "You *do* know there's a big-ass gap in the old bridge, right? And it hasn't exactly been maintained as a roadway. Hell, they even banned bikes on the bridge because of the structural issues, and the bit between the gap and Little Duck is mostly old train tracks barely held together by rust."

"Hence the challenge!" Thor bellowed. "It shall be glorious! We race tonight after the tavern closes!"

Which was how I wound up standing next to my truck on Little Duck Key at 4:30 in the morning. Thor and Tyr were seven miles away on Marathon, but Eitri had given me a set of what he called "special" binoculars, which enabled me to see the other end of the bridge clearly.

Larry, Bobbi, and Jana were standing next to me with binoculars of their own. We were all curious about how this absurd race would go. As we were driving across the *current* Seven Mile Bridge toward this idiotic race's finish line, Bobbi had been staring over at the darkened original bridge. "What do you think the over/under is on how soon they crash into the water and drown?"

Jana had snorted. "We ain't got that kinda luck."

"I don't know, ladies," Larry had said, "the pair of them were a few sheets to the wind."

Now I was peering through the dwarves' binoculars. Eitri was helping Thor into his Goat, while Tyr was clambering into a heavily modified stock car covered in corporate logos with

Brokkr's help. You didn't usually see a stock car on a regular road, but given that the Ivaldi brothers built this, it probably wasn't your average stock car anyhow. The frame looked vaguely like a Ford, but it didn't actually match any specific car I knew of.

Thor just sat in the car staring straight ahead while Tyr was having trouble keeping his grip on the steering wheel.

I shook my head. "Larry, those two aren't just a few sheets to the wind. More like the whole bedroom set." I looked at Bobbi. "I'll take the under—two minutes in."

Bobbi chuckled, but I was genuinely worried that the two jackasses were going to drown themselves.

Peering back through the binoculars, I saw that Eitri and Brokkr were standing between the cars with their hands up. Both cars were revving, but it was too far away for me to hear how the engines sounded. Of course, they were probably both purring—I'd never heard a hiccup from Thor's Goat, and Tyr's stock car just won the biggest race in NASCAR.

The dwarves lowered their arms, and the cars took off.

It was pretty hard to follow them from this far away, but as they got closer, it got easier. The stock car and the Goat went neck and neck, neither one taking the lead for more than a second or two before the other one overtook.

I took a look at the drivers. Tyr was grinning and looking like he was enjoying himself, while Thor was grinding his teeth and looked all determined. I could see sparks fly as the cars rubbed up against the guardrail, which was made from the old railroad tracks.

Peering through her own binoculars, Bobbi said, "Neither one of those idiots is wearing a helmet."

"Of course they aren't," I muttered.

"I don't think their heads could get any more damaged anyhow," Jana said with a snort.

I couldn't argue that particular point.

They were getting to the moment of truth: the gap near Pigeon Key, which was originally a swing-span to allow boat traffic across, but which was removed after the new bridge was built. They had to be getting close to two hundred miles an hour, and I just hoped it was enough to clear the gap.

Mostly because if it wasn't, I sure as shit wasn't diving after them...

When I was a kid, I never used to understand why they would show big moments on TV shows and in movies in slow-motion. It wasn't like time really slowed down, so why do that? Just let it play out in real time.

But time can be damned subjective, and as soon as the two cars hit the end of the road and flew into the air over the Moser Channel, time did seem to slow down. It was like I was watching a *Dukes of Hazzard* rerun with the General Lee flying through the air in slow-mo, except it was two cars and the drivers were even bigger dumbasses than the Duke boys.

They flew in a big arc through the air. We weren't close enough to hear anything, but I could tell looking that both gods were shouting at the top of their lungs.

Tyr landed first, the stock car bouncing on the rusty railroad tracks covered in wild overgrowth.

Thor landed second, but only with the front wheels on the road, the back half of the Goat dangling off the edge.

I winced. The '64 GTO had rear-wheel drive. I waited for Thor and his car to tumble into the ocean, which was only going to be a shame insofar as it was a really nice car.

But then the front wheels spun madly and the car took off onto the tracks.

"Sonofabitch."

Tyr was driving more cautiously on this stretch, as it was far more treacherous than the glorified bike path of the previous leg of the race. This had no paving, no solid surface, and an infrastructure that looked like it would fall into the water at any second. In fact, I could see bits of the bridge flying off it.

Thor, though, was flooring it. The Goat caught up to the stock car in short order, and by the time I didn't need the binoculars anymore because they were in plain sight, Thor had a length and a half on his brother.

Tyr put on a burst of speed at the end, but there was no doubt at the finish line: Thor was the winner.

The Goat screeched to a halt on the dirt and grass, tires spinning, dirt flying, the car doing a full 180. Thor leapt out of the car before it finished spinning, crying, "Ha hah! Again the thunderer is victorious!"

The stock car decelerated less spectacularly. Tyr got out looking all kinds of pouty. "Nicely done there, brother, though I betcher undercarriage's all messed up."

"Of what concern is that? I have won! The details are of no consequence! Thor has beaten his brother! Let those varlets claim that Tyr is stronger and smarter and faster and braver! They are all *fools*!"

I turned to Bobbi. "And here I was worried he was gonna gloat."

Thor walked up to Jana and wrapped one massive arm around her. "Ah, Jana, my sweet lovely minstrel! Come away with me and let us once again celebrate as only a god can!"

Somehow, Jana managed to extricate herself. She'd already gone to bed with Thor once, and that experience was disappointing enough to convince her never to bother again. "Sorry, chuckles. Got an early morning tomorrow."

Luckily Thor wasn't bright enough to figure out that, if that was true, she wouldn't have stayed up late to watch the race.

"Barbara Ann!" Thor cried to Bobbi, undeterred.

Since Bobbi was asexual, this was a lost cause. "My answer hasn't changed since the last forty times, Thor."

"Magnificent Dís?"

I just glared at him.

"Pity. And the taverns are all closed, thus depriving me of further options for celebrations. But on the morrow, the drinks in Mayor Fred's Saloon shall all be raised in honor of Thor! Thor the thunderer! Thor Odinson!"

"Thor the loudmouth, Thor the braying jackass?" I added.

Laughing, he replied, "Oh no, superlative Dís, your shrewishness shall not spoil my victory!"

"You don't mind if my shrewishness keeps trying, do you?"

Tyr walked up to Thor and put a hand out. "Good race there, bro'. Looks like you won fair and square."

"I accept your craven acknowledgment of my superiority, brother, and will allow you to buy the first round tomorrow night!"

The next night could charitably be called insane. Friday nights were crazy at the best of times, and we had the post-Daytona crowd and the pre-Bike Week crowd in addition to the usual tourists.

When I got to Mayor Fred's after my evening dive, Thor was, of course, the center of attention, and he made sure there was no danger of that changing any time soon. 1812 was between sets, and he was standing at the front of the bar, braying and laughing and hitting on every woman in the room. I saw Eitri amidst the crowd of cheering patrons, and Brokkr was probably in there somewhere, too. Larry was in his usual spot at the bar, laughing along with everyone else.

Tyr sat at the back corner of the bar near the pool table. Not really wanting a piece of Thor's insanity, I sought out the loser, who was nursing a bourbon.

Without preamble, I sat next to him and said, "So I thought the whole point of the exercise was to get to ask Ginny out. Yet there he is, hitting on every *other* woman in the bar."

"Ah, y'missed it before, little lady. Thor went a-courtin' soon as Sigyn showed her pretty face, and she turned him down faster'n snot."

"And I bet plenty of snot was involved."

Tyr laughed. "Yeah, prob'ly. It's all right, the big fella done earned it."

"No he didn't." I signaled Ihor, and ordered a beer.

Once he went off to pour my pint, Tyr said, "Now look, little lady, I know you ain't all that fond of my brother, but he *did* win the race."

"I'm not saying he didn't earn it because I don't like him, I'm saying he didn't earn it because you let him win."

Tyr shot me a look. "Excuse me?"

"Oh, don't give me that innocent look, you suck at it worse than you suck at that southern accent. Besides, I'm a fate goddess, remember? I can see shit most people can't. On the last leg, you went all cautious on the tracks."

"Them tracks was dangerous. Coulda ripped the heck outta my undercarriage, like I said afterward. And what's wrong with my accent?"

"Please, I've seen what Eitri and Brokkr did for Thor's Goat." Ihor handed me my pint and I gulped down a bit. "For starters, they gave it front-wheel drive, probably precisely to avoid what would've happened last night if he only had rear-wheel. Plus, the car's smart—hell, it's probably smarter than he is." I chuckled. "Well, okay, my beer is probably smarter than he is. And that's just a car they threw together for somebody they don't even *like*. You expect me to believe that your *pit crew* wouldn't magic up your stock car as much as they could? Your undercarriage would've been fine, and if it wasn't, they'd have it fixed up in time for Avondale."

"Yeah, we gotta hit the road for Arizona tomorrow." He shook his head. "Look, times've changed. Don't nobody worship us no more. Hell, if it wasn't for the comic books an' the movies, we'd prob'ly have no power left at all. But those of us who did survive, we got stuff to keep us goin'. I got my racin', Eitri and Brokkr got their tinkerin' and buildin', Sigyn's got her band. I hear tell Odin took up scuba divin'."

I nodded. The Allfather had actually been an excellent diver.

Tyr took a sip of his bourbon. "As for Loki, he was always schemin'. But Thor?" He shook his head. "He ain't got much goin'. He's just—well, he's just *Thor*, y'know? Thousand years ago he was stumblin' around, drinkin', bein' an idjit, and sleepin' with any girl that'd have him, and here it is a thousand years later, and he's still drinkin', still stumblin' around bein' an idjit, and still sleepin' with any girl that'd have him. We all found us a life. He didn't." He let out a long breath. "He's my brother. Hell, I'm his *big* brother. I been around a lot longer'n he has, an' I've seen stuff that'd turn his beard white. Especially with the Allfather not around no more, I gotta look out for 'im. So yeah, I let him win the race. I figured he deserved to have somethin'." He frowned at me. "You ain't gonna tell him, are you, little lady?"

"That depends. Can you, for fuck's sake, *not* call me 'little lady'? Seriously, what is it with you guys and your stupid nicknames? My name is 'Cassie.' It's just two syllables."

Tyr threw his head back and laughed. I noticed a complete lack of drawl in the laugh.

Then he held up his glass. "You got yourself a deal, Cassie. To Thor's victory."

I held up my pint. "To being a good brother."

We clinked our glasses and each took a sip.

A crashing sound came from the front of the bar. I looked over to see that Thor had fallen over and a crowd was gathered around him.

With a sideways glance at Tyr, I asked, "I don't suppose you can take him with you to Arizona?"

"I ain't *that* good a brother."

"Too bad." I got up and headed to the front of the bar, pushing my way through the tourists who were gawking at the drunken lout who'd gone from life of the party to rug. "Okay, folks, nothing to see here. C'mon, Thor, upsy-daisy."

Thor didn't budge.

The bar was too crowded to try to carry him out. So we just left him.

For the rest of the night, people danced around him, drank around him, tripped over him, and generally had a great time while he snored on the floor of Mayor Fred's Saloon. It was a fantastic party in his honor. Probably the best party he never saw. Well, okay except for that one time—

—but that's another story.

Introduction to "Editorial Interference"

Way back in 1993, Borgo Press published *Swashbuckling Editor Stories*, edited by John Gregory Betancourt, and featuring stories of science fiction editors and their grand adventures. (No, really!) I was actually working as John's assistant at Byron Preiss Visual Publications when the book came out, and he was talking seriously about doing a followup called *Two-Fisted Writer Tales*. It never actually came together, but the notion of *TFWT* prompted the following story.

Never really had a market for it, but it did get printed twice, once in an online "magazine" called *Fedoras Literary Review*. Back in the mid-1990s the world wide web as we know it didn't really exist, but there were online bulletin boards, and I was very active on one called GEnie. On the Science Fiction Roundtable on GEnie, we had a sort of virtual baseball team of writers called the Double-Breasted Fedoras. (I still have my jersey.) At one point, the Fedoras put out a literary magazine on GEnie, which didn't last very long (and didn't have a huge readership, as this was in the very early days of online zines...), and I decided to give them my story.

Years later, when my writers group, the Circles in the Hair, decided to put out a self-titled anthology of short stories we'd all written, this was my contribution.

It isn't *really* a two-fisted writer story. In fact, writers are the victims. But the story is one that—well, let's just say that my years of experience in the 1990s as an assistant editor who did a lot of work for almost no credit seriously informed the writing of the story, and let's just leave it at that.

(By the way, Wildside Press has a limited, numbered, hardcover edition of *Swashbuckling Editor Stories* available that is signed by many of the contributors. The anthology has stories by Greg Cox, Steve Rasnic Tem, George H. Scithers, David Bischoff, Bruce Bethke, and many more. Go to www.wildsidepress.com for details.)

Editorial Interference

The whole thing started when J.T. Corlear, my boss, requested my presence in his office. When I first joined the Federal Bureau of Investigation, I thought J.T. was in his 50s, but that was fifteen years ago and he doesn't look at all different. The wispy gray hair is still thinning, but not all gone, and his face has the same number of wrinkles. The only recent change was that he's started to slowly develop jowls.

He also kept the thermostat about six degrees lower than in the rest of the office, so when I entered, I pulled my white linen jacket tight around me.

As I sat in the guest chair, he picked up a green file folder that was overstuffed with various other manila folders from off his overcrowded desk. "I got a weird one for ya, Liz," he said.

J.T. always began his assignments by saying, "I got a _____ one for ya." Whatever adjective modified "one" was generally a good barometer for how the case would go. Most of them tended to be "odd" or "simple" (I liked those) or "confusing." Occasionally, I'd get a "complicated" or a "stupid." Once I got a "silly." The worst was the one time I got "gross"; I was a vegetarian for six months after that one.

"Weird" wasn't that common—it also wasn't very descriptive, so I prompted, "Weird in what way?"

"I got eleven murders, all across the country, all'a same MO, all in the last few months. Two of 'em are kinda famous—we got a best-selling novelist and a guy who writes for one'a those cartoon series. But we also got—" he checked through one of the papers in the file "—a librarian, a bookstore manager, a financial analyst, a lawyer, a housewife, a magazine editor, an engineer, a jeweler, and an artist."

"What's the MO?"

"All of 'em were strangled in their homes by a printer cord."

"Printer cord? You mean the ribbon?"

"No, no, the cord that connects the printer to the computer."

I nodded, understanding.

He handed me the folder, which nearly broke my wrist when I tried to hold it with one hand.

"These," J.T. said, "are all the police reports. Take a look at 'em, lemme know whatcha think." I got up, hefting the folders.

I spent the rest of the day reading through police reports from all over: three from New York, three from the Los Angeles area, two from Eugene (wherever the hell *that* was—Oregon, according to the file), and the rest from places in Maryland, Iowa, and Pennsylvania.

The novelist was a guy named William Radcliffe—wrote books about elves or something. I remembered seeing a story on his death on Headline News when I went flipping around between innings of an Oriole game. As for the other guy J.T. said was "kinda famous," not only had I never heard of him, I never heard of the cartoon he won an Emmy for. But then, I don't watch all that much television, unless there's baseball on.

I kept thinking there had to be some kind of literary angle, mainly because we had two professional writers, an editor, a bookstore manager, and a librarian. Then again, they were geographically pretty far removed—and that didn't explain the lawyer, financial analyst, etc.

An odd thing: in no case was there a sign of forced entry. Whoever did this knew the victims or faked knowing them real well—or something. In any case, it looked like the victims all let their killer into their homes.

Still, it bore investigation, so J.T. assigned me a team. I sent people out to New York, L.A., Iowa, Pennsylvania, and God-help-us-Eugene to talk to families, neighbors, etc., to see if there was some kind of link among the murderers that the local cops—who weren't looking for such a connection—wouldn't have seen.

I decided to take the local one—from Gaithersburg, Maryland, a Washington D.C. suburb—myself.

This was the engineer, a woman named Julie Lee. Born Julie Park, thirty-year-old MIT graduate, married, no kids, living in a nice little house that set my teeth on edge when I arrived at 7pm the following day. I've always *hated* suburbia. Should've sent Jones, she *loved* this idyllic stuff—but then, that was why I sent her to deal with the artist from Iowa.

Her husband answered the door, a short Korean-American man with dark hair who, if the mailbox was to be believed, was named Harold Lee. He was wearing a T-shirt with fresh creases on it, so he probably just changed into it after coming home from work. "Mr. Lee, my name is Special Agent Elizabeth Cooper," I said. I held my badge up long enough for him to actually get a good look at it, then continued: "Can I come in, please? I need to ask you a few questions about your wife."

Thankfully, he didn't wince or get defensive or do any of the other things bereaved spouses tended to do when this subject came up, but simply looked resigned, nodded, and opened the door all the way.

The house looked typically suburban—living room, staircase, hallway, kitchen, all the usual accoutrements. It was kept very neat, which either spoke well of the Lees or of their housekeeper.

"Can I get you something to drink, Ms. Cooper?"

"A glass of ice water would be nice."

Lee nodded and went to the kitchen, which had one of those counters that served as a window between the kitchen and the living room. As he fetched a jug of water from the refrigerator, he said, "I'm—I'm a little confused, Ms. Cooper—why is the FBI involved in this?"

"We think there's a possibility that your wife's death is connected to several other deaths around the country."

"Really?" Lee brought a glass of water into the living room and handed it to me.

"Thank you. Several people have been recently killed in the same manner as your wife, Mr. Lee."

"That's terrible." His mouth was twitching—he seemed to be fighting down his revulsion at the whole thing.

I proceeded to ask him all the usual questions, some of which the local cops had probably already asked, all of which had boring, normal, routine answers that wound up being of no use whatsoever. I found out that Harold Lee was a translator for the Korean Consulate, and he met Julie Park when she moved down here after graduating MIT.

Frustrated, though not completely surprised, at this lack of useful information, I decided to play a hunch: "Was your wife an avid reader, Mr. Lee?"

He actually smiled at that. He had a pleasant smile that seemed to brighten his entire face. "'Avid' doesn't begin to describe it. The attic is—was Julie's library. There are over a thousand books up there. She even did a little writing—some book reviews for a local magazine, that kinda thing. She even got a short story published somewhere."

"Do you know where?"

He shook his head. "'Fraid not. I'm afraid I don't read much outside the job—and what I do read for fun is usually in Korean. Just more comfortable with it. I do know it wasn't in a magazine—it was one of those books that's a collection of short stories."

I asked one or two more questions, thanked him again for the water, then took my leave.

The rest of the gang called in with endless variations on "Nothing new here," and they all flew back and turned in their reports.

It was Johanssen's report—he was the one who went to Eugene—that got the gears turning.

For one thing, both victims—a librarian named Martine Alphonse and a bookstore manager named Jack Martin—knew each other. They were part of a local writer's group called the Square Pegs, and had even written a short story together, under the cute pseudonym "Martin Martine." They'd also published a few stories separately. According to Alphonse's roommate, they were also collaborating on a novel, which Martin's wife confirmed. They apparently wrote the same kinda stuff that William Radcliffe wrote. Oddly, though, they were killed about a month apart.

One of the things that came up was that they both had stories in a new anthology.

After that, I turned to the Iowa artist, Lisbeth Eakins. According to Jones, she was getting into writing as well, having just sold two short stories, one to a magazine, one to an anthology, for which she also provided the cover.

Then I went to Stuart's report from New York. Sure enough, the lawyer, the magazine editor, and the financial analyst all had writing careers of some sort or other. The financial analyst, a woman named Rachel Klein, had published several science fiction novels and short stories, one of which won some kind of award—according to Stuart, the award was still prominently displayed in the apartment she had shared with her daughter. Bob McElroy, the magazine editor, worked for a trade journal where one of his duties was to edit the science fiction book review column—and he'd just sold his third story somewhere, but his coworkers couldn't remember where, and his family didn't even know he wrote. The lawyer, Miriam Bury, used to write, but had come out of "retirement," according to her boyfriend, to contribute to an anthology called *Cyberminds*.

Finally! A title.

"Markowitz!" I bellowed to our office coordinator—which meant, in real terms, that he did all the scut work no one else wanted to be bothered with. Fred Markowitz was in his first year with the Bureau and gave the general impression that he wouldn't make it to his second.

"Yo," he said with his usual dearth of enthusiasm.

"I want you to go to that bookstore down the street and pick up a book called *Cyberminds*. Should be in the science fiction section. It's a collection of short stories by different people, so it'll be under 'anthologies' or something like that."

"What if they don't have it?"

I sighed. "Then go to another bookstore."

"What if *they* don't have it?"

While I admired Markowitz's desire to plan for all possible occurrences, he was starting to get on my nerves. "Markowitz, we're in Washington D.C., one of the biggest metropolises on the east coast. Somewhere in this city there is bound to be a bookstore with this book in it."

"How'm I gonna know it when I see it?"

"Well, the word 'Cyberminds' on the cover should be your first clue. Then check the table of contents, make sure one of the authors is named Miriam Bury."

Markowitz rolled his eyes and shuffled out the door.

I didn't want to pursue this until I had the anthology in hand, so I did some overdue paperwork from other cases until Markowitz came back.

It took him three hours, but he finally returned with a copy. "Guy at the store said he only ordered two copies, and this is the first one that's sold," he said as he handed me the book.

The cover was hideous, all dark and foreboding, dominated by an image of a computer screen with a malevolent face on it. Subtitled, "Tales of Artificial Intelligence," it was edited by Kevin di Zuniga and featured "All-New Stories from WILLIAM RADCLIFFE, RACHEL KLEIN, CHRISTOPHER WOLFE, and many more!"

Christopher Wolfe was the animation writer. I quickly flipped to the table of contents.

They were all there.

Martine Alphonse, Christopher Wolfe, Miriam Bury, William Radcliffe, Rachel Klein, R. McElroy, Norah Janet Zimmerman, Julie P. Lee, Jack Martin, Lisbeth Eakins, Preston G. Alewife, and B.J. Levine. Cover by Lisbeth Eakins.

I frowned. Then I double-checked the file. Then I yelled.

"Stuart! Jones! Johanssen!"

They all whipped their heads around in surprise. "What?" Jones asked urgently.

"B.J. Levine. Author, contributed to this book." I tossed the paperback across two desks towards Johanssen, who caught it unerringly. "Find this person. I don't care how you do it."

"Who is he?" Stuart asked.

"He or *she* is one of two things. Could be the next and last target of our printer cord killer."

"What's the other thing?"

"The printer cord killer."

"Ah," Stuart said.

"If I'm right, someone's picking off everyone who contributed to this book."

Johanssen stared at the cover. "God, this is ugly."

Jones went over to Johanssen's desk and looked at it. "Geez, that's Eakins's work. I saw the original at her place in Iowa."

"We should contact the publisher," I said. "They should have files on all these people."

Johanssen added, "What about this editor guy, di Zuniga? He might be a target, too."

"Or he might be the killer," Stuart said.

I thought a moment. "Johanssen, get in touch with the publisher. I want a location on both di Zuniga and Levine."

"Got it."

The publisher was called Stellar Books, an imprint of some large multinational corporation or other that had just merged with another large multinational corporation the previous week. They were located in midtown Manhattan, and, according to Johanssen, they weren't allowed to release information on authors over the phone unless they had proof that they were *really* the FBI conducting a murder investigation—after all, we could be *anybody*.

Johanssen stinks at this sort of thing. I called them back, and got a prissy-sounding secretary-type. "Stellar Books," she said, "this is Susan."

"My name is Special Agent Elizabeth Cooper, I'm conducting a murder investigation for the FBI."

"Gee, there must be a lot of you going around."

"I'm Agent Johanssen's supervisor. He just told me some bullshit story about how the people at Stellar Books are completely uninterested in assisting in a murder investigation, that they are obstructing justice, and that they are making us very suspicious of their reasons for doing so, since they are the most obvious connection linking a series of rather grisly murders. I said to Agent Johanssen, 'This is ridiculous. The people at Stellar Books would *never* do something so unutterably stupid as be completely uninterested in assisting in a murder investigation, obstructing justice, and make us very suspicious of their reasons for doing so precisely *because* they are the most obvious connection linking a series of rather grisly murders. Let me call them back.' Now then, I, as a duly authorized representative of the Federal Bureau of Investigation, do humbly request that you release to me the address and phone number of Kevin di Zuniga and B.J. Levine. If you do not do so, I will go through the hassle of flying to New York, obtaining a warrant to search the premises of your office, and getting the information, as well as the equal hassle of having you arrested for obstruction of justice."

She gave me the addresses and phone numbers of Kevin di Zuniga (he was in New Jersey) and Bethany J. Levine (right here in D.C.). She even gave me di Zuniga's FAX number and Levine's e-mail address. I thanked her kindly, and hung up. Johanssen fixed me with a bemused look. I shrugged, and said, "You have to know how to reason with these people."

Johanssen called Levine's number, and got no answer. I tried di Zuniga and got his answering machine. I left an urgent message and told him to call me immediately. I decided to call Levine myself, swearing never to let Johanssen call anyone ever again.

"What?" came a frantic voice.

"Uh, may I speak to Bethany Levine, please?"

"Oh, *God*!" The voice was nearly screaming, and I couldn't solidly place a gender yet.

"My name is Special Agent Cooper of the FBI. It's urgent that I speak to Bethany Levine."

"Well, you're gonna need a goddamn fucking psychic, Special Agent Hooper of the FBI, 'cause the little bitch is dead!" The voice was male. I figured this out around the time he hung up the phone on me.

Great.

I led a team to the Levine residence, which was an apartment building in the northwest part of town. We showed up only a few minutes after the city cops, which shocked the hell out of the detective, a short Latino gentleman with sharply receding hair, a thick mustache, and a cigarette hanging from his mouth.

"The fuck're the fibbies doin' here?" he asked

"Fibbies, that's cute," I said. "My name's Cooper." I flashed my ID.

"I'm Detective Velez. Now that we're all nice an' introduced, whyn't you answer my fuckin' question?"

"Would I be right in assuming that the victim is one Bethany J. Levine, she was strangled by the cord connecting her printer to her computer, and that her body was found by her estranged boyfriend?"

Velez's cigarette fell out of his mouth when his jaw dropped. I picked it up and handed to him with a smile. "Jesus fuckin' Christ, lady, you some kinda fuckin' psychic?" He grabbed the cigarette out of my hand, placed it in his mouth, realized that it had been on the floor, then stubbed it out.

"No, just trying to follow a pattern."

"Pattern. Jesus. Don't tell me this is part'a some fuckin' serial bullshit."

"All right, I won't tell you. Where's the boyfriend?"

"Inna next room. You can't talk to him yet."

I scowled. "Why not?"

"'Cause he's givin' us his fuckin' statement, that's why you can't fuckin' talk to him, okay? Lemme get my statement, and take my fingerprints, and do all that other shit I gotta do that's gonna get ignored 'cause you fuckin' fibbies're gonna step all over my investigation and pull jurisdictional bullshit on me. That's why. Okay?"

I shrugged. "Fine. Let me know when you're done with him."

"And keep your fuckin' feds outta my people's fuckin' faces. Okay?"

I repeated, "Fine."

Eventually, I got to talk to the boyfriend, named Scott O'Sullivan. He was even more obnoxious than he had been on the phone, and competed with Velez for the Gold Medal in Most Uses of the Word "Fucking" in a Conversation. He was coming to the apartment to try to make up with Beth, with whom he'd had a fight. He found her dead on the love seat, strangled with printer cord. It turned out that when Johanssen called, he was calling the police and, for obvious reasons, ignored the call-waiting beep.

Jones was pocketing her cellular when she came up to me after I finished with O'Sullivan. "Just got a call from Markowitz. That di Zuniga guy called back. Said he's scared shitless. Apparently, someone's been makin' threats on his life. Local cops won't listen to him when he says he needs protection."

I let out a breath. "All right, get back to the office and get in touch with his local cops. I want a round-the-clock on this guy. And have Markowitz get us a flight up to Newark tonight. I want you and Stuart with me."

"Got it."

When I got back to the office, I had Johanssen run a check on every employee of Stellar Books and find out what he or she had been doing over the past four months. Then Stuart, Jones, and I flew to Newark, where a company car was waiting for us. We high-tailed it up the New Jersey Turnpike and across to the editor's West Orange house, where several local cops were already waiting for us. I had a bad feeling about this; in my experience, suburban cops were usually good for escorting "undesirables" out of the neighborhood, stopping speeding cars, and little else.

Di Zuniga, a short bald man with a beard who was in near-constant motion at all times, refused to leave the house, which certainly made it easier to protect him. He was completely unhelpful regarding who might be responsible for the murders.

"You must understand, Agent Copper," he said (this was his third variation on my last name since my arrival the night before), "I'm one of the most respected individuals in my chosen field. When readers see my name on a book, they know it's a quality anthology. When authors hear I am soliciting stories for a book, they flock because they know it will be a project worthy of their talents. I can't imagine *anyone* who would want to *kill* everyone involved with an anthology that *I* edited. It's simply inconceivable!"

I had checked his spacious home over fairly thoroughly, including an entire room full of books he was involved in—often several copies of each, and also different editions of the same book. He'd obviously been doing this for some time.

"The books in that back room," I said. "Are they arranged chronologically?"

"Yes, why?" he asked, getting up after having sat down for a full ten seconds.

"I notice that all the most recent books are from Stellar."

"Yes, I signed an exclusive deal with Stellar to edit six anthologies for them. *Cyberminds* was the last. Frankly, they'll probably be glad that it was, given the circumstances. When this gets out—"

"Is there anyone at Stellar who might be responsible?"

"I doubt it. You must understand, Agent Hooper, I hardly worked with anyone there. I mean, I spoke often with Peter

Blake, the publisher, and that assistant fellow who did all my office coordinating, but that's it. I did most of the work out of my home office here."

Another night passed, and nothing happened. Johanssen called in to say that the checks on Stellar employees turned up negative. Only two of them were out of town during any of the murders, and they weren't anywhere near the murder victims.

In the morning, I went to New York to talk with the good people at Stellar Books.

I forgot what a nightmare it was driving in midtown Manhattan. Stellar was located on Sixth Avenue in the 50s. Both Sixth and all the side streets are no-standing zones during the day. Ordinarily I could park a FBI vehicle there anyhow, but Sixth Avenue was being repaved, so there was literally nowhere to put the car on Sixth, and despite the illegality, all the spots on the side streets seemed to be taken.

Eventually I put the car on 56th, and walked to Sixth in a foul mood. When I'm in a foul mood, I tend to analyze things. But this case was defying analysis—or maybe I was in *too* foul a mood. I wasn't even sure why I was checking into Stellar personally, since they were all clean.

Then again, maybe someone there wanted all the contributors killed as a way of drumming up sales. If they'd invested a lot of money in the book—

No, that didn't wash. For one thing, if no one there did it, it means they would've had to have hired someone, and these hits were *not* professional. A pro wouldn't leave so obvious a link among the victims. Besides which, this was the final book in a six-book contract; I could see going to the effort if it was the first and sales stunk, but why bother when there wouldn't be any more books anyhow?

Still, it couldn't hurt to check them out personally—and the alternative of spending the day with Mr. Hyperactive didn't appeal.

Of course, it was possible that di Zuniga was the killer. But he seemed too legitimately spooked by this whole thing. Unless it was an act. Well, if any evidence to support that cropped up, he'd be easy to arrest...

Peter Blake, publisher of Stellar Books, interrupted a meeting to talk to me, which was the least he could do, or so he said.

"I must admit, Agent Cooper, I'm very distressed by this whole business. I had no idea our authors were being murdered. This sort of thing—it's just *appalling*."

"Mr. Blake, do you know of any of your employers who might have had reason to want these authors dead?"

"Not really."

"Did any of them hold a grudge against Mr. di Zuniga, and were perhaps using this as a way to get back at him?"

"I doubt it. I was the only person who dealt directly with him. The book's publicity rep might've spoken to him once or twice, but that's it."

Something clicked. "Mr. di Zuniga said the only people he dealt with here were you and an assistant who did his office coordinating."

"Oh, yes, well, Tony did deal with him quite a bit." At my questioning stare, he added, "Anthony Pascazzi. He was an associate editor here for a couple of years."

"But not anymore?"

"No, he resigned about three or four months ago. Said the pressure was too much for him. A pity, he was a decent editor—had a lot of potential."

I asked Blake a few more pointless questions, then went to his secretary, Susan McElhatton, the one I'd intimidated two days earlier. "Can you give me anything on a former employee named Anthony Pascazzi?"

"Uh, when did he stop working here?"

"Four months ago or so."

"Well, I've only been here for a few weeks. Patricia would be able to help you—she's been here *forever*."

I found Patricia Goldblume, the office manager, on the phone. After several minutes, she got off and snappishly asked, "Yes?"

"Ms. Goldblume, I'm Special Agent Cooper of the FBI. I'm investiga—"

"Yes, yes, I know who you are. What is it, I'm busy?"

After the eager-to-please Peter Blake, this was like ice water in the face. "It's a murder investigation, Ms. Goldblume. I need to know how I can find a former employee of this company, an associate editor named Anthony Pascazzi."

"That's privileged information, Agent Cooper. And even if it wasn't, I'm far too busy—"

"I already went through this once with Ms. McElhatton. Now I *can* go to the trouble of obtaining a court order to search the premises and having you arrested for obstruction of justice. It's up to you to decide which one will take less of your precious time."

"I don't like your tone, Agent Cooper, and I don't appreciate being bullied. How would your superiors feel if I told them you were engaging in such tactics?"

"You're welcome to report me, Ms. Goldblume, though I suspect that would take even more of that time you're trying so hard to keep a rein on, since you'll be asked to fly to Washington to testify at my disciplinary hearing." I ran my hand through my curly blonde hair. "Look, I'm trying to catch a serial killer, Ms. Goldblume. That's the kind of thing that strains my politeness muscles. Now will you give me a way of getting in touch with Anthony Pascazzi or not?"

She gave me a way. She even let me use one of the office phones to try calling him. Unfortunately, the phone number had been disconnected. This didn't encourage me.

He also had an e-mail address. When I got back to di Zuniga's, I called the guy in our office who patrols the various computer networks. I identified the online service Pascazzi used and asked if his e-mail address rang any bells.

"Uh, lemme check." I heard the clicking of a keyboard. "Uh, okay, this guy's pretty active on the skiffy BB."

"The what?"

"Sorry, the science fiction board. But he hasn't been on much the last few months."

Of course, he wouldn't be if he was travelling across the country killing people.

Stuart and Jones went to Pascazzi's last known address to find it occupied by two men (a couple, apparently), who'd been living there for four months. They didn't know who had it last, though one complained that whoever he was, he didn't do anything about the roach problem.

I was about to have them check hotels when one of the West Orange cops told me that there was a light blue Pinto with New York plates that had been parked near the house several times for an hour or so at a time each of the last couple of days. No one had seen anyone get in or out. He even copied down the license plate number. He added, "I wouldn't've thought much about it, ma'am, except, uh, we don't get a lot of Pintos 'round here."

I pointed out that no one does—there's few of that brand of Ford around these days—and commended him on his observation. That'll teach me to stereotype suburban cops.

The license plate went with a car reported as stolen by the NYPD, as it was the one piece of property belonging to Robert McElroy that was missing when he was found murdered.

Sure enough, it turned up the next day, but this time only for a moment. I couldn't get a good look at the driver from where I was observing—West Orange didn't get enough traffic for me to stay close without him noticing. When he drove off, I followed, Stuart and Jones in the car with me. He led us to a condo complex, finally settling in one of the houses (identical to all the other houses in the row) toward the rear of the complex.

When we burst in, guns blazing, a 5'8" man in his twenties with longish brown hair and wearing wire-rim glasses laughed and said, "Well, it's about fucking *time* you people showed up!"

I straightened. "Excuse me?"

"My next step was going to be a neon sign on the car that said, 'Hey, the killer's in here!'"

"You *wanted* us to catch you?"

He laughed again. "Of course I did! Christ, why do you think I left so obvious a trail? Not that it went right. I was expecting a huge media event—'Printer Cord Killer Strikes Again!' 'Next *Cyberminds* Author Lives In Fear Of Being Next Victim.' Instead, I got jackshit."

Stuart frowned. "'Next Author'?"

Pascazzi rolled his eyes. "Christ all-fucking-mighty, you didn't even get that, did you?" At our quizzical glances, he said, "I killed them all in the order that their story appeared in the anthology!" I frowned, then realized he was right. That was why Alphonse and Martin were killed so far apart despite both living in Eugene, and why Levine was killed last. "Figures—once again I work my ass off to accomplish something and no one notices."

"Is that what this was all about?" I asked. "Getting noticed?"

"Not just noticed—recognized! Jesus, you think di Zuniga's responsible for those books? All he did was call Bill Radcliffe and ask him to send in a story. *I* was the one who got Chris Wolfe and Rachel Klein, *I* was the one who got Miriam Bury out of retirement to write a story for the book, *I* tracked all the others down, *I* rejected the stories that sucked worms—including every single one that Kevin goddamn di Zuniga sent me from his idiot friends with a note saying, 'Is this any good? Let me know.' *I* line edited, *I* pitched the book at sales conference, *I* made sure publicity sent review copies to all the right places, *I* did *all of that!* And for *all* this, *all* I got was my name in with four other people in the 'special thanks to' part of the book—and the only reason I got *that* was because I did the 'special thanks to' part, just like I did every other fucking thing for that goddamn book.

"So what happens? All the reviews say 'Kevin di Zuniga this' and 'Kevin di Zuniga that' and 'Isn't Kevin di Zuniga a genius?' and 'Another winner from Kevin di Zuniga—this is his best book in *years!*' and *it's all because of me!*"

Pascazzi had been gesticulating madly throughout his diatribe. He finally put his arms down, and I slapped the handcuffs on him. "Read him his rights, Jones."

I walked out of the house—which I later found out belonged to a colleague of Pascazzi's who was letting him housesit until he found a new place in New York, and who was unaware of his friend's criminality—and sighed. Here I was trying to ascribe a financial motive or a lunatic motive, and it was just a guy who wanted credit where it was due.

A little more investigation revealed that Tony Pascazzi had done a lot of travelling in the four months since he left Stellar, and it all matched up with the murders. He'd drained his savings account doing it, but he was obviously a man with a mission. He had no trouble gaining ingress, since all he had to do was knock on the door, say, "Hi, I'm your editor on *Cyberminds*, I was in town, thought I'd drop by," and he was in.

Jones mused at one point what he would've done if one of them worked on a typewriter.

The case was a jurisdictional nightmare, but ultimately it was tried in New York, since Pascazzi was still officially a New York City resident, as were three of the victims. The best moment of the trial was when di Zuniga testified, and almost got Pascazzi acquitted. We tried to puzzle out what the Assistant District Attorney was thinking letting di Zuniga anywhere near the stand, since he was such a pathetic witness. He kept carrying on about how he knew Pascazzi was trouble the moment he was assigned to coordinate *Cyberminds*, and how he knew something was wrong with him, and he encouraged Blake to have him fired, though he resigned instead. When Pascazzi's lawyer ripped into him, I almost smiled: as a hostile witness, di Zuniga buckled, admitting that yes, Pascazzi did much of the work, and no, he didn't *really* try to get him fired, and no, di Zuniga in fact couldn't remember his name half the time, and no, Pascazzi didn't get much credit, but that was just the way the industry worked.

By the time the lawyer was finished, the jury was almost ready to strangle di Zuniga with a printer cord themselves.

After that, though, things went as expected. Once the show was over, the piles of physical evidence against Pascazzi pretty much did the trick. Not that this surprised anyone. Indeed, after leaving such a large trail, Stuart and Jones both expressed surprise when he pleaded not guilty. I replied, "This whole thing was orchestrated to get him recognized for what he did, and even that failed. So he pleads not guilty, he gets a trial that the entire publishing industry and everyone who watches Court TV will know and talk about. He finally got his credit."

J.T. was right. This *was* a weird one.

Introduction to "Sunday in the Park with Spot"

This short story came about entirely due to my (earned) reputation for writing very fast. One of the reasons why I've been able to thrive as a writer of media tie-ins is due to my ability to hit deadlines, even when those deadlines are insane. I wrote *Sleepy Hollow: Children of the Revolution* in two months, I wrote *Goblin Precinct* in one month, I wrote *Gene Roddenberry's Andromeda: Destruction of Illusions* and *Command and Conquer: Tiberium Wars* each in three weeks, and I wrote the novelization of *Serenity* in two-and-a-half weeks.

So when Jean Rabe and Brian Thomsen found themselves short on word count for their *Furry Fantastic* anthology that was being published in 2006 and needed a story very very fast, Jean called me. I gave her this story. (This also led to Jean asking me to contribute to her next anthology, *Pandora's Closet*, for which I wrote the *Dragon Precinct* story "A Clean Getaway," which can be found both in that anthology and in *Tales from Dragon Precinct*.)

Sunday in the Park with Spot

"Can I hear a story? Please?"

"All right—*one* story, and that's it. Then you must sleep."

"Just one?"

"Yes, just one—and be thankful for that."

"But— Okay, just one, then."

"You promise to go right to sleep after that?"

"Yes, ma'am."

"Good. In that case, I will tell you a story that takes place in a mythical land called 'The Bronx.'"

"Where's the Bronx?"

"It's in a magical city known as New York. The Bronx is the northernmost region of that fair city, populated by a good portion of the Folk, as well as many other strange beings—fish and fowl, mammal and invertebrate. Perhaps the most baffling are the ones called humans. They are charming, peculiar creatures, who believe themselves to be the only intelligent people in the world when they in fact have very little to do with the day-to-day reality."

"Why do they think that?"

"That is one of the great mysteries. However, they do perform several useful functions—they provide food and shelter for many of the Folk, and they also have produced some remarkable healers. In particular, they have done much to aid the cat and dog population."

"Cats make sense, but why dogs?"

"That is another of the great mysteries, but this one has a likely solution: dogs are fiercely loyal. Humans tend to reward such behavior."

"But cats aren't loyal to *anything*."

"True, but cats treat those who provide for them well. Humans are not particularly bright specimens, and they probably mistake that kind treatment for the same loyalty they observe in dogs."

"That makes sense."

"Now please, don't interrupt anymore."

"Sorry."

"Our story takes us to one house in a neighborhood in the Bronx known as Riverdale. Many Folk lived in this region, including the Chief Chaos Wrangler, Mittens. On one fine Sunday afternoon—a day when most humans remain at home to care for their domiciles and tend to the needs of the Folk—Mittens received a sign.

"Now Chaos Wranglers, you must understand, cannot always predict when they will need to ply their trade. By its very nature, Chaos is random and indefinable, and so the times when it must be curtailed can come at the most inconvenient moments.

"On this day, Mittens found himself with the usual indicator that there would be a shift in the Chaotic Winds—an itch behind his left ear—and that he would need to move quickly. The first thing he had to do was confirm the shift by tracing the sigils.

"Naturally, Mittens's humans did not understand this behavior. They were a pair who had mated, male and female, named Bob and Sue."

"Those are really weird names. So's Mittens, actually."

"Humans have very bizarre customs regarding nomenclature. Unfortunately, the rules of hospitality state that the one providing shelter also provides the names for those who dwell under that shelter—no matter how ridiculous those names might be. So it has always been."

"That's a silly rule."

"What did I say about interruptions? Especially foolish ones."

"You didn't say anything about foolish ones."

"But I did tell you not to interrupt. Now be silent.

"Sue saw that Mittens was tracing the sigils, but humans are not terrifically bright creatures, and so she said, 'Oh, Mittens, what's gotten into you *this* time?'

"From another room, Bob said, 'What's the little guy doing now, sweetie?'

"'Just his usual gadding about. I swear, I don't know what gets into that cat sometimes.'

"'You did feed him, right?'

"In a long-suffering tone, Sue said, '*Yes*, dear, of *course* I fed him.'

"'Just checking. You want me to take out the pooch?'"

"What's a pooch?"

"If you stopped interrupting, I'd tell you. 'Pooch' is a human term for a dog. You see, Bob and Sue sheltered a dog as well as a cat. While Mittens lived inside their abode, their dog, who was called Spot, spent most of his time in the outdoor expanse behind their shelter. He had his own small shelter, which Sue had constructed for him. The humans, whatever their other failings, are fine craftspeople.

"In response to Bob's question, Sue said, 'Let me give him his food, first, then you can take him out.'

"'Good—that gives me time for a shower.'

"Before you interrupt again, I will explain—a shower is something else the humans have built. It is a device they use to groom themselves by pouring water on their persons."

"Pouring water? That's icky! Why do that on purpose?"

"It is yet another mystery about humans. May I continue without interruption?"

"Sorry."

"Sue poured food into the receptacle designated for Spot. In his shelter behind the abode, Spot heard the distinctive clank of the dry food against the metal of the receptacle and immediately forgot whatever he was doing and ran for the abode, with thoughts only of food dancing in his head.

"Meanwhile, Mittens had been paying very close attention to the exchange between Sue and Bob even as he collated the data from his tracing of the sigils. The news that Bob was planning to take Spot out heartened Mittens, as it meant he himself would not need to sneak out. Mittens had clandestinely left the shelter a few times, and it only served to worry the humans unnecessarily. They tended to obsess over Mittens's safety when he wasn't in their domicile—as if cats could not survive on their own away from their humans. Still, Mittens knew that Bob and Sue's hearts were in the right place, misguided though their fears might be, and he was loath to put them in such a position.

"Spot would make that unnecessary. Though there were attendant risks in trusting a dog.

"After Spot ran in and shoved his face into his receptacle—dogs have *no* sense of finesse when it comes to matters culinary; it's rather embarrassing, really—Mittens finished grooming himself and waited for Sue to finish patting Spot on the head and saying, 'Good dog, Spot.' Humans tend to praise Folk for doing what comes naturally for some odd reason.

"Once Sue left, Mittens approached Spot while the latter was gorging himself. 'I have a task for you,' the cat said.

"The dog looked up from his food. 'A job? I like jobs. Jobs are fun. Thank you for trusting me with a job! What's the job mean? What do I do? When do I do it?'

"'I will tell you,' Mittens said patiently. 'Bob will be taking you to the park for a run.'

"'A run? I love runs! Runs are great fun! I get to run this way and that, and sometimes if I'm really lucky, I get to chase a stick or a ball! I love doing that!'

"'Yes, and you should enjoy it as much as you want—especially as it will make Bob happy as well.'

"'You think so?' Spot seemed thrilled by the very idea. 'That'd be great!'

"'However, you must do something else.'

"Spot was confused for a moment, then said, 'Right! The job! I remember now, you want me to do a job!' Spot then realized he was parched and padded over to the water dish. After lapping up some water, he turned back to Mittens. 'I will do this job for you.'

"With that he started to walk off, but Mittens stepped in front of the dog before he could go out the door. 'I haven't told you the job yet, Spot.'

"'Oh, right! I'll need that, won't I? Okay, tell me what the job is so I can do it for you.'

"Grateful that he now had Spot's undivided attention, Mittens explained the job. 'When Bob takes you to the park, you must find the squirrel named Tail-Drop.'"

"That's a different name. Are the squirrels' humans smarter?"

"I'm afraid not. For whatever reason, humans do not shelter squirrels. They are self-sheltering by nature, and also tend to prefer the outdoors more often than not. As a result, they choose their own names. However, it also makes them useful helpmeets for the Chaos Wranglers.

"Mittens explained to Spot: 'You must find Tail-Drop and then tell her to trace the Order Sigil at the World Tree at precisely the time of sunset.'

"'Order Sigil, World Tree, sunset. Got it. Won't be any problem. I'll do just what you ask, Mittens, youbetcha.'

"'There's one important thing.' Mittens hesitated then, because too much information might be rough on the dog, but he needed to know this. 'The information can be passed on to any gray squirrel you meet, in case you don't find Tail-Drop. But it's very important that you do *not* share this with the black squirrel.'

"'Not the black squirrel.' Spot nodded. 'No problem. I'll do it. Youbetcha.'

"Mittens was concerned, but Spot had a good heart and a noble soul. He would do the right thing.

"When Spot was done eating, and after Bob had altered his protective covering, he attached a tether to Spot's collar and took him out of the abode to a grassland that the humans had named Ewen Park."

"Why a tether?"

"More of that worrying that humans indulge in so much. They fear that their Folk will be endangered if they are not physically linked. Bob, however, only kept the tether on until they arrived at Ewen Park. This grassland has several sections, one of which is bordered by fences and intended for dogs to roam free. Most humans don't have wide-open spaces for dogs to run in, and they are Folk who enjoy such, so some humans will bring their dogs to such grasslands.

"For a while, Spot was happy to run after a stick that Bob would toss across the grassland, intending for Spot to retrieve it. And this action made Spot happy, as Bob was happy, and he got to run free.

"After the fifth time he retrieved the stick, the sight of a squirrel running across reminded Spot that he had a job to do. Unfortuntely, Spot found he couldn't remember the specifics, beyond the fact that he had to talk to a squirrel.

"He thought back to his conversation with Mittens even as he ran to fetch the stick another time. For sure, he knew he had to tell a squirrel to trace the sigils for Order at the World Tree. Spot had no idea which one *was* the World Tree, but he also knew that such matters were not for dogs. That was the type of thing cats worried about—dogs had much more important jobs, like fetching sticks and running in circles.

"Finally, Spot remembered something very important—the black squirrel. Spot didn't know the squirrel's name, but there was only one black squirrel that made its home in Ewen Park, and Spot now knew with complete certainty that the black squirrel was the one he had to talk to. Mittens had made a very special point of it.

"Unfortunately, the black squirrel was nowhere to be found. Spot kept searching every time he fetched the stick, but no black squirrel. Plenty of gray ones—including one who looked familiar, though Spot couldn't for the life of him remember who it was—but no sign of the black.

"Bob started talking to another human by the name of Louie, who sheltered Buford and Cello. Spot always liked Buford, who was big and friendly and loud. Cello was small and annoying, though, and Spot didn't like him very much.

"Spot started thinking about how much he liked Buford and didn't like Cello, until he caught sight of a pigeon, flying down toward the benches where humans sometimes sat and threw food to the ground. Although Spot found pigeons to be vile Folk, he also knew that they saw things nobody else did from the air. So he went over to one pigeon and asked her, 'Have you seen the black squirrel?'

"The pigeon gazed up at him with confusion. 'What are you talking about, Spot? Why do you want to talk to Fan-Tail?'

"Spot remembered that that was the black squirrel's name, and that he never liked that name. But he never liked Mittens as a name, either. To answer the pigeon's question, Spot said, 'Mittens told me to!'

"'I doubt that very much,' the pigeon said, cooing with laughter.

"'He did too! Mittens was very specific! He told me to tell Fan-Tail to trace the Order Tree in the Sigils World! Or, rather, the Order Sigils in the World Tree!'

"Cautiously, because she didn't want to anger the dog that was so much bigger than her, the pigeon said, 'I doubt that very much, Spot. Mittens is the Chaos Wrangler. Fan-Tail is an agent of Chaos. He is absolutely the wrong person to give this information to.'

"'Hmph.' Spot looked down his muzzle at the pigeon. 'That shows what *you* know, you stupid pigeon. Mittens was very precise, and made sure to mention Fan-Tail *by name.*' Spot knew that was a slight fib, as Mittens hadn't given the black squirrel's name, but the pigeon didn't need to know that. She just needed to tell Spot where Fan-Tail *was.*

"But the pigeon was much smarter than the dog."

"Wouldn't take a lot."

"You'd been doing so well with the interruptions."

"Sorry, but the dog is just so *dumb.*"

"It's not the dog's fault. It is in their nature to be easily distracted. Still, Spot was Mittens's best option, despite the risks. After all, time was of the essence. It was already midafternoon, and if Tail-Drop didn't trace the Order Sigils in the World Tree, the consequences would be very dire indeed.

"In any event, the pigeon was smarter than the dog, but the dog didn't appreciate that. Pigeons are not among the birds sheltered by humans."

"Why would anybody shelter a *bird*?"

"Oh, plenty of humans do. It's another of their mysteries—they shelter beings whose purpose is to fly through the air and then put them in cages so they cannot roam free. But pigeons, for whatever reason, are not among those they so imprison. In fact, most humans view them as necessary evils, not appreciating their value as scouts and observers among the Folk. They are always watching, and when necessary marking those items or people that warrant further attention from the Folk."

"So then what happened? Did the dog find the black squirrel?"

"Sadly, yes. Though the pigeon did everything she could to dissuade him, Spot was convinced that Fan-Tail was the squirrel he needed to talk to rather than the one he should avoid. So when he caught sight of the black squirrel, he ran to him as fast as his paws could take him.

"Bob was engaged in his conversation with Lou and did not notice Spot's bolting. The pigeon took matters into her own wings by flying close to Bob's head, which distracted the human and enabled him to observe Spot running away from the fenced area and down toward the paved pathway that humans use to walk through the park."

"Why would anyone pave a park? Or is that another one of those human mysteries?"

"Are you continuing to ask ridiculous questions in order to avoid sleep?"

"No! Honest, no! Is it just that humans don't make sense?"

"Yes. Humans are incomprehensible and not very bright. It's usually best to simply accept the offerings they provide and otherwise try to ignore them.

"Now then, Spot had sighted Fan-Tail and so ran toward him. The black squirrel was surprised—he was usually shunned by the canine population, but this one was galumphing toward him with enthusiasm usually reserved for retrieving a round ball thrown by a human. Fan-Tail twitched his nose in anticipation. He saw one of two possibilities: The first was that the dog had switched sides and wanted to help Fan-Tail. The second, and more likely, was that the dog had made a terrible mistake.

"'Hello! You're Fan-Tail, right? Aren't'cha? I hope so! I've got something I need to tell you!'

"'Yes, that's me,' Fan-Tail said. 'I'm that squirrel. Yes, I am. Please go ahead. Tell me. Go on.'

"'This is *really* important! I've got a message for you, and it's from *Mittens*, the Chaos Wrangler.'

"The black squirrel's nose twitched again. It was definitely option number two: Mittens would never send an emissary to talk to Fan-Tail. They were mortal enemies, serving opposite masters. The black squirrel was on the side of chaos, after all. He assured Spot, 'I'm listening. Go ahead. Tell me. I'm rapt.'

"Spot paused a second. He knew this was very important to Mittens, and he hated the idea of letting anyone down, so he wanted to make sure he got the message *exactly* right. 'Okay, here it is—you need to go to the World Tree and trace the Otter Sigils.'

"Fan-Tail managed to resist the urge to rub his claws together and bob his tail up and down. It wouldn't do for this dog, regardless of how dim he seemed, to be aware of just how spectacularly he had screwed up. 'World Tree. Otter Sigils. Good. When?'

"That brought Spot up short. 'When?'

"'Yes,' the squirrel said. 'When? Need to know. Tell me. When?'

"Spot panicked. He couldn't remember that part. Most of it, he remembered. He remembered that Mittens told him to tell the black squirrel about the sigils and the World Tree and that he had to fetch the stick every time Bob threw it and that he was hungry again. He remembered all of that. But when had fallen right out of his head.

"Just then, Bob cried out, 'Spot! What're you doing over there? C'mon, boy, we gotta get home before it gets dark!'

"Those words brought it home for Spot. 'Midnight! I remember now, Mittens specifically said that at the precise moment of total darkness—right at midnight. That's it.'

"This time, Fan-Tail didn't bother stopping himself from rubbing his claws together. The stupid dog had played right into his hands. Obviously, the Chaos Wrangler had divined the black squirrel's spellcasting tomorrow morning, and planned to counter it at midnight with the Otter Sigils. Fan-Tail would simply go to the World Tree at midnight and trace the sigils himself. As an agent of chaos, the sigils would have a much different effect if he traced them than they would from one of those annoying gray squirrels."

"There are really Otter Sigils?"

"Of course. Why do you think that otters swim in such precise patterns?"

"Then how can the black squirrel trace them at a tree?"

"If you stop interrupting, you'll find out."

"I'm sorry."

"Now then—Bob put the tether back on Spot when he caught up to the dog, and the pair of them went back to Bob and Sue's shelter. Spot was barking happily, thrilled that he had fulfilled his mission."

"But he didn't! I'm sorry to interrupt again, but Spot *didn't* fulfill his mission! He helped Chaos win!"

"What have I told you about judging a story before hearing its end?"

"That isn't the end of the story?"

"No. You see, Mittens is no fool. One does not become Chaos Wrangler without learning a few tricks, and being aware of your surroundings. You see, what Mittens saw was that Fan-Tail had planned to cast a spell that would bring chaos into the Bronx—and the Bronx has enough of that as it is."

"If it was so dangerous, then why entrust the dog to convey so critical a message?"

"Because the message was not as critical as Spot was lead to believe. When Bob brought Spot back, the dog immediately found Mittens and started running around the cat, encircling him several times. 'I did it! I did it, I did it, I did it! I told that black squirrel exactly what to do, *just* like you asked! He'll be at the World Tree at midnight tracing the Otter Sigils!'

"Mittens meowed affectionately, and said, 'Well done.'"

"But it wasn't well done! It was all wrong! Dogs are stupid!"

"Yes, dogs are. They mean well, but they are forgetful and easily distracted, and tend to mangle what they've been given. Which was exactly why Mittens gave the instructions to Spot that he did, with special mention of Fan-Tail—he knew that the dog would muck it up. That Spot used Otter Sigils instead of Order Sigils made the jest even greater, because the only way to re-create Otter Sigils on land is to writhe in the dirt, an amusing visual image that Mittens would treasure."

"So Spot was *supposed* to tell the black squirrel instead of the gray one?"

"Not necessarily. If he got it right, no harm would be done. If Tail-Drop did trace the Order Sigils on the World Tree at sunset—or at midnight, for that matter—it would only strengthen the counterspell that Mittens himself was going to cast at dawn to stop Fan-Tail. But now the black squirrel would be distracted by Spot's news, and be even easier for Mittens to defeat."

"Mittens is a very clever cat."

"He has to be in order to be a proper Chaos Wrangler. So that is how Mittens was able to use Spot to stop Fan-Tail from bringing more chaos into the world."

"What about the pigeon?"

"What?"

"The pigeon? What happened to her?"

"Oh, eventually, Mittens was able to explain to her what was going on. The pigeon was not pleased that she had gone to all that effort for nothing, but Mittens assured her that her objections to Spot only reinforced Spot's determination to do the right thing—that is to say, the *wrong* thing, by talking to the black squirrel. That mollified the pigeon, and she continued to do her job of scouting and observing and marking those things that warranted attention.

"And that ends the story. The sun's all the way up, so it's time for you to wash up and go to sleep. Make sure you groom between each one of your claws before going to bed."

"I will. Thank you for the story!"

"You're welcome, little kitten."

Introduction to "Wild Bill Got Shot"

Back in 2004, the World Science Fiction Convention was in Boston, Massachusetts. One of the program events was called "Two Beers and a Story," and it was conceived by Laura Anne Gilman and the late Jay Lake. It included Laura Anne and Jay, myself, and David Levine and Janna Silverstein. It involved each of us sitting in the bar, along with a big audience, being given a pint of beer, opening our laptops, and writing a story in the time it took us to drink that pint as well as a second. Folks in the audience were randomly shouting, "DRINK!" and we had to partake of the beer when that happened.

In the end, we each read our stories. They were all pretty entertaining. I honestly don't recall now, with the distance of more than a decade, whether or not David, Janna, Laura Anne, or Jay did anything with their stories. I certainly know that mine languished on the ol' hard drive until now.

Prior to the publication of *Without a License*, the only people who "read" this story were the people to whom I recited it at "Two Beers and a Story" in a Boston hotel in 2004. All I can say in my defense was that I was drinking (and also that I'd been watching a lot of the HBO show *Deadwood* at the time...).

Wild Bill Got Shot

"I was there when Wild Bill got shot."

"Shut up and deal, wouldja?"

"I am dealin'. I'm just sayin' that I was there when Wild Bill got shot."

"I been playin' poker in this here bar for the last year. If all the folks that said they was there when Wild Bill got shot actually *was* there when Wild Bill got shot, you'd have enough to fill up the entire Montana territory."

"You callin' me a liar, Jay?"

"I'm callin' you a man who's doin' a fair piece'a talkin' and a damn sight less dealin'."

"Fine, fine. The game's five-card draw. Jacks'r better t'open."

"Good."

"Want proof that I was there?"

"Only if'n you can do it while dealin' the damn cards."

"I reckon I can walk an' chew gum at the same time."

"I'd like to see some proof'a that."

"Hang on a spell—anyone openin'?"

"Nope."

"Nope."

"I'm in for twenty."

"Call."

"Call."

"I been with two-nickel whores that got more life'n this damn hand. Fold."

"Fold."

"I'm in."

"So I was in Deadwood. Now mind you, this was back in the days before there was law in Deadwood. See, them injuns had it as their land an'—"

"I want two."

"I'm tellin' a story."

"Thought you could walk'n chew gum at the same time, there, Al."

"Maybe, but I'm gettin' to the part where I provide the background. Scene-settin', that's what the dime-novel boys call it."

"Al, I'm fair to convinced you can't even read, much less would know a dime-novel boy if'n he bit you."

"'Sides, you think we give a good goddamn 'bout Deadwood, Mississippi?"

"Well, Deadwood's in the Dakota Territories, f'r one."

"You gonna let me tell m'damn story?"

"I'm willin' to throw in my entire stake if'n you don't."

"I'm just waitin' for m'damn two cards."

"Here you go. Anyhow, them injuns was given the Dakotas by treaty—but then Custer found gold. Everybody and his damn brother was harin' off to Deadwood—so, since they couldn't break the treaty with the injuns, they made Deadwood lawless."

"I'll take three, an' wish I'd known about Deadwood back then. I'd'a been whorin' 'till the cows come home."

"Y'idjit, they still had money."

"One for me."

"None for me."

"Y'mean, you had to *pay* for whores? What's the damn point'a bein' lawless if'n you gotta *pay*?"

"Trent, you opened."

"Check."

"Check."

"Twenty."

"Hell with that—I'm out."

"Call."

"Anyhow, Wild Bill come into town. Everybody was wonderin' what all he was doin' there. We all figured he'd be prospectin', but he never commenced to buyin' no equipment. 'Stead, he kept playin' poker an' losin' each time. Coulda opened a new bar with the credit they was extendin' 'im. Jack McCall, now he kept—"

"Dammit all, Al, we *know* Jack McCall done killed Wild Bill, an' I'm in with twenty an' twenty more."

"Hell, I fold."

"Jay?"

"I'm thinkin'."

"That explains the wood-burnin' smell."

"While Jay's thinkin', I'm gonna keep tellin' my story. See, Jack played goin' on fifty games with Wild Bill."

"I never heard that."

"'Course not. Didn't nobody talk 'bout that, just talkin' 'bout how Jack killed Wild Bill 'cause Wild Bill done killed his brother. But what I gotta be askin' myself is why Jack was playin' so many of those games with a man who killed his brother."

"An' what I gotta be askin' myself is when Jay's gonna tell us his damn bet."

"I fold."

"Coulda done *that* five minutes ago, an' we wouldn't have to listen to Al's damn story."

"Got me a straight."

"God-*dammit.*"

"Take the damn money."

"See what interests me is why Jack decided t'kill Wild Bill."

"Thought it was because Wild Bill killed his brother, an' let someone else deal the damn cards."

"Five-card."

"See, Jack was playin' all them games, but never once said nothin' to Wild Bill. Sometimes he won, sometimes Wild Bill won, but nothin' really happened. Then, all of a sudden, one day, outta the damn blue—"

"I can't open."

"Me neither."

"Nope."

"Nope."

"—outta the *damn* blue, Jack comes in an' shoots Wild Bill in the head. An' what's *real—*"

"You gonna open or flap y'damn gums, Al?"

"I'm openin' with fifty, an' what I'm sayin' is there wasn't no good reason for Jack to be shootin' Wild Bill in the head."

"Fold. An' I gotta ask, Al—did he have a reason to be shootin' Wild Bill anywhere else?"

"Y'know Trent, there's times when you're funny—then there's now."

"I want me two cards."

"So if'n Jack had reason to be shootin' Wild Bill, I gotta wonder why—"

"Three cards."

"—he killed Wild Bill when he did."

"If'n you were there, Al, then what cards did Wild Bill have when he died?"

"Don't nobody know. See, that's why you know I was there—nobody saw Wild Bill's hand. I know some damn fool went 'round claimin' he had aces over eights, but the stone cold truth is we didn't see his cards, and that crazy woman that followed Wild Bill around knocked over the damn table, so didn't nobody else see no cards, neither. But I did see Jack McCall come in an' blow Wild Bill's head off. An' you know what else?"

"I know I'm sorry Jay asked the damn question, that's what *I* know. An' I'm foldin'."

"Me, too."

"Yeah, I'm outta this crap."

"I'll take three."

"What else is that Wild Bill didn't sit in his usual spot. Normal-like, he sat with his back to the wall so he could be seein' the whole place. I remember one night, someone tried to shoot Wild Bill and Wild Bill done shot him instead."

"I'm in for fifty."

"Fold."

"So what I'm thinkin' is that somethin' else was goin' on. I'm thinkin' that Jack McCall was under th'influence'a somethin' else. An' so was Wild Bill."

"I think Al's so full of it his eyes're turnin' brown, an' I think Trent's bluffin' so much it's comin' outta his ass. I call the fifty an' raise another fifty."

"Ain't anyone gonna ask why I think that?"

"First off, Al, we wanna know if'n you're gonna call."

"See, I think that 'cause both men was actin' outta character. Fact'a the matter is, Wild Bill been actin' outta character the whole damn time he was in Deadwood. An' Jack started acted all crazy-like the day he shot Wild Bill. An' I call the hundred an' raise fifty."

"I'm out."

"Fifty to you, Jay."

"Raise a hundred."

"That's a hunnert t'you, Al."

"See, what I think—"

"You gonna call the damn raise'r not, Al?"

"See, what *I* think is that Wild Bill was possessed by spirits."

"Only spirit anyone's possessed by is the ones behind th'bar, an' you gotta call the damn bet, Al."

"'Cause th'only thing that makes sense to me is that Wild Bill was possessed—by someone who'd sent him to Deadwood so nobody'd be findin' him. Ain't that right, Jay?"

"Don't know what you're goin' on 'bout, Al. I'm just playin' poker."

"I'm sayin' that you missed the chance there, Jay. By the time you were catchin' up to the spirit that took Wild Bill, he was gone. He'd fled t'somewhere else, an' poor ol' Jack McCall was stuck with a gun in his hand and a murder charge. Funny thing is—Jack don't have no brother. But he done made that story up so they wouldn't be chargin' him with murder in Deadwood."

"Thought Deadwood was lawless."

"Shut up, Trent."

"Something you wanna be doin', there, Jay?"

"I'm just playin' poker, Al."

"Oh yeah? I think you've been followin' me. An' I think you gotta be makin' your move."

"Really?"

"Yeah, really."

"Al, what're you—? Sweet Mother'a God!"

"Aaaah!"

"My eyes!"

"What the hell?"

"Al, where's Jay? What just happened?"

"Al? Al, wake up!"

"Anybody got'nee smellin' salts?"

"What?"

"I didn't say nothin'."

"No, I mean, Al. He whispered somethin'."

"I didn't hear it."

"I did—he said, 'Wild Bill's ghost can rest easy now.'"

"The hell's that mean?"

"Damned if *I* know. I just wanna know what happened to Jay."

"Somebody get the doc f'r Al, willya?"

"Anybody know what that was about?"

"I'll tell you what it was about—Al just had aces high."

"You mean—?"

"Yup—sumbitch was bluffin'."

"So what'd Jay have?"

"Where the hell *is* Jay?"

"Dunno, but you ain't gonna b'lieve what he had."

"What?"

"Two pair. Aces over eights."

Introduction to "-30-"

I first met Steve Savile when we were on a *Doctor Who* panel together at Dragon Con in 2008. We stayed in touch, and in 2011, he decided that it would be cool to release a series of thrillers pulled from the day's headlines, to wit: the CIA engaging in a program that uses third-world vaccination programs to further their own anti-terrorist agenda. The miniseries was called *Viral*, and we saw this story from several different viewpoints in Pakistan, Kenya, and New York City, through the eyes of journalists, doctors, agents, and operatives.

The range of viewpoints on the authorial end was pretty wide, too. Steve, a Brit living in Sweden, got together four writers: me, Alex Black (both American), Jordan Ellinger (Canadian), and Jason Fischer (Australian).

One of the notions Steve had in mind was an American journalist who breaks the story, and what he might have to go through, and I leapt at that one.

The result is "-30-," which was published as the first part of the miniseries. Each of us did a novella that was released individually, and later we put out an omnibus. For the first month, it was a Nook exclusive, sold only by Barnes & Noble for their e-reader, and it did very well during that month. It was my first time writing a thriller, and I gotta say, I enjoyed it, and would love to some day revisit the genre in general and two-fisted reporter Joe Lombardo in particular again.

Perhaps some day I will...

This story was and is dedicated to my dear friend Elizabeth Donald, who is always there to remind me that newspaper reporters are awesome.

-30-

Joe Lombardo had been in the middle of the dream when the alarm woke him.

He was getting an award, he always remembered that much. Whenever he had the dream, the entire thing was just like when he won the Pulitzer back in 1998 for the series he did on the horrors of Kosovo. But the award he got varied from dream to dream—sometimes the second Pulitzer that had eluded him in real life, or the Nobel Prize for Literature for one of the books that he'd never actually finished, or a trophy for one of the many fighting tournaments that *Kaicho* had tried and failed to get him to sign up for, or an Academy Award for the screenplay he'd never gotten around to starting.

But every time, no matter what award his dream-self had earned, he always got it at the luncheon on the Columbia University campus where they gave out the Pulitzers.

He fumbled for his smartphone on the nightstand, but he couldn't locate it, though he did manage to knock his glasses onto the rug.

Sweet Christ, don't let me step on them, he thought as he gingerly set his feet down on the throw rug that protected his bare feet from the cold hardwood. Then he felt around while the phone kept up its insistent beeping.

Finally locating the glasses, he snatched the wireframe spectacles off the floor and put them on. Able to see actual objects instead of fuzzy shapes, he now saw his phone dancing across his bureau thanks to the vibrate function even as the beeping continued to fill the air.

Right, I left it on the bureau so I wouldn't just snooze it and fall back asleep. He stumbled toward the bureau and switched off the alarm.

Why the fuck did I set the damn thing for eight?

As if on cue, Kane came loping into the bedroom on all fours, looked up at him with his big eyes, and mewed.

"Right," he said down to the cat. "It's your fault. Stupid diabetes." He reached down to the floor and picked the fifteen-pound Tortoiseshell up. Kane rubbed his head into Joe's neck, and Joe absently scratched behind the cat's ears as he wandered out of the bedroom—navigating carefully through the minefield of dirty laundry, half-read books, and DVD and CD cases that were strewn about. One of these days, he was going to clean the place.

Right after I finish the book and start the screenplay. He wandered down the hall of his one-bedroom apartment to the kitchen, where the insulin was stored in the refrigerator.

After filling one of the syringes with four units and sticking Kane in the back with it, he dug out the special food that the cat, as a diabetic, had to eat now and dumped two scoops of it into his bowl—Kane's reward for allowing a human to shove a needle into his back. After checking the fountain to make sure there was enough water for the cat, he got the coffeemaker going and then stumbled back into the bedroom, his brain having finally acknowledged what he saw on the phone when he turned the alarm off: he had voicemail and three missed calls.

He checked the latter first: Edward Jackson, his editor at the New York *Daily News*, the trunk line for the MTA, and a 347 number he didn't recognize.

Putting the phone to his ear, he ambled back to the kitchen and played the voicemail.

There was, conveniently, one for each missed call. He played the first one just as the coffeemaker started making the B-movie monster sounds indicating that it was working properly.

"Lombardo, it's Eddie. There's gonna be a presser at City Hall at noon announcing the new snow emergency plans for Mass Transit. You will be there. Call me when you wake your lazy ass up."

"Like I wouldn't be there?" he said to the kitchen as the phone went to the next one. That would be someone at the MTA, and the first message now made the second one's source more understandable.

"Yo, Joe, it's Afeo over at Transit. Listen, I got somethin' for you. Hit me back on my cell."

Joe sighed. Afeo was a convenient "source in the MTA who wishes to remain anonymous," but he wasn't going to stay that way if he kept calling reporters from his office phone.

Then came the mystery number.

"Joseph, this is Nik Rugova. I don't know if you remember me, but— I am in New York, and I thought perhaps we should meet. I know it has been a few years, yes? But I've got something for you. I'll be at the Dunkin Donuts on Broadway and 96th all afternoon. Do not call this number back."

"Sweet Christ," Joe muttered, staring at the phone for a second, then replaying the message to make sure he wasn't going completely crazy.

Nope, that's definitely Nik's voice. And we always met at a Dunkin. But why the fuck is he calling me from a local number? Besnik Rugova was a CIA analyst who had been a useful deep-background source back in the day. In a lot of ways, Nik was responsible for Joe's Pulitzer. An Albanian American who wrote reports for the CIA on his family's homeland and its environs, he had been more than willing to help a reporter bring the atrocities committed against Albanians to light.

But he hadn't heard from Nik in at least five years.

On a whim, he called the number Nik called from.

Three beeps, then: *"The number you have reached is no longer in service."*

Joe frowned as he pulled a mug that had the dictionary definition of *coffee* written on it down from the cabinet and poured the freshly brewed beverage into it. Nik had never been the type to use disposable cell phones, yet he had apparently come to New York and purchased a burner for the express purpose of leaving a message with Joe.

Sipping the hot black coffee, he wondered what it was all about. He had the press conference at noon over at the Hall, then he'd need to schlep all the way up to 96th on the 2 or 3 train to meet with Nik. He couldn't remember the last time he'd been back up that way. Since moving to the lower east side, he'd rarely ventured north of Houston Street, much less up to the old neighborhood.

But he could worry about that later. He called his boss back next. "Jackson."

"Hey there, Ed-Ed, it's Joe."

"Don't fucking call me that," Eddie said automatically. Joe was one of the few in the city room who still used that nickname, as the others had all been frightened into dropping it. But the others were all younger and hadn't worked in a war zone, so they were easier to intimidate. "You get my message?"

"No, I just like hearing the dulcet tones of your voice first thing in the a.m. Yeah, I got it. Also got a call from my guy at the MTA, so there may be a wrinkle."

"What'd he say?"

Joe blinked. "I haven't called him back yet."

"Motherfucker. What'd I always tell you, Lombardo? Call your source before you call your editor. The source may not wait."

"I don't want to have that conversation until the coffee kicks in."

Eddie made a weird kind of noise that sounded like a radiator letting out steam. "You called me before coffee?"

Shrugging, Joe said, "I don't need to be coherent to talk to *you*, and I don't need to remember what you say 'cause I never listen to you anyhow."

"Well, *that* shit's certainly true. Hold on." Eddie then distantly yelled at someone in the bullpen, having moved the phone far enough from his mouth to make the words indistinct. Then he came back. "All right, listen, I need something for the web site soon's the thing's over, all right?"

Joe winced. He hated cobbling together pieces that fast. "I—"

Eddie wouldn't let him complain. "Yeah, I know, you need time to mull over your words and pick the right semicolon, and all that other shit, but we need hits on the damn site, so you will shut the fuck up about how computers killed journalism—"

"I never said that, I said *the web* killed journalism."

"—and write the damn piece," Eddie continued as if Joe hadn't spoken. "You can do your froofy op-ed shit for the morning, but I need the news in there right off."

"So why not send a reporter to do that, while I—"

"Because your ass is the only one I'm sendin'. Mia's still covering the Bronx DA race, Freddie's on vacation, Juan's tracking down—"

"All right, all right." He sighed. "Remember when newspapers had, y'know, a budget?"

"No." Eddie made the radiator noise again. "Go call your MTA guy."

There was a time when Joe wouldn't have taken his laptop onto the subway. It was like wearing a sign saying PLEASE STEAL THIS EXPENSIVE PIECE OF EQUIPMENT. But one day a year earlier he looked around and realized that there were at least a dozen people in the subway car who were holding a piece of electronic equipment that was both smaller and worth more than his battered old laptop.

So as he sat on a 3 train that rumbled uptown from Chambers Street, he opened up his netbook and started turning the notes he'd taken during the press conference, as well as those he'd taken when he'd called Afeo back, into something resembling a news piece suitable for the hallowed pixels of nydailynews.com.

He kept at it until the train decelerated into the 96th Street station. Cursing that he hadn't finished the piece, he actually sat with the laptop on one of the 96th Street benches and typed until he got to the end of the article.

Not bothering to proof it, or even spellcheck it—that was his editor's job, and if there were infelicities in the writing, well, that was all the people who insisted on reading newspapers on computers deserved—he saved it and closed the laptop. Once he got aboveground, he'd be able to cadge a wireless signal and e-mail the article to Eddie.

The cold winter air sliced through him as soon as he stepped onto the 96th Street platform, and it only got worse when he jogged up the stairs and went outside, the November wind whipping viciously down Broadway. *Shoulda worn gloves.*

Wandering into the donut shop, Joe looked around to see a bald man with a hawk nose sitting reading a copy of the *New York Times*. He looked up at Joe's entrance, and then smiled, showing teeth that had been yellowed from years of cigarette smoking.

Joe held up a finger and then went to the counter, ordering a large black coffee and a chocolate frosted donut. After receiving and paying for the order, only then did he join Nik, clutching the coffee in the hopes that it would restore feeling to his hands.

"What happened to your hair?" he asked with a grin.

Pointing at Joe's belly, Nik said, "It transformed into fat and moved from my head to your stomach, yes?"

Joe chuckled. "Yeah, well. Things have slowed down a bit."

Nik had meticulously folded and set down the paper while Joe ordered, and now he put a hand on it. "I couldn't find your byline in today's paper, Joseph."

"Firstly, it's Joe. I know I went by Joseph when we first met, but I was young and pretentious, and now I'm older and crankier. Joe suits me better. Secondly, I haven't been with the *Times* in a few years. They wouldn't let me leave the foreign desk. I'm at the *Daily News* now."

His expression getting sour, Nik said, "Truly?"

"Yeah yeah," Joe said with a dismissive wave, "I know, it's not the *Times*, but at least I don't have to use honorifics all the fucking time."

"True, but you also must spell 'kidnapped' with only one P, yes?"

Joe laughed and then took a sip of his coffee.

"It certainly explains the change from Joseph to Joe. So you're no longer a foreign correspondent?"

"*No*, no no no no. Had more than enough of being shot at, thanks. Now I cover local politics. Usually I only have to travel to City Hall, which is all of a mile from my apartment. It's calmer and more conducive to surviving to retire and bounce my grandchildren on my knee."

Nik's eyebrows raised. "You have grandchildren?"

Joe winced. "Well, I have to have kids, first."

"You and Elissa are—"

Knowing he was going to say something like, "trying," Joe cut him off. "Divorced for three years now."

It was Nik's turn to wince. "I'm sorry." He let out a long breath. "It may be that you're not the right person to give this to, yes? But I do not know any other reporters well enough to trust them."

"Why don't you tell me what it is, and I can tell you who at the *News* to pass it on to?"

"No." Nik shook his head sadly, staring down at the battered Formica table. "It must be you, Joseph." He allowed himself a small smile and corrected himself. "Joe, rather. I know you'll do right by this information, and use it to help people rather than sensationalize. It's why I was willing to keep being your source after Kosovo. You proved with that story that you would do the right thing given a choice, yes?"

Joe sipped his coffee to cover up a derisive snicker. The only thing he was after was the Pulitzer that he got. While it was all well and good that people were helped, that had never been the objective. At best, it was a fortuitous side effect.

Of course, Joseph Lombardo would have agreed wholeheartedly with Nik. He was an idealistic little twerp. A year in Kosovo, two years in Afghanistan, and another year in Iraq pretty much cured him of that.

Not that he was going to tell Nik any of this. *No sense letting the poor bastard do anything but think well of me.*

"One of the methods by which the agency is performing some of its covert operations is to piggyback onto existing vaccination and immunization programs, yes? Operatives will pose as doctors or nurses with Doctors Without Borders or some such, or perhaps they co-opt someone local. They give inoculations, but it's a means to an end."

Frowning, Joe asked, "How's helping people aid an op?"

"In Pakistan, they were mishandling the needles so that some blood comes out onto the syringe—then they do a DNA test to see if it matches the profile of a terrorist's brother, who was already captured. And that's just one example."

First, Joe sipped his coffee, trying to properly compose his next words. "I'm not sure what the problem is. I mean, people are still getting the immunizations, right?"

"Some are. But the inoculations are not always complete or properly administered, making them less than useless. Plus, there's a great deal of propaganda and paranoia against these inoculations in the first place, yes? Something like this just makes it worse. The World Health Organization constantly tries to convince people that vaccinations are safe and helpful, and things like this just undermine it."

Visions of another Pulitzer luncheon dancing in his head, Joe tried not to sound overenthusiastic. "Isn't it risky, you giving this to me?"

Nik gave another small smile. "I have not yet actually given it to you, yes? I was not aware that you weren't on this beat anymore."

"Yeah." That was the biggest problem. Joe had only even met the *News* foreign editors a couple of times, and wasn't even sure he knew their names. They probably knew of his history with the *Times*—though it was several years and many sets of layoffs ago, so they might not have. *Would they even take a story from me?*

He could always go back to the Times with it. It wasn't entirely ethical, since they were a direct competitor of his current employer, and it might cost him his job, but this—

This was huge.

Potentially. "What, exactly, do you have?"

"Interdepartmental memos, authorizations, a few photos, one or two field reports. It's all on an encrypted jump drive, which is back in my hotel room, yes? I can give you the drive and the decryption software."

It took all of Joe's self control not to do a spit-take with his coffee. This wasn't just a source with a rumor he heard around the watercooler. Nik was talking about giving him the motherlode.

If everything worked out right, Joe could write his own ticket.

But the number of ways it could go wrong were legion.

"Won't this jeopardize your career?" Joe asked, legitimately concerned. True, he hadn't spoken to Nik in years, but he still considered the older man to be a friend—or at least a treasured acquaintance.

That got a bitter chuckle out of Nik. "What career? I have been marginalized. I began my career in the CIA under President Reagan. Everyone thinks me a relic, that my ideas are 'too twentieth-century.' I write reports on Canada, yes? There is no duty less useful to the Central Intelligence Agency than my reports on Canada." Nik leaned forward. "I no longer *have* a career. And if this is what the CIA believes to be a viable strategy, then I no longer *wish* to have a career."

Alarm bells started pinging in Joe's head. *How much of this is a legitimate problem and how much is Nik's midlife crisis?*

Sweet Christ, how much of this is my *midlife crisis?*

Nik put a hand on Joe's shoulder. "But this is something that can *make* your career."

"Yeah." Joe took a deep breath. Nik removed the hand, and regarded him intently. Finally, Joe said, "Look, Nik—I need to think about this, okay?"

"Of course, Joseph. Joe. I understand."

After slugging down the rest of his coffee, he added, "Plus I've got an op-ed to write about the MTA's new snow emergency plan." Joe then remembered that he never actually cracked open his laptop in order to e-mail the news piece for the web site. *Hell with it.* "Can we meet tomorrow morning?"

"I cannot wait that long, Joe. I must have a response tonight, yes?"

Of course—you don't steal a smorgasbord of confidential CIA material and sit on it for days on end. "Fine, why don't we meet at midnight? I know a place where—"

"No, we shall meet at my hotel." Nik then gave Joe the name and address of the no-tell motel he was staying at, a dump down in Chelsea that charged by the hour.

Joe frowned as he put the name and address in his phone. "If you're staying down there, why'd we meet all the way uptown?"

"I had remembered that you and your wife lived on West End Avenue, yes?"

That got a sigh out of Joe. "Yeah, we lived up at 102nd." He shook his head. "That was a long time ago." He rose to his feet and held out a hand. "Whatever I decide, Nik, it's been great seeing you again."

"I wish I could say the same, Joe."

"Excuse me?" Joe thought that to be a bit insulting.

"I would have preferred to see you under *good* circumstances."

"Oh, right." Joe nodded, then shook his head, then headed out the door, the weight of this decision heavy on his mind.

Normally, Joe would write a five-hundred-word op-ed piece on the mendacity of the mayor and the incompetence of the Mass Transit Authority in an hour or two, especially given that he'd done a draft of the thing on the subway earlier that day.

But as he sat in the small dining room of his apartment, he kept allowing himself to be distracted by the view of the Williamsburg Bridge out the window. Never mind that he'd been seeing that view for the past three years to the point where he had every strut of the damn span memorized. He'd been futzing around with the op-ed piece for four hours, and now it was creeping toward eleven and he'd only squeezed two hundred words out, pausing only to give Kane his shot and feed him at eight.

What is wrong with me?

Of course, he knew the answer. Nik's story kept crowding the MTA one out of his brain.

He was also feeling woozy, which made him realize that, while he'd remembered to feed his cat, he hadn't done likewise for himself. Grabbing his smartphone, he called the pizza place across the street

"Hey, Val, it's Joe. Yeah, the usual small. Thanks." He ended the call, grateful for having regular eating habits with a place that was open until two in the morning, and then saw a dialogue box pop up in the lower-right-hand corner of his screen telling him that Elissa Albanese was online on Skype.

Yes! It was seven a.m. in Baghdad, so his ex-wife would just be getting up.

He Alt-Tabbed over to Skype and clicked on her name. *Can you do a vidchat? I need to talk to you about something.*

-30-

After an eternity, she finally replied: *And good morning to you, too. Give me a minute to freshen up.*

Seriously? I've seen you naked. Worse, I've seen you first thing in the AM. Not sure which is more frightening.

Hardy har har.

Then he got the request for the video chat, and Joe let out a long breath, accepting the request.

A moment later, a slightly pixellated version of Elissa's face appeared, taking up most of the screen. His own image appeared in the lower right-hand corner, which he minimized. It always freaked him out to see himself on his own web cam.

Elissa was obviously fresh out of the shower, as her brown hair was stringy and wet, and she wore a well-battered bathrobe.

"Sweet Christ, didn't I give you that robe as a wedding present?"

Her voice came out of the laptop's tinny speakers. "Joe, I've got to get dressed and get to the clinic. What do you want?"

"Don't let me stop you. I haven't seen a naked woman in ages."

"Please. I've seen your web browser history, and that was when we were married. Or did you mean you haven't seen a naked woman with the tits she was born with?"

Joe swallowed. "Now that's just mean."

"I'd say I'm sorry and I couldn't resist, but I'm not sorry and I could easily have resisted. I just chose not to."

Defensively, Joe said, "I haven't been to those sites in weeks." That was mostly true.

Elissa brushed a lock of wet hair out of her face. "Much as I'm enjoying this re-living of the final year of our marriage..."

"Right, right." Joe took a breath. "You guys do vaccinations, right?"

"Yeah, when we can." Elissa worked with *Médicins Sans Frontières*, currently assigned to Iraq. "It's hard because a lot of the people are taught that vaccinations are evil and that they don't work, and all the other bullshit. Of course, those same people want to know why we can't keep their kids from getting polio."

"It's a vicious circle." Joe nodded, hoping he sounded at least vaguely sincere. "How would you feel if, say, the CIA used an inoculation program to find a terrorist?"

"I would try desperately to summon up the energy to be surprised, and probably fail. If I wasn't so exhausted all the time, I'd even get outraged. Why?"

Joe heistated just long enough for Elissa to see where he was going.

"Hell, no. Joe, do you know—"

He held up a hand. "I don't *know* anything. I've got a possible source that might have something."

"You need to find out, Joe. Seriously, I am not fucking around, you have to find out, and if you do find out, you have to stop it from happening."

"Uhm..." Joe shook his head. "I can't really do that. I mean, I can report it, but—"

"Oh God, no, Joe, that'd be a disaster! Didn't you hear what I just said?"

"Which part?"

Elissa actually got up and started pacing. "If word gets out that the vaccinations are CIA plots, we'll never be able to inoculate anyone. We'll..."

She started pacing away from her laptop. "Uh, Elissa?"

Realizing what she'd done, she sat back down in front. Joe tried not to notice that the bathrobe had started to fall open a bit. "Joe, listen to me very carefully. If you report this, millions of kids will *die* because their parents won't take them to a clinic. It'll justify every single dumbshit conspiracy theory out there. Sure, they may capture one terrorist, but they make it easier for the next hundred terrorists—and for their recruiters, who'll go on about the great deceivers of the West." She pointed at the camera to accentuate her words. "You have to get them to stop it."

Joe leaned back. "And how am I supposed to do that?"

"How the hell should *I* know? I couldn't even get you to clean the toilet."

"Hardy har har," Joe muttered, throwing her favorite retort back at her. "Look, I need to get back to an op-ed piece. I'll let you know what happens, okay?"

"You'd better." She glowered at him through the computer screen, and the connection hiccupped so her face was frozen there for several seconds. "This is some bad shit, Joe."

"Yeah." He hesitated, then asked the question he'd been wanting to ask her for years. "Elissa, I came back from Iraq for you. So I gotta ask—why'd you go there?"

She just stared at the camera for a couple of seconds. Then Joe realized it was frozen again. "Goodbye, Joe," she finally said, and ended the connection.

Joe tried to retype the question in the chat window, but Elissa went offline while he was in the midst of typing. He decided to go ahead and send it—she'd see it when next she came online.

He stared at the same paragraph of the op-ed piece for the next ten minutes, changing that to which and back again four times, before the buzzer rang with his desperately needed pizza.

It took him from the time he paid for the pizza to his finishing of the second slice to make his decision.

Saving and abandoning the op-ed piece, Joe placed the pizza box in the oven—it didn't fit in the fridge, and he needed to keep Kane out of it somehow—and grabbed his leather coat.

There were no cabs to be found, so he hopped on the F train, which was only a few blocks away. The entire time he jumped up and down to keep warm while waiting for an F to finally show up, he wondered if he was doing the right thing.

He also wondered what, exactly, he was doing. Was he meeting a source for a story? Or was he going to do—well, whatever it was Elissa thought he should do. Scold Nik? Tell him to go back to the CIA and stop it?

Right. If he could do that, he wouldn't come to me for the first time in ages. He said he'd been marginalized, which meant I was his last resort, not his first one.

In retrospect, Joe realized he probably should have said some of that to Elissa.

The F finally clattered into the station. The heat was a massive relief, and he took off his gloves and unbuttoned his coat. He had no trouble finding a seat—while there were plenty of people coming in from Brooklyn (East Broadway was the first Manhattan stop on the northbound F), there were still seats available.

By the time the train pulled into 23rd Street, he knew what he had to do.

It took him another ten minutes to walk across from Sixth to Eighth Avenue, where Nik's crummy hotel was. The place was one of those Manhattan buildings from a hundred years ago that was probably really nice when it was built. What Joe didn't know about architecture was a lot, to paraphrase one of his favorite movie quotes, so he had no idea what all those fancy designs on the façade were all about, but he did know that they probably weren't supposed to be cracked and broken.

He pushed open the dirty glass door that looked like it belonged to a 1970s high school, and was confronted by a lobby that had last been painted during the Carter Administration. Cheap, split linoleum squeaked under his sneakers, and cracked leather sofas sat against the south and east walls. The west wall had what was once a grand staircase, with an elevator right next to it. Next to the door on the north wall was an alcove protected by bullet-proof glass, behind which sat a young man of Indian descent reading what looked like a medical textbook. The clerk barely looked up from his studies to acknowledge Joe, who went straight to the elevator.

He noticed a security camera as he waited for the elevator. A closer look revealed that it wasn't actually hooked into anything, and its indicator light was dark. Joe recognized the make and model—it wasn't battery-powered. It was cosmetic security, enough to make the clients feel safe, but not actually requiring the expense of maintaining video surveillance.

The elevator clanked down to the lobby and the door rumbled aside. Joe stepped in and pushed the round plastic button for the sixth floor. *You really didn't spare any expense on accommodations, didja, Nik?*

After a sudden lurch that almost brought Joe's pizza back into his throat, he was carried up six flights. He practically leapt out of the door as soon as it slid open, resolving to take the stairs back down.

When he arrived at the end of the hall, he knocked on 6C. He knew it was 6C because the impression from the number and letter was still left on the wooden door. The "6C" itself—probably tarnished brass, based on the residue and what he'd seen on other doors—was long gone.

-30-

The door creaked open from the impact of his fist knocking on it. "Nice lock, Nik," he said with a chuckle. "Seriously, there's a Comfort Inn just a few blocks from here. Couldn't you have—"

Joe cut himself off, as he realized that Nik wasn't going to be replying to him. His erstwhile informant lay on a thin stretch of ugly carpet between the hotel room's bed and bureau. Nik's eyes stared lifelessly upward, right hand on the foot of the bed, legs splayed as if he fell.

The room was small and cramped, but the lighting was poor enough so that you couldn't see what a dump it was. Or, at least, could avoid thinking about it. The bed had a hideously patterned bedspread, the wall over the bed had the single ugliest painting Joe had ever seen—and this after covering modern art openings when he first broke into journalism—the carpet was a really unfortunate shade of brown, and the TV on the bureau looked like it was purchased brand-new in 1987.

His years covering wars on foreign soil had provided him with ample opportunities to look at dead bodies, and he had quickly learned that the main difference between the living and the deceased was that the latter didn't move *at all*. Living people moved in so many subtle ways, but the dead were utterly motionless.

Nik's body was utterly motionless.

Unbidden, his mind went back to his first day in Kosovo. American soldiers had found a house that was filled with corpses. Seventeen people, members of two families, all Albanian, all slaughtered. They'd been dead a while, their flesh and decaying organs giving off a horrid stench—he hadn't just smelled it, he'd tasted it.

With him had been a reporter from the London *Times*—Clive, or Colin, or something like that. He was in his sixties, and he'd just smiled, showing teeth that were even yellower than Nik's had been at Dunkins, and elbowed Joe in the side. "Could be worse, mate," he'd said. "Could be *you* over there."

Joe shuddered at the memory. Biting his lip, he stared more closely at Nik's body on the hotel room floor. There were no visible signs of trauma, no petechial hemorrhaging, no bruises, no obvious bleeding, no discoloration except for those smoker's teeth.

Then he did the only thing he could do: he called 911.

A CIA analyst was dead in a cheap motel in Manhattan. There was no way the agency was going to let the local cops handle this for long, but Joe wanted to make sure they were there and started their own paperwork, so there was at least a chance that Nik would get a proper death investigation by a detective who might possibly give a shit about something other than politics. His years of covering Washington had convinced him that federal agents were useless when it came to actually solving crimes.

Besides, he had no faith that this wouldn't be covered up by the agency. Getting NYPD here might at least forestall that.

Joe went back to the lobby via the staircase, which only creaked some from his weight, and walked up to the medical student behind the scratched bullet-proof glass.

Without even looking up from his textbook, the young man asked, "May I help you?"

"You should know that the police are going to be here shortly. There's a dead body in 6C."

That got his attention. "I'm sorry?"

"The occupant of 6C is dead. I called the police."

"Why would you *do* that?" The young man was panicking now. "This is terrible!"

Joe just stared at the clerk. "Out of curiosity, what's the alternative to calling the police?"

"Calling the owner! He'll know what to do." The clerk snatched the phone off the hook and punched in several numbers. "He's going to kill me."

"No problem—the police'll be here already to investigate your murder, too."

The clerk just gave him a nasty look at that.

By the time the detectives arrived, the sun was coming up. Joe had waited for the officers, a pair from the 10th Precinct, who went over the scene before calling it in. Right around sun-up, two middle-aged guys entered the lobby: one white, one black, both with thick mustaches of the type that only cops could still get away with. Both were dressed in cheap suits and had receding hairlines, though the white guy covered it up by shaving his head. He hadn't done it in a couple of days, though, as Joe could see the stubble on his scalp.

The white guy introduced himself and his partner when they all sat on the cracked leather sofa in the lobby, under the nervous eye of the clerk, who'd left a voicemail message with the owner that was as yet unreturned.

"I'm Detective Jones, this is Detective Smith. Yeah, I know," he added, shaking his head.

"Joe Lombardo." He shook both detectives' hands firmly. Both men had calloused fingers.

"Officer Pérez says you're a reporter?"

Joe nodded. "For the *News*."

"How did you know the deceased?"

"I used to work for the *Times*, and he was a source when I covered the foreign beat. He was in town, wanted to get together. We met for coffee this afternoon, and he said he wanted to show me something."

"And what was that?" Smith asked that question, and he was the one taking notes in his pad.

Hesitating only for a second, Joe said, "Dunno. He never got the chance to show me. If you find a flash drive in here, well, then you'll know more than me."

It wasn't Joe's first felony, this lie to the police, and he suspected it wouldn't be his last, either. But there was no way he was going to tell the cops the specifics, especially since Nik hadn't really provided any.

Besides, he was hoping to prompt a response, and sure enough, Jones looked over at Pérez, the officer who'd first questioned him, who was standing at the base of the stairs. "Harry, you guys find a flash drive?"

Officer Harold Pérez shook his head. "Nah, just an overnight bag with a change'a clothes and shit. Didn't have no cell phone, no electronics, nothin'."

Smith regarded Joe. "You sure about this flash drive?"

"Nope," Joe said honestly. He hadn't actually seen it, after all. "Nik just talked about it, but didn't show it to me or give me any specifics. For all I know, he was talking out his ass."

Or the flash drive is somewhere safer than a shit motel in Chelsea.

"You said he was a source," Jones said. "What did he do for a living?"

Joe tried not to smile, because he knew how these guys were going to respond. "He's an analyst for the CIA. I covered Koso—"

"Oh, *shit*," Smith said.

Jones put his head in his hands. "That's just fucking great. All right, go on."

Joe told him what more he could about Nik, but the detectives' hearts were no longer in it. They knew what Joe knew—as soon as the feds found out that an agency analyst was dead, the FBI was going to come in and piss all over their investigation.

If Nik died of natural causes, it won't matter.

He had been hoping the cops would find the flash drive, because then it would be out of his hands. The truth would either come out or it wouldn't, depending on whether or not NYPD could get the drive decrypted before the feds snatched all their evidence.

But now he wasn't sure what would happen. Or what Nik did with the flash drive.

He gave Smith his contact info, put Smith's own contact info in his phone (refusing Smith's business card, as the last thing he needed was more random pieces of paper in his coat pocket), and then left the hotel, the morning sun blazing in his face as he walked eastward on 23rd toward Sixth and the F train home.

Oh, fuck that. An empty cab was coming up Eighth and he raised an arm to flag it down. He climbed in, giving his address while muting the display, since he didn't really need an update on what was happening in New York City and the world, what with working for a newspaper and all.

As the cab turned onto 23rd and then again onto Seventh to head south, Joe yawned and realized he should have stopped for coffee before grabbing the taxi. At least he was likely to make it home in time for Kane's shot.

The next thing he knew, the cab was slowing down as it approached the corner on which his building lay, pulling in behind a Federal Express truck that was just pulling out into

East Broadway's traffic. *I totally zoned out. Sheesh.* Shaking his head and blinking a few times, he pulled out his credit card and ran it through the scanner.

I'm going to take the world's longest nap, he thought as he stumbled out of the cab and fumbled in his pocket for his keys. Instead, he found his smartphone. Frowning, he took it out and saw that the display was dark, even when he pushed the button. *Shit, let the battery die down again.* He usually charged it overnight when he went to bed, but not having actually *gone* to bed...

Upon entering the lobby, the doorman looked up and said, "Mr. Lombardo! You *just* got a FedEx."

"Okay." Joe wasn't expecting anything, but he got unexpected overnight packages all the time. "Thanks, Ivan."

It was a 9x12 flat envelope. Joe took it and felt the sides as he walked to the elevator.

The first thing he was able make out was a square, flat shape—probably a CD or DVD jewel case.

He stopped dead in his tracks when he felt the other object: a small rectangle.

Flipping the envelope over, he stared at the airbill, but the return address was a stationery store with a Broadway address in Manhattan. The ZIP put it on the upper west side.

Oh, Sweet Christ, no.

Looking around the lobby, he saw a couple of other tenants—that brunette with the small dog, that Wall Street guy who was waiting for his car service to pick him up—plus Ivan, and an Asian guy sitting on the lobby bench wearing a shiny New York Yankees windbreaker that looked like he just bought it. *Too many witnesses.*

He rang for the elevator, waiting not-very-patiently for one to arrive. When it did, he waited for another neighbor to disembark, then got on, stabbing the metal button with "21" on it. The number lit at his touch.

Once he got to the twenty-first floor, he practically ran down the hall to his front door, fumbling for the keys.

Kane was greeting him at the door, mewing. "In a minute, cat," he said, absently bending over to scritch him on the head before going into the dining room.

He stared at the package for several seconds, standing in the shadow of the Williamsburg Bridge, suddenly deathly afraid to open it.

Nik's dead. It could've been natural—and it could've been an assassination made to look natural, Christ knows I saw worse overseas.

Joe stared at the white envelope for several more seconds, hoping it might provide some sort of insight or wisdom.

After it became blindingly obvious that it would do neither, he finally yanked on the pull tab and ripped it out, then reached in.

His Braille-like check of the envelope was accurate: a CD jewel case with a silver CD with the word decrypt marked on it with a black Sharpie; and a silver flash drive, unlabelled.

Sweet Christ. He must have sent this right after we had coffee. Hell, maybe he sent it before we met up.

Then he heard the distinctive click of his front doorknob being turned.

He did three things at once: he dropped both the flash drive and the jewel case into the pocket of the leather coat he hadn't yet removed; he turned into a defensive posture that was one of the first things *Kaicho* had taught him; and he cursed his stupidity in leaving his front door unlocked.

The door opened to reveal a man wearing mirrorshades and a black knit wool cap. A rather fake-looking beard covered his cheeks, and he wore an all-black bodysuit that looked suspiciously like Kevlar under a leather jacket, as well as leather gloves. The only identifiable body part was his nose, which was strictly average.

"Two choices, Lombardo," the man said in a whisper. "You can hand over the package that Rugova sent you and we forget that any of this ever happened."

"What package?" Joe asked unconvincingly.

The man's head inclined toward the dining room table and the open FedEx envelope, then he looked back up at Joe.

"All right, fine, that package. What's behind door number two?"

He smiled under the fake beard. "You're found dead of a heart attack. That hard-drinkin' journalist lifestyle just did you in. *Such* a shame..."

-30-

Wishing he had some kind of recording device, Joe said, "So first you kill Nik, then you—"

"Rugova died of a heart attack, too. That's what the M.E. will say—if it even goes to autopsy. Probably not. Looks natural, after all, and it's not like anyone gives a flying fuck about an over-the-hill analyst."

The man was moving slowly closer to Joe, probably thinking that he was using the cover of the conversation to get close enough to make his move.

Which was exactly what Joe wanted him to do.

His smile growing into a wide grin, the man modulated into a raspy voice reminiscent of the knight at the end of *Indiana Jones and the Last Crusade* as he said, "Choose wisely."

Joe knew that he could take the first choice. Hand the flash drive and CD over and never have to worry about it. He didn't really know anything, after all, and he'd seen enough of the agency's work to know that they wouldn't do anything to him if he cooperated.

And then nobody would know that the CIA was using humanitarian medical aid to pursue their agenda.

His potential assassin had moved pretty close. Joe noticed that, while his torso was covered in body armor, he was wearing ordinary black sweats, probably for the freedom of movement.

"You have to get them to stop it."

Elissa's words echoed in his mind all of a sudden, and he realized that there was no way he could just hand this over.

The operative had moved within a couple of feet now. He seemed to be palming something in his left hand, which he was holding gingerly as he moved. *Probably where he's keeping the syringe that has whatever he's going to fake my heart attack with.*

"Well?"

Kaicho had always taught that a kiai—yelling as you made a particular move—served several functions. It showed spirit, it got your blood boiling, it added oomph to your technique. But it also could serve as a distraction, as your opponent is likely to be sufficiently surprised by you yelling that he misses your technique entirely.

So when Joe shouted, "Hai!" at the top of his lungs, the operative hesitated for a split-second, which was more than enough time for Joe to lift his leg and bring his foot down hard on the man's left leg just below the knee. It was, he felt, a pretty darned good joint kick given that he was wearing sneakers and was sleep deprived.

Joe heard a very satisfying snap of bone at the impact of foot on leg, and his opponent cried out, "Augh!"

A syringe fell to the hardwood of the dining room floor with a light *clink*.

The operative shoved an arm toward Joe's chest, which he managed to deflect somewhat, but the impact still pushed him back a bit, and he stumbled on one of the dining-room chairs.

As Joe struggled to his feet, the operative—now hopping on his right leg—pulled out a Luger .22 with a suppressor from a shoulder holster under the leather jacket. *That would be Plan B,* Joe thought grimly.

The .22 didn't have enough recoil for the bad guy to lose his balance, to Joe's disappointment. *Right, like he's going to bring a Desert Eagle for a covert kill in a gigunda apartment building in the biggest city in the world.*

As he raised the Luger, Joe reached out with his left hand and grabbed the weapon by the suppressor and pushed it so that the barrel was facing the window. The operative's finger squeezed on the trigger, and a bullet flew out of the barrel with a *phut,* tearing the crap out of his windowsill.

Heat seared into Joe's left palm as the suppressor got very hot, and he had to let go. As he did, he slammed his right elbow into his attacker's jaw, followed quickly by a palm-heel to his nose. The operative screamed in pain, but not from the strikes to the face—right afterward he stumbled back, accidentally putting weight on his shattered left leg.

The palm-heel might have been a better idea if Joe's hand hadn't just been burned. He hissed in pain, shaking his hand as the operative fell backward, latching onto the kitchen counter for support with his left arm.

He still held the Luger in his right.

"Mrow!"

Joe had never been so happy to see Kane in his life. The cat wandered in, wondering what all the fuss was about, and why it was disturbing his nap.

-30-

The operative looked away for just a second, before turning back, but Joe took advantage of the oh-so-brief distraction to jump feet first toward the operative. His feet crashed into the body armor, and the pair of them fell to the hardwood in a tangle of arms and legs.

It was, quite possibly, the worst jumping side kick he'd ever delivered, but he'd take it under the circumstances.

Using his right hand, he pushed himself to his feet. The assassin was now on the floor, unhurt—Joe kicked him in the Kevlar—but now on the floor, and with the busted leg, he'd have a hard time getting up.

Better yet, he had dropped the Luger. Joe couldn't see where, but at this point, he didn't give much of a damn, as long as the assassin wasn't holding it.

In the movies and on TV, people punched folks in the jaw. In the real world that was ill-advised, as it didn't hurt the person you were punching all that much, and it did a number on your fist.

The temple was a different story, as the skull was softer there, and you could do serious brain damage.

Having only half a second to mull, Joe considered and rejected a punch, as he'd have to bend over. Better to keep with what was working: his feet.

So he stepped on the guy's head.

Joe stood over the man who tried to kill him, blood pouring from his nose and mouth and from cuts all over his head, particularly near the left temple. He was moaning incoherently. Somewhere in the room there was a .22 caliber pistol that Joe could use to shoot this man down.

His years in the killing fields of Kosovo and the brutal desert of the Persian Gulf had taught Joe that life was very cheap. People killed for much worse reasons than this—Joe was defending himself, after all, against a man who broke into his home and tried to end his life. Had already ended the life of a friend.

The Luger was sitting on the kitchen floor, frighteningly close to where Kane was mewing, demanding to know what was going on.

Joe walked over to where the pistol was and picked it up with his right hand.

Flexing his left hand, which was stinging badly from the burns, he held the .22 with his right, aiming the suppressed muzzle right at his opponent's face.

The assassin moaned a few more times.

Although he'd used firearms any number of times in his life, they'd always been under controlled conditions at ranges and such, and he always aimed the weapon at an inanimate object.

This was the first time in his life he'd aimed it at a human being.

And if he pulled the trigger, he would be taking a human life.

The moaning stopped.

Now Joe could only hear the sound of his heart slamming into his ribs and his own rather labored breathing. His left hand stung like a sonofabitch, and his mouth was filled with the bitter-almond taste of adrenaline.

"Could be worse, mate. Could be you over there."

Joe could not squeeze the trigger.

He turned and ran out of the apartment. Tall, dark, and violent probably had people expecting a check-in, and when they didn't get it, they'd likely send in backup that would be less susceptible to his mad karate skills.

Making sure the safety was on the Luger, he dropped it in his right coat pocket, hoping to hell he wouldn't need it, completely unsure if he'd be *able* to use it if he did.

Unwilling to wait for the elevator, nor to be in an enclosed tin can where he'd be trapped with any more potential assassins, he took the stairs down all twenty-one flights of stairs. At least on the staircase, he had somewhere to run.

Of course, there were security cameras in the elevators and none in the stairwells, but Joe preferred to survive an attack by a foe the cops couldn't identify than die in an attack by someone who was easily caught.

By the time he reached the bottom of the stairs, sweat was dripping off his forehead, his breathing had become even more labored—something he wouldn't have believed possible when he was pointing the Luger at the assassin—and his leather coat felt stifling.

-30-

Having gone all the way to the basement, he fell more than walked through the metal door. *No sense in letting Ivan see me leave. Better for him to tell the backup, "Why yes, Mr. Lombardo went up to his apartment." Then they'll waste time going up twenty-one flights and finding their colleague on the floor.*

He jogged through the uneven concrete floor of the narrow basement hall, past the laundry rooms and the lounge with the ping-pong tables and vending machines. Two old people, one male, one female, were in the laundry room, babbling at each other. Joe heard the words "chemo" and "hip replacement" as he passed by. Unsurprisingly at this early hour, there was nobody in the lounge.

As he pushed in the long metal bar that opened the door at the end of the hall, he remembered that he left without giving Kane his shot.

For a brief, insane instant, he considered going back upstairs for Kane, then wiser instincts prevailed. *Well, he can miss one every once in a while. Won't kill him. Probably.*

He walked out onto Pitt Street next to his building. *Sweet Christ, I need to tell somebody about this.*

Reaching into his pocket he pulled out his smartphone, trying to figure out who it made the most sense to call—

—and then he remembered that he hadn't charged the damn thing. And he left his laptop upstairs. *Nice job, asshole.*

He walked down Pitt Street, trying so desperately to look casual that he knew he had to be failing, dabbing his forehead with the sleeve of his coat. It was a chilly fall morning, it wouldn't do to be sweating like a stuck pig. The worst thing he could do right now was be noticed.

Or is it? Maybe if I look like a homeless person—

Joe shook his head and laughed at the very thought. *People will just ignore me, like they do all the other homeless. Get your head out of your ass, Lombardo.*

Walking north on Pitt Street, he looked in vain for a working pay phone. He hadn't even *touched* a pay phone in who knew how many years. The advent of cell phones had significantly reduced their usefulness. Once upon a time, the pay phone had been the newspaper reporter's bread and butter. Hell, there was a time when Joe could tell you the location of every working pay phone in Manhattan, including each of the last four remaining full phone booths with the sliding doors that enclosed you completely. (They were all on West End Avenue. Joe used to walk all the way to West End just to use one.)

Now, though, he was nowhere near West End, and intact pay phones were rarer than a spotted owl. Here the mouthpiece missing, there the earpiece ripped out, here the wire cut, there the entire unit missing.

When he finally found a phone in one piece on the corner of Pitt and Grand, he realized that, even if he had the first clue *who* to call, he didn't remember anybody's number. They were all stored in his smartphone. Even Detectives Smith and Jones were in his phone. *Good job declining to take their business cards, dumbass.* He couldn't even remember what precinct those two were from. There was always Ed—but Joe realized with a shock that he had no idea what Ed's direct line was, either.

Still, he made a beeline for the phone, almost crashing into a guy wearing a blue Yankees jacket, who in turn nearly bumped into a woman with a stroller. The woman cursed the guy out while Joe snagged the phone from the metal hook. *Gotta love this town.*

And then Joe recalled that he could call 411, get the main *Daily News* number, and get transferred to Ed. *Good, good, that'll work.*

He put the phone to his ear—and heard nothing. *Fuck.* He slammed his finger on the hook a few times to hang it up and release it again, but there was no dial tone.

Then, suddenly, he couldn't move. His legs had turned to rubber, the sweat continued to gush out of his forehead, and his heart felt like a fist was clenching it. *What the fuck is happening here?*

He was having trouble breathing. For a moment, he closed his eyes, tried to inhale through his nose, hold it for a few seconds, then exhale through his mouth. This was how he always felt about an hour after a sparring class ended. Of course, his usual solution under those circumstances was to pour a glass of Jim Beam, lay down on the couch, and watch random TV channels until he fell asleep.

-30-

After he felt his breathing was, if not under control, at least somewhat manageable, he opened his eyes.

The first thing he noticed was a giant red edifice about a block away, at the corner of Pitt and Broome. The 7th Precinct.

Good. Yes. Go to the cops. Report the crime. Somebody did break in to my apartment, after all, and I think I'll be a pretty convincing hysterical person who had to get out of his apartment in a hurry with an uncharged phone. This will work.

He walked up Pitt, trying to hold it together.

His knees had other ideas. At one point, they buckled, and he stumbled to the sidewalk.

Just as he did so, he heard a distinctive whistle go over his head, followed by a small but powerful *clink*. Too many years in war zones made Joe intimately familiar with those two sounds: a sniper bullet.

FUCK!

The whistle had started to his right and gone over his head to hit the sidewalk to his left. Whirling his head around, he saw a red-brick building across the street, with a low roof. He saw the glint of the early-morning sun on metal, and a figure kneeling.

Sniper!

Dimly, he registered that other people had noticed, too. There were a few dozen people on the street, and they were either ducking or screaming or shouting or something.

Suddenly, the crash reversed itself, and Joe found himself bursting with energy. He devoted this to a single action: running.

To his dying day, he would never know why he picked the direction he chose to run in, nor would he remember any details from when he started until he came to a sweaty, exhausted stop in front of a beautiful red-and-white-brick neo-Renaissance edifice. Looking around, he saw no signs of any snipers, nor anybody chasing him. All he saw were people glancing at him with slightly confused or annoyed expressions before moving on with their lives.

He also realized that he was exactly where he needed to be. Because the beautiful building he was standing in front of was the Seward Park branch of the New York Public Library. They had computers with internet connections. He could e-mail Ed.

Unfortunately, the library would not actually open until ten. With a couple of hours to kill, he wandered over to Canal Street to a dim sum place that served breakfast. He ordered a large, desperately needed coffee and banana French toast.

Not realizing how hungry he was until he walked in and smelled all the food, Joe practically inhaled the French toast when it arrived, and only didn't do likewise for the coffee due to its temperature.

After wolfing down the last of the banana French toast, he leaned back in his chair and his eyes fell on a pay phone. Relieved, he started to get up before he remembered one important detail about pay phones: you had to *pay* to use them. Joe had no cash on him whatsoever—it was why he'd used his card to pay for the cab ride. In the old days, he'd have just used his calling card to pay for it, but that account had long since lapsed.

There were ATMs around, but he was suddenly wary of using them. It was why he'd considered and rejected the notion of getting a phone charger from an electronics place (as soon as one opened, anyhow). Right now, he was scared shitless of leaving any kind of trail. Eventually he was going to have to pay for this meal with his card, but he rather desperately needed the caffeine and calories. Giving anyone trying to find him an easy way to track him—say via an ATM withdrawal or turning on his smartphone—would just make another assassin or sniper be likely.

Pay phone was his only bet. But with no actual cash, he had no way of making that call.

The library has internet. It'll open at ten. Just sit tight until then.

The next two hours were among the most grueling of Joe Lombardo's life. Every time someone walked into the dim sum place, he flinched. Every noise was cause for jumping half out of his seat. *Where's the next assassin going to come from?*

His left hand wasn't badly burned, but it stung like crazy, to the point where flexing it hurt. Luckily he was right-handed, but eating proved a challenge, since operating a knife and fork for the French toast proved an annoying challenge.

By the time ten o'clock rolled around, he was on his fifth coffee and was practically vibrating from a combination of nerves and caffeine. He had spent that time convincing himself that using his card would be a terrible idea. When the check came, he stuffed a few paper napkins into the padded folder to make it look like there were a wad of bills inside, and simply walked out the door.

The Luger felt heavy on the right side of his coat as he exited, heading back down Canal Street to East Broadway, past Seward Park to the library on the other side of it. There was a queue of people outside waiting to get in, and just as Joe joined the throng, the front door opened from the inside and a smiling, middle-aged African-American woman said, "Come on in, folks."

Joe went straight for the computers, which were already turned on and showing a Windows desktop image with the New York Public Library logo and a picture of one of the lions that sat in front of the main building on 5th Avenue and 42nd Street. He also noticed a set of headphones next to the monitor.

He double-clicked on the icon for the internet browser, and was about to type in the domain name for the web-mail version of his e-mail—and then hesitated. *If I didn't want to use my ATM, do I really want to log into my e-mail? The address is pretty publicly known, and if these guys can hire assassins and snipers, they can probably trace the IP address of where I log on.* He closed the browser by clicking on the X in the upper-right-hand corner.

And then he saw the Skype icon on the monitor.

Smiling, he put the headphones on, plugged them into the jack on the front of the CPU, and double clicked on that icon.

He first got the Skype account when a podcast asked to interview him, and it shortly thereafter proved a useful way of staying in touch with Elissa. The account wasn't linked to an e-mail address or phone number—he never even got around to establishing an icon, traditionally a picture of oneself. It was just the generic default icon.

If someone dug deep enough, they might be able to find that account, but he doubted that anyone who'd only been even looking for him for the past twenty-four hours would even know it existed.

So he felt safe logging on.

A perfectly good idea right up until it asked for his password. His laptop signed him in automatically, and it had been almost two years since he last logged on manually—when he got the current laptop.

Sweet Christ, what the hell did I use for my password?

He tried his e-mail password and his password that he used for the *Daily News* web server, neither of which worked.

That was when he remembered that he never finished the damn op-ed piece. Ed must be spitting nails. There were probably half a dozen voicemails piling up from him alone.

Voicemail! It finally hit him—he used the same password for Skype that he used to access his previous phone's voicemail. (His current phone didn't require a password.)

After entering 2246—a number that had absolutely no significance in his life, which was why he chose it—in the password field, he was logged into Skype.

Please let her be home, please let her be home. Sure enough, Elissa Albanese was among the names listed among his (very few) contacts who was online.

He clicked on her name and then typed in the chat field. The pain in his left hand had subsided into an ache, and he was able to push past it in order to touch type. *I need to talk to you NOW. Can you vidchat?*

As he typed, he noticed that his question from the last chat about why she went to Iraq after he came home from there to be with her was still in the window, unanswered.

It seemed like an eternity later—though the clock in the lower right-hand corner of the monitor insisted it was only a minute—that she responded. *Is it about the CIA thing?*

Kinda. I'm at a library, so I can't do voice, but I need to see and hear you. I've got headphones.

A long pause. *Okay. I'm betting there's a story there.*

The window came up offering a video chat, and Joe accepted. Elissa's slightly pixellated face appeared once again, but this time her hair was tied in a bun, she was wearing a plain black T-shirt and cargo pants, and looked haggard and exhausted. The bags under her eyes had bags under them.

"Well," her voice said into his headphones, "*you* look like hammered shit."

You don't know the half of it.

And then, furiously touch-typing, he spelled out everything that happened to him after their last conversation.

"Jesus, Joe, you walked out of a restaurant without paying your check? That's just so—so—so I don't know what."

Joe rolled his eyes. *Seriously? THAT'S what you're taking away from this? I was almost killed!!!!*

"Right, I know, I'm sorry." She waved an arm back and forth. "It's just this is so— I mean, I knew it was big, but— Jesus."

I know, I know. I don't know what to do or who to trust. I only got in touch with you because my Skype account isn't exactly common knowledge.

She smirked. "Bet you've never been more grateful to forget to charge your phone, huh?"

Something like that.

There was an interminable pause.

What do you think I should do?

"What is it you want, Joe? I mean, what do you want to get out of this?"

Right now, I'd settle for seeing tomorrow's sunrise.

"Okay, fine, but—well, what's the upside for you here? You can't write this story."

I dunno, given what they're going through to cover it up, writing it may be my only key to survival.

Elissa leaned forward in her chair, making it look as if she was going to come through the monitor. Joe actually flinched. "Don't you *dare*, Joe! Do you know how much time I *waste* here trying to convince parents to let their kids be inoculated? And how many of them still don't do it after I talk until I'm blue in the face?"

Joe found he couldn't resist. *Well, to be fair, I never listened to you, either.*

"Very funny—and start now. Is getting another fucking Pulitzer so goddamn important that you just throw everything else away?"

Angry, Joe started typing as soon as she said, "Pulitzer." *I could give a shit about awards right now, Elissa, I'm trying to stay the fuck alive!* It was even almost true, though he had to admit that one of the things that made this story so attractive was the awards potential.

"All right, fine, maybe I'm being a little unfair."

A little?

"Joe, dammit, this is *important!*"

So's my

He stopped typing when he noticed an Asian man walk in wearing a shiny new Yankees windbreaker. The same windbreaker that he saw in the lobby of his building, and again on Pitt Street.

Erasing what he'd typed, he replaced it with: *Gotta go—one of the guys after me is in the library.*

"Oh no you don't, Joe, no, come on, you can't—"

Whatever Joe couldn't do was lost as he hit the red phone icon that hung up the call. Pausing only long enough to shut the computer down, Joe moved toward the back of the library. Shiny Jacket hadn't seen him yet, and it wouldn't do to draw attention to himself.

Snaking his way between several bookcases, he worked his way around to the exit, thinking, *I still haven't gotten an answer to that question I asked Elissa. Maybe I don't even want to know.*

He nodded at the guard, there to inspect packages, of which Joe had none. *Thank Christ they don't check people's pockets. Don't think the Luger would go over too well.*

As he exited onto East Broadway, he contemplated the efficacy of losing himself in Seward Park. Just as he rejected the notion as silly, a short, bald African-American man wearing a beige trench coat over a navy blue suit approached him. He was wearing mirrorshades of the same brand as that of those worn by Joe's would-be assassin back at the apartment, and sported a Van Dyke.

"Excuse me, Mr. Lombardo, but do you think we can go somewhere and talk? I'll buy you a cup of coffee."

Joe tensed up, hands raising upward into a defensive posture.

The short man regarded him with amusement. "Really, Mr. Lombardo? In the privacy of your own apartment is one thing, but we're in public now. Prolonged hand-to-hand combat would only draw attention."

Grinning, Joe said, "You say that like it's a bad thing. First of all, I'm a reporter. Drawing attention to things is what they pay me for. Secondly, who needs prolonged hand-to-hand combat? I've got a Luger in my pocket."

The man shook his head. "And here I thought you were merely glad to see me. At least now I know where Mr. Kornetzki's weapon got to." With a sigh, the man held out his hand. "You may call me Agent Johnson."

Pointedly not accepting the handshake, Joe said, "I'm guessing you're saying I may call you that 'cause it's not your real name—which is smart, since you're in violation of the agency's charter by operating domestically."

"Johnson" kept holding the hand out. "I'm not operating at all, Mr. Lombardo. I'm just offering to buy you coffee."

For a moment, Joe seriously considered the possibility of really shooting Johnson in the face. It was blindingly obvious that he was the point guy for the CIA on this—but he was also offering to take him to have coffee in a public place.

"So now you want to talk?" Joe asked.

"Yes."

"Because actions haven't been working so hot for you."

Johnson sighed. "Look, today has hardly gone according to plan for either of us. So let's sit down and see what we can work out."

All at once, Joe felt the fatigue slam down on him. He'd been going on adrenaline and fear for several hours now, and that would only go on so long before he'd crash. The banana French toast and coffee had forestalled his collapse, but it really only was a matter of time, and then the guy in the Yankees jacket or Johnson here or one of their other guys would take care of him.

And if things went sideways, he still had the Luger.

"Fine, Agent Johnson, let's have us some coffee."

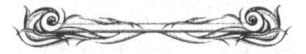

Agent Malik Canizius, codenamed "Agent Johnson," had been having a good day right up until Kornetzki told him he couldn't find Rugova's flash drive.

It had all started when Sandoval called Malik into his office. "We got us a situation. Rugova's gone batshit."

Malik sat down in Sandoval's guest chair, trying not to be nauseated by the miasma of cheap cigars that always hung around the older man. "What does 'batshit' mean in this context, exactly?"

"He's gone whistleblower. He's up in New York, gonna talk to a reporter. Your job is to keep that from happening. Take care of him."

At that, Malik winced. He hated vague instructions, because they usually were for ops that needed to be wholly deniable. "Take care of him how?"

"How do you *think*, dumbass?" Sandoval reached into his drawer and pulled out an antacid, popped it in his mouth, and washed it down with cold coffee. "Hire some local talent, make it look natural, get back the flash drive he brought with to give to whichever reporter he's going to see. Even money it's that Lombardo asshole he fed shit to in the nineties. Joan already e-mailed you everything you'll need."

Nodding, Malik got to his feet and straightened his tie. As he turned to leave, Sandoval added, "Oh, and we've got, like, no budget for this, so keep the team to two or three, 'k?"

Malik just shook his head as he left. Within twenty-four hours, he was in New York with three freelancers, who were the best he could get for the money he had: Kornetzki, who would stage the scene and make it look natural; Opper, the sniper who was there to back up Kornetzki if things went bad; and Hsu, a surveillance guy.

Initially, everything went according to plan. Kornetzki took care of Rugova, it would look like a heart attack if there was any kind of investigation, especially given that the analyst was staying in a fleabag so crummy that they wouldn't even notice the smell of a dead body. Opper was on a roof across the street, Hsu was walking up and down 23rd Street, and Malik was in a company car parked two blocks away. Ideally, he'd have a tricked-out van for an op like this, but this was off the books and on the cheap, so a Lincoln Continental had to do.

Then Kornetzki's voice sounded in Malik's ear with the fateful words: "Boss, I can't find the flash drive."

This was very bad. "Check again."

"I've checked three times. We—"

-30-

From his post on the street, Hsu interjected, "Kornetzki, get out. Someone's approaching. Agent Johnson, check your phone."

Pulling out his smartphone, Malik saw that Hsu had sent him an image: a grainy photograph that nonetheless looked very much like the picture in Joseph Lombardo's file. "The reporter."

After Lombardo found the body, Hsu said, "He's calling 911."

"Fuck," Opper said.

"It's fine," Kornetzki said. "The local yokels will call it a heart attack."

Malik shook his head. "Yes, and now we know where the flash drive wound up. Everyone back to the car, please. We're about to set up on Lombardo."

They all got back to the Continental right around the time that the first blue-and-white responded to Lombardo's call. Malik told everyone to read the dossier on Lombardo in their tablets while he drove in silence to the lower east side.

By morning, they were as ready as they could be. Kornetzki was waiting for Lombardo to come home, and Hsu was in the lobby. Opper, though, had returned to the Lincoln. "Only place I've got a shot on his place is the Williamsburg Bridge. Mind you, it'd be a perfect shot, but—"

"No," Malik snapped.

"Calm down, Johnson, I know that's too public. Kornetzki'll take care of him."

Opper's prediction had proven optimistic, as Malik heard a lot of cries of pain that all sounded like Kornetzki rather than Lombardo.

After another moment: "Target... gone..."

"Kornetzki?" A long pause. "Kornetzki!?" Malik slammed the steering wheel with a fist. "Dammit!" He took a breath. "Hsu, find him. Opper, you go, too." Climbing out of the Lincoln, Malik locked it as soon as Opper was out, the case with his rifle in hand.

Malik went into the lobby. The doorman tried to stop him, but Malik flashed his badge quickly, said, "Federal agent," and went to the elevator.

Upon arriving at the twenty-first floor, he saw that Lombardo's door was wide open. Pulling out his agency-issued

Beretta, he went in with weapon raised before quickly seeing that the kitchen-dining-room-living-room space that took up the front part of the apartment was clear but for Kornetzki in his silly disguise writhing on the floor, clutching one leg, and bleeding from head wounds.

"What happened?"

"Kicked..." Kornetzki seemed to be fading in and out.

Rubbing the bridge of his nose between two fingers, Malik asked, "Did you even *read* the dossier, Kornetzki? It said *right there* that Lombardo's a black belt." He threw up his hands, then put a finger to his ear. "Hsu, Opper, do either of you have—"

"Got him," Hsu said. "He's going up Pitt. Looking at phone booths for some reason."

Malik nodded. That made sense if he was trying to stay under the radar.

The longer this went on, the harder things got. Ops happened domestically all the time, for all that they were not allowed, but they were only successful when they were quick and efficient. This particular op was becoming rapidly less of both.

Hsu continued: "I've got Opper heading up to a short rooftop to set up. Lombardo's working his way in that direction."

"Good." A sniper shot in the middle of a Manhattan street wasn't ideal, but Lombardo had spent the early days of his career in war zones. Those kinds of journalists made enemies. They'd be able to cook something up for NYPD if needs be, allow them to close the case with a minimum of fuss and panic.

Malik went back downstairs. As soon as the elevator deposited him on the ground floor, he said to the doorman, "I need you to call 911. There's an injured man in 21F. It looks as if Mr. Lombardo had a prowler."

"Uhm—okay." Ivan squinted. "Are you—"

"I'm sorry, I have to leave." Malik exited, ignoring the continued pleas of the doorman. Kornetzki may not have read dossiers, but he knew to clam up. He'd even serve time if he had to—it wouldn't have been the first time, and they'd be able to pull strings so it was only a couple of months.

As Malik walked back out into the cool air of the New York morning, Opper's voice sounded in his ear. "Set. Just waiting on a clear shot." A second later: "There he is."

-30-

"Take the shot, please." Malik tried and failed to hide the urgency in his voice as he got into the Lincoln. His laptop was still in the passenger seat. It was connected via secure modem to a CIA satellite that fed him all kinds of information. At present, it was seeking out uses of any of Lombardo's credit or debit cards, or a ping on his cell phone. Thus far, all he'd gotten was Lombardo's payment for the cab down from the hotel. The reporter was keeping his phone off.

"Fuck!" Opper's exclamation nearly blew out Malik's eardrum.

"What happened?"

"The sonofabitch stumbled right when I threw my shot. Dammit!"

"Can you get another—"

Before Malik could finish the question, Hsu said, "He's running. And, uh, we've got another problem. Cops at twelve o'clock."

Malik winced, then grabbed the laptop, calling up a map of the area. His heart sank when he saw that Opper was set up all of a block from the 7th Precinct.

"Hsu, go after the target. Opper, are there any witnesses?"

"No, but I got cops comin' right at me—I ain't got time to clean up."

For a few moments, Malik only heard Opper's footsteps and labored breathing as he ran. Then, distantly, came the word he really really didn't want to hear: "Freeze!" Then Opper's channel went blank, so the sniper had trashed the earbud, as he was supposed to.

"Hsu, *please* tell me that you have eyes on Lombardo."

"Not yet."

Malik ground his teeth in frustration. This was now officially a disaster.

For the next several hours, Hsu and Malik both searched the area, expanding their search radius, and getting more and more frustrated. Malik stared at his laptop in vain for a sign of a credit or debit card, of his cell phone pinging. He expanded the search parameters to cover him logging into his e-mail, the *Daily News* web site, or his Facebook, Twitter, MySpace, or Skype accounts. The latter two were long shots, as Lombardo hadn't used MySpace in years (but then, who had?), and his Skype use was sporadic.

Malik also had made some phone calls to get Opper and Kornetzki taken care of, though it wouldn't be easy.

At 9:32, Sandoval called. With the utmost reluctance, he answered it, only because letting it go to voicemail would result in an ass-chewing of legendary proportions.

"What the fucking *fuck*?"

That made Malik wince. Sandoval only used profanity when he was unhappy. "Things have gone a trifle—"

"No, asshole, this not a fucking 'trifle.' This is a clusterfuck of epic fucking proportions. We're gonna have to burn Opper—no fucking loss, you ask me, why the fuck you sign up his pathetic ass?"

Through clenched teeth, Malik said, "You said I had no budget, remember?"

"And ain't that bitin' us on the ass?" Sandoval sighed. "All right, fine, look, I'm getting shit from on high and it hasn't even been two hours. Pull the plug on the op."

"Sir, Lombardo has the flash drive."

A pause. "All right, keep trying to locate him, and then talk to him. See if he'll give it up willingly."

Malik let out a muffled snort of skepticism, but said nothing.

Sandoval continued: "But from here on, it's just talking. We'll both be up on charges otherwise. It may happen anyhow. McIntyre's shitting bricks."

"Understood."

At 10:07, Malik hit paydirt, as Lombardo's Skype account was accessed. Pulling the Lincoln over in front of a fire hydrant on Allen Street, he grabbed the laptop. "Hsu, the target is on a computer near Seward Park. It's not his laptop's IP." He called up a map. "There's a library branch at the east end of the park. He's probably on one of the computers there."

"On it. I can be there in three minutes."

Malik nodded, even though Hsu couldn't see that, put the laptop back on the passenger seat, and pulled into traffic and worked his way down to the Seward Park Library.

"I think he made me. He's moving away."

"Let him go." Malik was tired of playing cat-and-mouse, and this op was now officially more trouble than it was worth.

He found a place to park on the south side of East Broadway that had metered parking. Sticking his government credentials on the dashboard to forestall any tickets, he then crossed the street and walked toward the front entrance, just as a very harried-looking Joe Lombardo walked out.

This was Malik's first look at Lombardo in person, and it wasn't a pretty picture. His brown eyes were bloodshot, his receding brown hair was a mess of disorganized curls, and he was walking very unsteadily. It was no wonder he'd stumbled when Opper tried to shoot him.

Malik walked up to the reporter as he stepped onto the sidewalk. "Excuse me, Mr. Lombardo, but do you think we can go somewhere and talk? I'll buy you a cup of coffee."

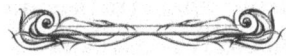

Joe gulped down the espresso as if he'd never had any before, never mind that it was something like his fifth.

He and "Agent Johnson" were seated at a high-end coffee place on Essex Street, one of those places that everyone told him he *had* to go to when he moved down to the lower east side and had never actually gotten around to trying. The CIA agent had already paid for both drinks.

"So Agent Not-Really-Named-Johnson, you've already tried to poison me and shoot me. What's next?"

"Nothing, Mr. Lombardo." The agent sipped a cup of jasmine tea. "Agent Rugova sent you a flash drive, did he not?"

Joe just sipped his espresso.

"Johnson" smirked. "Of course. Either way, I am returning to Washington. The man who tried to poison you is in the hospital, the man who tried to shoot you is under arrest. This operation has provided a casualty rate far in excess of what is acceptable for a mission of this type."

"So that's it? Two shots and you give up?"

"Honestly, giving up after one would have been more prudent. As you said, the CIA is forbidden from operating domestically, and those who do tend to pay a dear price."

Joe grinned. "Like going to the hospital and being put under arrest?"

"Touché." The agent reached into the inner pocket of his suit jacket and pulled out a business card, handing it to Joe.

He took it, and saw that it only had a phone number with a 202 area code written in black on an otherwise blank white card.

After sipping the last of his tea, Johnson said, "We're fighting for freedom, Mr. Lombardo. So you're free to do whatever you wish with the information on the flash drive that Agent Rugova sent you." Another smirk. "If he sent it to you. You may call me at that number if you wish to talk further."

With that, Johnson left.

Joe sat and sipped some more espresso, wondering if it was truly over or not.

It turned out not to be: as soon as he got home, he was greeted by detectives from the 7th Precinct who had questions about his break-in, especially regarding why he wasn't home. He said he panicked and ran and it took him a while to get his head together and come home. Making up for that disappearance, he gave a statement in which he, for the second time in twenty-four hours, lied to the police.

After telling the detectives that he had no idea why this guy broke into his apartment and attacked him, they all left.

For several seconds, Joe just stood and stared at his apartment.

There was dust all over everything from the cops' attempts to lift fingerprints, his windowsill was a shattered mess, there was blood on the dining room floor and the counter, and the dining room table and chairs were on their sides or turned over.

Then, finally, he plugged his phone in.

After that, he grabbed his laptop—currently on the dining room floor—and placed it on the kitchen counter. Flipping it open, he slid the CD tray out, then reached into his coat pocket.

He found the Luger, and took that out and stared at it for several seconds.

Gonna need to get rid of this thing.

Unwilling to think about that, he put the weapon down on the counter and reached into the other pocket, which had the flash drive and the decryption CD, as well as "Agent Johnson's" minimalist business card.

Setting the card aside next to the laptop, he plugged the drive into a USB port and placed the disc in the tray and closed it.

The CD ran automatically, and put up a status box that showed that the decryption process was 0% complete with seven hours remaining. After two seconds, it was 1% complete with six hours and fifty-eight seconds remaining.

Joe let out a very long breath and finally, for the first time since he went out to Nik's hotel room, he shrugged out of his leather coat and tossed it onto the couch. He stared at his phone, plugged into the charger and sitting on the end table in the living room. The battery was up to 2%. He could try turning it on, but he decided that nobody could possibly have a phone message for him that was more important than the very long nap he was about to take.

So he went into the bedroom and fell facefirst onto the bed at a forty-five degree angle and immediately fell asleep.

By the time he woke up again, it was dark out. Drool fell from the corner of his mouth to the comforter. He rolled off the bed, clambered into an upright position, wiped his mouth with the back of his hand, and then stretched, his muscles and bones popping and crunching.

Taking a deep breath, he instantly regretted it. *How long have I been wearing these clothes anyhow?*

That he couldn't come up with an answer to that question off the top of his head told him all he needed to know. Before he did anything else, he was peeling off his clothes and showering.

A good fifteen minutes later, he exited the shower, refreshed if pruney, and walked out into the living room while toweling off.

He stood in front of the laptop and saw that the decryption was 98% done. Nodding at the laptop, he went back to the bedroom and threw on a T-shirt and sweats.

As he walked back to the counter, he noticed that the phone was fully charged. But he wasn't ready to turn it on *just* yet.

So much relied upon what was on that flash drive.

With a ding, the laptop announced that the decryption was done. Sitting on a stool next to the counter, Joe clicked on the "OK" tab.

Then dozens of PDFs and graphics files all started to open on his screen.

His jaw slowly fell further and further open as he continued to read. Nik had mentioned an operation in Pakistan, and here were the details, involving a clinic in a small town near where a terrorist was believed to be hiding. Another in Kenya, which had far less noble a goal than tracking an enemy of the U.S.. A false vaccine being developed for another operation. And on and on and on.

It was too much.

He didn't know where to start.

He didn't know what to do.

"But this is something that can make your career."

"You can't write this story."

"So you're free to do whatever you wish."

Suddenly, his dream of the other night came back to him: winning another Pulitzer, proving that he wasn't just a flash in the pan with the Kosovo story. And this would absolutely do it. This would shatter the CIA, displacing the rock that exposed the ants underneath to the sun and forcing them to run and hide.

Then he thought about the kids Elissa was talking about. How many kids would die because their parents wouldn't let them get immunizations after his story proved that the Americans were just using doctors for their own vicious ends? Hell, one of the files he had showed that they were co-opting a *Médicins Sans Frontières* station.

He could run the story. He could bury the story.

Looking to the side of the laptop, his eyes fell on the plain white card with the 202 phone number on it.

And he smiled.

There was a third choice. He'd already lied to the police twice, why not lie to a CIA agent? Agent Not-Johnson didn't need to know that Joe didn't want to run the story.

Jumping down from the stool, Joe walked over to the end table. He turned his phone on. After a few seconds, it booted up. Immediately it informed him that he had voicemail, that he had thirteen text messages, and that he'd missed nine calls.

He ignored them and went to the dialer, entering the number on the card.

"Agent Johnson, this is Joe Lombardo."

"I was not expecting to hear from you, Mr. Lombardo."

"Then you're an even bigger idiot than I thought," Joe said harshly. "Look, you know what I have. You know what I can do with it."

"Yes."

"So make it worth my while not to do anything with it."

"How am I supposed to do that?"

Joe grinned. *He wants me to spell it out, I'll spell it out.* "With Nik gone, I need a source in the CIA. You just got elected."

"That seems reasonable." Johnson agreed very quickly, which confirmed what Joe had figured—Johnson was expecting a *quid pro quo.*

"Good. I'll be in touch. And don't fuck me on this, Johnson. This flash drive paints a *nasty* picture."

"No doubt. Good day, Mr. Lombardo."

"Johnson" ended the call.

Joe wasn't sure how long he'd be able to milk this. But he intended to do so for as long as he could. He was gonna get scoops up the wazoo.

He didn't even bother playing the voicemail or seeing who the texts or missed calls were from, instead just calling Ed.

Caller ID betrayed him. "Lombardo, where the *fuck* have you been?! You still owe me a fucking transit story, and you will apologize for dropping that fucking ball even though I guaran-damn-*tee* that I ain't *never* gonna accept it."

"Later, Ed-Ed, I promise."

"Don't fucking call me that, and give me *one* good reason not to fire your sorry ass."

"Fire me all you want, but first, I need you to tell me what're the names of the editors on the foreign desk."

"Say *what?*"

"The foreign desk." He smiled. "I think I need to go back to international."

Introduction to "Behold a White Tricycle"

Jay Lake—who died in 2014 after a protracted battle with cancer—was a twisted genius in so many ways. He was a wonderful writer, a great person, a delightful presence, and a brilliant intellect. He was also an atheist and a rationalist, so it just figures that he would come up with something like the never-actually-published anthology *44 Clowns: 11 Stories of the 4 Clowns of the Apocalypse*.

Following the experience of "working" together on "Two Beers and a Story" at WorldCon in Boston, Jay invited me to play along and be one of the eleven contributors to *44 Clowns*.

The problem was that what I came up with was a story that really could *only* be published in an anthology about the Four Clowns of the Apocalypse. Or, well, in a collection of my own short fiction. Which is why "Behold a White Tricycle" has not seen the light of day at all, following Scorpius Digital Publishing failing to actually publish *44 Clowns*, until now.

While Jay did not live to see this volume, he did live long enough to see my announcement of it with a table of contents, and he was thrilled to see that "Behold a White Tricycle" was finally going to be published. I think it's a fitting end to this tour through my non-licensed work, and I hope you enjoy it, as you have, with luck, enjoyed at least some of the other ten stories in this volume.

Behold a White Tricycle

a story of the Four Clowns of the Apocalypse

And I saw when the Ringmaster opened one of the tent flaps, and I heard, as it were the noise of thunder, one of the four clowns saying, "Hiya hiya hiya!"

And I saw, and behold a white tricycle: and he that sat in it had a tooty horn; and a red nose was given unto him: and he went forth laughing, and to induce laughter.

And when he had opened the second tent flap, I heard the second clown say, "Vootie!"

And there went out another tricycle that was red: and power was given to him that sat thereon to give candy to the children, and that they should hit one another over the head with rubber mallets: and there was given unto him a seltzer bottle.

And when he had opened the third tent flap, I heard the third clown say, "Hotcha-cha-cha!"

And I beheld, and lo a black tricycle; and he that sat on it had a pair of rubber balls in his hand.

And I heard a voice in the midst of the four clowns say, "A pie in the face for a penny, and three pies in the face for half a dollar; and then get sprayed with this big bottle of seltzer."

And when he had opened the fourth tent flap, I heard the voice of the fourth clown say, "Whaddaya say, whaddaya say, whaddaya *say*!"

And I looked, and behold a pale tricycle: and his name that sat on him was Bozo, and tigers followed with him. And power was given unto them over the fourth part of the circus grounds, to tickle with feathers, and with hunger for cotton candy, and with kids dying laughing, while watching the beasts of the earth tramp about.

And when he had opened the fifth tent flap, I saw under the big top the souls of them that died laughing, and for the testimony which they held.

And they cried with a loud voice, saying, "How long, O Lord, holy and true, dost thou not let these clowns hurry up and stop acting like idiots so we can see the cool stuff, like the trapeze artists?"

And greasepaint was given unto every one of them; and it was said unto them that they should rest yet for a little season, until their acrobats also and their jugglers, that should be as silly as they were, should be fulfilled.

And I beheld when he had opened the sixth tent flap, and, lo, there was a great earthquake; and the tent became black as sackcloth of hair as the lights went out; and the tent then became as blood as the red lights went up.

And the stars of the circus fell unto the earth, even as a fig tree casteth her untimely figs, when she is shaken of a mighty wind.

And the circus departed as a scroll when it is rolled together; and every tent and stand were moved out of their places.

And the ringmaster, and the great jugglers, and the rich backers, and the chief owners, and the mighty weightlifters, and every roustabout, and every clown, hid themselves in the dens and in the rocks of the mountains.

And said to the mountains and rocks, "Fall on us, and hide us from the face of them that want us to perform six shows a day, and from the wrath of the bosses that write our checks."

For the great day of the circus is come; and who shall be able to juggle?

About the Author

KEITH R.A. DECANDIDO has also written some longer fiction, including a bevy of tie-in novels in the universes of TV shows (*Star Trek, Supernatural, Orphan Black*), movies (*Alien, Cars, Serenity*), games (*World of Warcraft, Summoner's War, Dungeons & Dragons*), comics (Spider-Man, the X-Men, Thor), and bunches more. If you liked "Partners in Crime," check out the "Precinct" books, including the novels *Dragon Precinct, Unicorn Precinct, Goblin Precinct, Gryphon Precinct,* the short-story collection *Tales from Dragon Precinct,* and the forthcoming *Mermaid Precinct, Phoenix Precinct, Manticore Precinct,* and *More Tales from Dragon Precinct.* If you liked "Seven-Mile Race," check out more Cassie stories in the collection *Ragnarok and Roll: Tales of Cassie Zukav, Weirdness Magnet,* as well as *Buzzy Mag Online* and the anthologies *Apocalypse 13, Bad-Ass Faeries: It's Elemental, A Baker's Dozen of Magic, Out of Tune, Tales from the House Band* Volumes 1-2, and *TV Gods: Summer Programming.* If you liked "Under the King's Bridge," check out *A Furnace Sealed,* coming soon from WordFire Press. If you liked "The Ballad of Big Charlie," check out another story featuring Mia Fitzsimmons, "Streets of Fire" in *V-Wars: Night Terrors.* His other recent and forthcoming work includes the *Tales of Asgard* trilogy featuring Thor, Sif, and the Warriors Three; fiction in the universe of the online app game *Summoner's War;* the *Alien* novel *Isolation;* short stories in the anthologies *Aliens: Bug Hunt,* the two *Baker Street Irregulars* anthologies, *Joe Ledger: Unstoppable, Nights of the Living Dead,* and *Release the Virgins!* In addition to all this, Keith is an editor of long-standing—he has more than a dozen anthologies to his credit, and he also edits manuscripts for clients both personal and corporate. He has been writing about popular culture for Tor.com since 2011, covering *Star Trek, Stargate, Batman, Wonder Woman, Doctor Who*, Marvel's Netflix series, and many more, plus he's doing a weekly rewatch for the site of every live-action movie based on a superhero comic book. Keith is also a third-degree black belt in karate, which he both teaches and trains in. He's probably done some other stuff, too, but he can't remember due to the lack of sleep. Find out less at his web site at DeCandido.net, which is a gateway to his entire online footprint.